Old

Sisters of Circumstance

A Novel

by

P.J. Rhea

Published by
Brighton Publishing LLC
501 W. Ray Road
Suite 4
Chandler, AZ 85225

Old Harbor
Sisters of Circumstance

A Novel

by

P.J. Rhea

Published by
Brighton Publishing LLC
501 W. Ray Road
Suite 4
Chandler, AZ 85225
www.BrightonPublishing.com

Copyright © 2012

ISBN: 13: 978-1-62183-003-0
ISBN: 10: 162-183003-9

Printed in the United States of America

First Edition

Cover Design By: Patricia McNaught Foster

All rights reserved. No part of this publication may be
reproduced or transmitted in any form or by any means,
electronic or mechanical, including photocopy, recording, or
any information storage retrieval system, without permission in
writing from the copyright owner.

Old Harbor - Sisters of Circumstance ~ P.J. Rhea

❧ *Dedication* ☙

I dedicate this first novel to Glenda, for going above and beyond friendship. You were my sister of circumstance and I couldn't have done it without you. And to Mike for always being my rock and my support. You believed in me when I didn't believe in myself.

Acknowledgments

*A*lthough *Old Harbor* is written as fiction, the story is very true-to-life as far as the inherent desire and need for friends in our lives. The encouragement and help of my many dear friends who are—to me—like sisters, as well as the support and love given to me by family has been invaluable. These are the things which helped me breathe life into this town and the charming characters who live there.

I will forever be grateful to the people who believed in me enough to help me find my way through my first novel and also have been more proud of me than I could have ever imagined.

Nancy Nix: Thank you for the insight you were able to give me of the Alaska you lived in for twelve years. You helped me paint a picture of a place I had never seen so well, that I felt I was actually there.

Glenda Jones and Nancy Cochran: Thank you for the long hours sitting around the kitchen table helping me figure out timelines.

To my husband, my children, and my six awesome grandchildren: Thank you for your patience with me as I stressed over something new and foreign and also for the excitement we shared as we watched Old Harbor come to life on the pages.

And to Brighton Publishing and Kathie McGuire: A big thank you for giving me this opportunity to fulfill a dream. You are the best.

❧ Chapter One ❧

Seasons

When I was a little girl my grandmother, Ruth, used to tell me people lived by seasons. She'd say, "You're in the spring of your life, Allie. You're a young plant that needs to be fed knowledge and love in order to grow properly. When you're an adult, old enough to be on your own and maybe with a family of your own, then you'll be in your summer. People who have raised their families and are becoming grandparents are in their autumn and, well, I am in the winter. That's the part of a person's life for reflection and sharing the knowledge they've acquired with others, if they are willing to listen. To look back at your life and remember what you have accomplished and to just enjoy the people who are a part of you. Not everyone makes it to winter, and for some it can be a cold dark time unless they have family to surround them and keep them warm."

Then she would cup my chin in her loving hand and smile down at me. "That's my wish for you, little Allie, that you live long enough so you can enjoy the winter."

I loved my grandmother; and when she passed away, I missed our time together. She had a sparkle in her eyes and lots of spunk, and my mom, Carol, took after her. They were the type of women who would light up a room when they entered it. People took notice and listened to what they had to say. I was more like my dad, both in personality and feature: quiet and often unnoticed. As I got older, I wondered if I would be able to enjoy those winter years if I lived to be old like my grandmother. My mother was Grandmother Ruth's only child and I was my mother's only child. My father was the youngest of three children. He had a brother who had died in a war at the age of nineteen and a sister who never married and who died of cancer. So I guess he may as well have been an only child. I had no aunts, uncles, cousins, and no more living grandparents. It would be up to me to make sure I had people to keep me warm in my winter.

Old Harbor - Sisters of Circumstance ~ P.J. Rhea

My dad was a drinker—and by drinker, I mean an alcoholic. My mother loved him and I suppose she never stopped, but she hated the drinking, and even more, she hated the small town life. We lived in a small town near Nashville, Tennessee.

"Everyone knows your business here in this dreary town," she would complain. "I need noise and people and things to do." She tried to talk my dad into moving at least a hundred times. "Roger," she would say, "I'm smothering here, please, can we move somewhere with personality?"

But his answer was always the same. He would always kiss her softly on top of her head and say, "Carol, I can't, I have roots here and it's a good place to raise kids."

With most of his family gone, I think he needed to stay there to feel connected. His drinking increased with each passing year, and by the time I was ten, mom couldn't stand it anymore. She didn't divorce him; she just left, taking me with her. She packed what she could in a van and the two of us headed to New York. My dad just sat there on our porch with his head in his hands as we drove away. I felt so sorry for him and wondered why he didn't try to stop her. Why he didn't beg her to stay. I knew I would miss him, but I also knew I would never see him again. That first year he would call my mom, asking her to come back, sending her money when he could, and asking to see me.

"Please Carol, I love you both and I miss you."

She would respond by letting him know he was welcome to come to New York and live with us as long as he was willing to stop drinking. In the beginning he would ask to speak to me whenever he called. He would try to sound happy for me and I would attempt to sound excited about New York, but we were both just pretending. As time passed he called less and less, and there were times he wouldn't ask to speak to me at all. I knew from my mother's voice that he was in one of his crying moods and didn't want me to know. My mother missed him too. She kept their wedding picture on her nightstand till the day she died. It was sad that two people, obviously in love, would not compromise to keep our family together. When I was a child I couldn't understand how he could pick alcohol over me. How could a

2

person let a drink be more important than his daughter? By the time I turned twelve, he drank himself to death. We didn't get the news about his passing until the day after his funeral.

"I didn't even get to tell him goodbye!" I screamed at my mom as if it were her fault, but I knew he was a prisoner of his addiction and she had done the right thing by removing us from that environment.

An uncle of his found him sitting at his kitchen table slumped over a bowl of potato soup. The table was covered with empty beer bottles and there was a picture in the center of the table of the family he had lost. It was the only family picture we had ever had taken. I remember when Grandma Ruth took the picture. We were posed in front of our Christmas tree and my dad was holding me up so I could place the star on the top of the tree. It broke my mother's heart when they called to tell her, and she cried for a very long time over his passing. It was the only time I had ever seen my mother sad for more than a day. Even when Grandma Ruth died, she only cried at the funeral and then it was as if all was done and that was that. I hated that she had taken me so far away and that my father had to die all alone. But I knew I belonged with my mother.

I wasn't sure if I would ever like living in such a large city, but mom loved New York from the first day we arrived. It was busy and exciting to her. We found a tiny apartment in Greenwich Village and she found a job in a restaurant as a hostess, which was perfect for her. She was what some called a character. She was a beautiful woman, with dark blonde hair that encircled her oval face like a frame. Her eyes were blue and wide with long lashes, and they sparkled with excitement over everything. She was full of life and often too outspoken for her own good, but I adored her. She was my best friend, and often my only friend.

I was the complete opposite of her. I wasn't really shy, just quiet. I wasn't afraid to speak my mind, but I often deliberately stood back and observed. I was a people watcher. I was a strawberry blonde, like my dad. My blue eyes were clear and bright like my mother's, but lacked the sparkle of excitement that lived in hers. Mine were full of curiosity. Mom would tell me that I over-analyzed

Old Harbor - Sisters of Circumstance ~ P.J. Rhea

everything, and I guess she was right. I made a few friends while in school, but none I really continued to talk to after my school years ended. I mostly hung out with Mom. We loved going to shows and movies together. In our tiny apartment, we would laugh and talk for hours. She was the one person who loved me for exactly who I was, and I saw no fault in her. But there was one habit she had that I was not happy about. It was the only thing we ever argued about and it was the one thing that, as it turned out, would take her from me. Mom was a smoker. Her habit had grown to almost three packs a day.

I would beg her not to smoke, but she felt it helped her keep her figure; not that she needed help. She was slim and glamorous, but always afraid she would get fat. She could be a little vain when it came to her appearance.

I was angry when she told me about the cancer. When she finally went to a doctor the cancer was too far along to place much hope on a cure. She agreed to the chemotherapy in hopes to buy a little time. She kept it from me as long as she could, and by the time she let me in on it, the end was way too soon. I stayed by her side for weeks and watched my beautiful mother, my friend, waste away. Her bright eyes dimmed and her beautiful hair was falling out. When she died, I barely recognized her.

One of the last things she said to me: "Don't take me back to Tennessee when I'm gone, Allie. I never really belonged there and I left nothing behind."

My dad was buried in a small family cemetery, along with his parents and his brother and sister. His remaining relatives had not cared much for my mother after she left my dad. She was right, she didn't belong there. So, when I was nineteen years old, I was left alone.

She died on September 11, 2001, the day the twin towers fell and the nation was in shock. Since mom had always loved being around lots of people, I imagined that maybe she saw the spirits of all those people leaving that day, and followed them. All of New York was experiencing grief, so mine went unnoticed. No one knew my world was crashing down around me just like the towers. I cried for days, and people would look at me with sympathetic eyes and tell me

Old Harbor - Sisters of Circumstance ~ P.J. Rhea

it was going to be okay. They thought I was grieving the same loss they were, weeping over the thousands of victims of this tragedy. It was a sad and scary time in this city and I was struggling with a hole in my heart that would never be filled. I was empty and lonely and afraid to be by myself, and I couldn't think of a single person I could go to for comfort. There was no one to just sit and talk to about the wonderful woman who had left her beloved city so quietly, while the world was falling apart.

I had her cremated and placed her ashes in several locations throughout the city—places I knew she loved and were a part of her. Now she would be a part of them, too. I was glad she didn't see her city like this. She loved it here and this would have broken her heart. I felt I was the one who was dead, numb, and so very alone. In a city of millions of people, I felt as if I was stranded on an island with no one to talk to. I kept thinking about the fact that Mom had only lived through her summer. She never really got started with her fall. I thought of all she would miss. I had dreamed of her helping with my wedding, if that day ever came. And what a fantastic grandmother she would have been. Would Grandma Ruth be the only person in my family to have lived to see her winter?

My attempt to be normal, to feel alive, was futile. My job didn't offer much opportunity to make friends. I'm a photographer, something I actually love to do; that is, anywhere but at my job. Taking pictures at a portrait studio in a department store does not make you a photographer. Day after day, it was the same thing. It was the same basic backgrounds to choose from, plus one background depicting whatever holiday was near; place each child in the same pose, the same white wicker chair or fake grass carpet to sit on. Any effort to branch away from the required standard poses was quickly shot down.

"Miss Davis, we have limited time with each client and in order to stay on track, you must stick to the poses offered on our contract."

The manager refused to have more than one person on the clock, so there was no time to get to know the person who took your place at the end of your shift. I saw hundreds of people every day as they passed by the studio's entrance, but never got to know anyone. I watched them as they went about their lives: errands to run, families to care for, partners to love. I wanted that so badly. I was at work a few weeks after my mom's death taking a picture of a mom and her grown daughter. They told me that what happened to the towers had brought them closer, and they wanted to be sure they had a recent picture of each other.

"You just never know when something could happen to someone you love," the mom had explained.

I couldn't help it. I broke down and cried in front of them, and they both ran over to me and hugged me. I clung to them for as long as I could. I desperately needed to grieve and to feel compassion from another person. They asked me if I had lost someone in the towers. I knew it wasn't the complete truth, but I just said yes.

I noticed my boss was watching from his office and he did not appear to be happy about the time I was using for my own benefit. He was not a cruel man, but he was all business and made it clear to all his employees that he wasn't interested in our personal life. The closest he had come to showing any feeling was sending flowers to the hospital when I knew my mother's time was short and I had to ask to be off for a while. When I returned a few weeks later he said he was glad I was back and he hoped I realized I had been out more days than I had built up and would not get paid for the last week I was off.

I thanked the ladies for their sympathy and told them to go freshen up in the ladies' room so we could proceed with their session. I felt bad for lying to those ladies, but I had no one else. No shoulder to lean on, no ear to hear my memories of her and what she had meant to me. I promised myself that day I would not die alone. My winter would be warm because I would be surrounded by people I loved and who loved me.

My mom never divorced Dad, she never even considered getting remarried after he died, but she had no problem making friends, no problem getting dates. She had male friends who were important to her, and one she may have loved, but she never wanted to feel obligated to a relationship again.

Old Harbor - Sisters of Circumstance ~ P.J. Rhea

"Just friends for me, that's all I need."

I needed friends too, but I wasn't my mother.

Making friends was something I didn't do well. I was tired of being lonely and I wanted so badly to have a family. Someone I could come home to, someone who needed me. I had always taken care of Mom, even before she grew ill, and I wanted to be needed again. I was half a person now and I wanted to feel whole again. I tried to meet people by going to clubs and sitting at the bar. I quickly found out that the men I met there were not for me. I wasn't the one-night-stand type, and they weren't wife shopping.

I played the online dating game, too. I tried to sound interesting in my profile, without being dishonest. After all, this was to find my soul mate, right? I already knew from watching my parents that marriage wasn't easy, and I didn't want to start off a relationship with lies. I would be honest and he would have to like me for who I was. I didn't want to be shallow either, but I refused to consider one without a photo. I mean, there has to be some attraction to the person or you never make it past "hello." I'm not unattractive myself, so I had plenty of responses. I must have gone a year with a date every weekend, but never one who felt like *the one*.

There was this one guy who seemed to have potential. He was nice looking and funny. I allowed the relationship to become a physical one and it lasted a few months, but I realized I was trying too hard to make the wrong thing seem right. I was raised believing you should be married before you had sex, so I wasn't sure if it was my attitude toward sex outside of marriage or the poor effort put forth by him, but I never felt satisfied even one time. I was starting to believe it was me who had failed him and not the other way around. I just wasn't meant to be happy, to have a family and a life that was full. Mom had always made her happiness.

I remember she would tell me, "Allie, you have to make your own destiny. Don't wait around to see what happens; decide what you want and make it happen."

I'm trying mom, but it just isn't meant for me.

Old Harbor - Sisters of Circumstance ~ P.J. Rhea

She had been gone almost nine years now. Would it be my fate to be alone? To never marry, have children or grandchildren to warm my winter? I was just beginning to accept the idea that I may never see that winter. After all, I was struggling with a sad excuse for a summer.

❧ Chapter Two ❧

Taking a Chance

I knew my grandmother would think I was crazy for what I was about to do. Mom may have considered it exciting. *Way to grab the future by the horns and choose your destiny, Allie.* The few people I called "friends" in my life would probably never notice I had left town. My job would be filled before I finished packing, and the apartment that had been home to me for over nineteen years was already spoken for as soon as I was gone and it could be cleaned and painted. This city I had spent most of my life in would never miss a beat once I left. My absence would not affect anything I had touched. But my leaving could change my life forever.

It was September 10th and I was thinking about my mom. As I sat in the waiting area provided by my dentist's office, the television that hung on the wall was telling about the scheduled ceremony planned for tomorrow to honor the victims of 9/11.

"They won't call your name," I said aloud, without thinking. This drew the attention of everyone in the room and I felt embarrassment creep into my cheeks as all eyes locked on me. "Sorry," was all I knew to say.

I grabbed the magazine on the table nearest me so I could hide behind it till the attention passed. It was a *Travel* magazine from the travel agency next door. These were the only magazines that were ever current here, probably replaced every month. Everything else had been here at my last check up six months ago. As I looked through the pages at all the wonderful places a person might travel to, I couldn't help but think about my mom again. She had always promised we would go on exciting vacations when we could afford it. I reached the back cover of the magazine and was about to lay it down when something grabbed my attention. It was a small article with nothing special to draw your attention, like pictures or bold print. But the first two words hit me hard and demanded that I take notice:

Object: Matrimony!

*Single men, seeking brides. For more
information contact the Minister of the
Community Church in Old Harbor, Alaska.
Your future awaits you.*

There was also a website listed. I started to tear the ad from the magazine, but at the first sound of paper ripping, the lady behind the counter looked at me with disapproval while clearing her throat. Instead I wrote the information down on the back of a gum wrapper and stuck it in my pocket. When I got home, I pulled it out and looked at it for a long while. *This is insane, I can't do this,* I thought. I tossed the little paper in the trash, only to retrieve it, as if saving a life from a fire. I laid it beside my computer for safekeeping. For the next seven weeks, I would look at it while using my computer. Sometimes I would touch it, as if I could get the answer to all my doubts by the feel of this piece of paper. *Your future awaits you*—how could I even think about doing this? What century was it, after all? I just needed to try harder to find the person I was meant to be with. Go out more, and maybe try to be more approachable. Weren't mail-order brides a way for foreigners to get citizenship? Something desperate women did? I had to laugh at my own analogy. *Let's face it Allie, you are a little desperate here.* But was I really that desperate? People didn't arrange marriages anymore, did they? Not in this part of the world. To even consider the idea of going to a new place to marry a total stranger, I must be completely out of my mind. *And Alaska of all places; like the winters in New York are not bad enough. Why couldn't the men of Hawaii need a bride?* I had to laugh at my own ranting: *It's not like I'm considering this!*

One afternoon, as I contemplated the piece of paper which now ruled my life; I again started to laugh at the very idea of doing this. It was a rainy, cold day and I wasn't scheduled to work, so I was feeling extremely sorry for myself. *Why not? I can at least see what it's all about.* I keyed in the website address given and hit the enter key. As I read the introduction, a strange feeling came over me and I knew in my heart that my life was about to change.

Old Harbor - Sisters of Circumstance ~ P.J. Rhea

The first sentence was all it took. *Are you tired of being lonely?* It was as if they were talking directly to me. I was almost surprised not to see my name at the end of the question. There was a picture of a little church building, painted white with light blue trim, a darker blue roof, and a beautiful, rounded white steeple at the top. The scenery in the background was breathtaking. The tall snow-capped mountains were like something painted by an artist. There was also a picture of the minister who had placed the ad. He was younger than I expected—probably early thirties—and very pleasant looking. He had bright eyes that smiled as wide as his toothy grin. I almost expected he would be one of the grooms, but his explanation began with introducing his lovely wife, Gwen:

I am Brother Carl Bible. I had to be a minister with that name, right? He must have a sense of humor, I reasoned. *I am located in a small town in Alaska, population around 300 people. Old Harbor is beautiful and friendly, and full of nature's gifts. We have several men in our town who want nothing more than to have a family to share this with. There are no eligible women left in our small town, and the men are too busy with their jobs to go to other cities to meet someone. I feel there is no finer place to live on God's earth, and the men who are seeking brides are hard-working and capable of providing a nice home and companionship to someone willing to give them a chance. If you are interested in becoming a wife to one of these fine gentlemen, and live in this lovely place, fill out the attached application and send it to me.*

He continued to explain the way this all came about. He was tired of seeing all the sad men in his congregation and wanted to bring the laughter of children back to this church. He had called a meeting of all the single men who would like to find a wife. Almost every single man came to the first meeting. Some left after hearing his idea, and some backed out just prior to him placing the ad, so there was a total of five men who were willing to give this a try.

Here is the deal, ladies. You must be willing to marry within a few weeks after you arrive. From the information required on the form, I will hopefully be able to match each couple. Once you have been matched, you will correspond by email and phone for two months, at least once a week, more often if you would like. This will

Old Harbor - Sisters of Circumstance ~ P.J. Rhea

help you determine if you are compatible and would like to come to our lovely town and continue the relationship. The prospective grooms are required to pay for a one-way ticket for the ladies, but if you change your mind after you arrive, you will be expected to pay for your own return ticket. You will spend your first four weeks in Old Harbor as guests of Gwen and me, getting to know your future grooms in supervised activities. So far, we have a dance planned, several dinners, and a movie night. This will also give the ladies an opportunity to get to know each other. You will be like family because of your common choice to do this—sisters of circumstance, you might say.

I really liked that. I had always wanted a sister and now I could possibly have four.

The deadline for applications is October 31, 2010

Oh no, It's October twenty-ninth. No time to think it over. I had to do this now.

The application was much like the ones I had filled out for the online dating sites I had used.

> **Name**: Allison Ruth Davis; Allison because my mom liked the name, and Ruth after my grandmother. I prefer to be called Allie.
>
> **Age**: I will be 29 on November 20.
>
> **Occupation**: Photographer.

Okay, those were the easy questions. Now I had to put likes, dislikes, hobbies, beliefs, and what I was looking for in a mate. Write a few lines telling more about myself. I had to make myself sound interesting. Say something that would catch the attention of someone I had never met. "I have never done a lot of cooking but I am willing to learn. I love to read and I especially like mysteries. I love nature. My favorite thing to do for fun is take pictures of the animals I spot in the park or the zoo. I try to be kind to people and I am the kind of person you can trust." *Oh great, Allie, you just bored yourself with*

Old Harbor - Sisters of Circumstance ~ P.J. Rhea

your own life. You just may be doomed to be alone, girl, because there is nothing interesting about you.

Please include a recent photo. No problem with that. I had a camera with a timer that I could set up to take my picture. I put on my only decent dress. It was emerald green and not only accented the red in my hair, but showed my petite figure. My hair was long, past my shoulders, and I let it hang down my back with part of it pulled back in a clasp. I had never worn a lot of makeup, but I did put on just a little to bring out the blue in my eyes and a soft shade of lip gloss to give shine to my lips. I would just have to hope the picture took his mind off of my answers. When I finished the application I uploaded the picture to my computer and copied it to the last page. Then I took a deep breath, closed my eyes and hit the 'send' button. *Okay, Mom, I'm choosing my fate. Let's see if it chooses me back.*

For several days, I waited. I would check my online mailbox every time I passed it. What did I think would happen? *Get a grip on yourself, Allie. This was a crazy idea, after all. It just wasn't meant to be. Just get out of this apartment and meet people, for goodness sake.* I decided I just wasn't what they were looking for and stopped checking every day.

∽

It was November 20th. It was my birthday and I was sitting home alone, reading a book. Every day was lonely for me. Holidays were empty and boring, but for some reason my birthday was the saddest of all. My mother had always made a big deal out of my birthday. We would celebrate all day long, so I was feeling especially lonely and sad. I had been staring at the same opening in my book for about half an hour when my computer made the "ping" noise it makes when I receive an email. *Just some store advertisement letting me know of a sale,* I thought to myself. I glanced over, prepared to hit "delete." I dropped my book to the floor and it hit my foot. Despite the pain it caused, I just stood there, frozen. The email heading read "Happy Birthday from Old Harbor!" I sat down at my desk and stared for several minutes at those words, but then like a child who just realized they had a gift under the tree, I excitedly opened it.

13

Old Harbor - Sisters of Circumstance ~ P.J. Rhea

Hi, Allie, my name is William Hickman. I am a 30-year-old tour guide from Old Harbor, Alaska. Mostly, I take tourists fishing. I am a widower. I own my own home. I liked the answers on your application and can see by the picture, you are very pretty. I hope to get to know you better, if that's okay with you. My email address and phone number are on the application I have attached. If you are willing to give me a chance, please call or write. Hope you have a nice birthday.

Widower. I wondered what had happened to his wife. He offered no explanation, which seemed odd to me. How long had she been gone? I read his application, word for word, and he never mentioned it again. He did sound very nice and I wanted to know more about this widower from Alaska. I waited until the next day and replied to his email. We "talked" back and forth for several days by way of email messages, and finally one day he said he wanted to hear my voice if that was all right with me. I agreed on a time for him to call and instantly went into a panic. I have trouble holding a conversation with people I know face to face, so how could I possibly expect to have a conversation with someone I have never seen? Sure, we had a few nice sessions chatting on the computer, but there are no uncomfortable long periods of silence on computers.

I jumped when the phone finally rang. He had said he would call at eight o'clock on Sunday evening and the phone rang at exactly eight.

"Hello, this is Allie speaking. Is that you William?"

"You have a sweet voice," he said. "I am so glad to finally have the chance to hear you."

I couldn't believe it. We talked for over three hours that first time. It came so easy. This was not happening. He was too perfect. *He must be a serial killer, trying to get me to come to him. Maybe that's what happened to his wife; he cut her up into a million pieces and tossed her in the ocean for the sharks.* Well, no one could accuse me

14

of not having an imagination, and mine was going over the limit. Or, just maybe, it was for real; maybe he was really that nice. I could really finally be happy. Maybe the reason I had been lonely all these years was because my soul mate was in Alaska and I hadn't gone after him until now. If I'm dreaming all this, well, it's the best darn dream I have ever had and I do not want to wake up.

We talked every day after that for two weeks straight. One day he called and seemed different. He was quiet and I felt like he was trying to think of what he wanted to say. *Oh please don't be growing tired of me,* I thought.

"William, are you okay? Because you seem a little quiet today." I heard him take a deep breath as if finding his nerve.

"Oh, I'm sorry if I seem quiet. Everything is fine, just fine." He stumbled over his next few words but finally he found the courage he had been looking for. "Allie, would you consider coming to Old Harbor to be my wife?"

I took in a deep breath, shocked at what I had just heard. It was what this was all about, after all. It was the reason for the ad in the magazine. I sat stunned for a few seconds, swallowed hard and in almost a whisper, I answered him.

"Yes, I think I would like to do that."

We both laughed for a while to relieve the nervous tension. It was hard to start the conversation back up, but finally he said, "You just made me a very happy man, Miss Davis."

I couldn't believe this was happening to me. I must have still been in shock or something because I don't remember what he said for the next few minutes. Then I heard myself agree to when I would leave.

"I'll put your ticket in the mail first thing tomorrow. The other ladies are coming in two weeks. Will that give you enough time to get things wrapped up there?"

"Sure," I said, "two weeks will be fine."

Old Harbor - Sisters of Circumstance ~ P.J. Rhea

Did I really just agree to move my entire life in such a short period of time? Once I hung up the phone, sheer panic would be an understatement to describe what I was feeling. I had two weeks to make arrangements to leave my home of nineteen years and move my whole life to another state. Sure, no problem. I lay across my bed with my head spinning, thinking about all I had to do. I realized that tears had been falling down my face, but these were happy tears. I was so happy, I could pop. A big smile came across my face. *Well, Mom, what do you think? Your daughter is moving to Alaska and getting married!* I knew that if she were here right now she would be bouncing off the walls with excitement. Making plans for my wedding, helping me pack. She would be so happy for me. I could almost hear her saying, "No way could I live in that small town, though," and I laughed out loud thinking about the way she was. My only sadness was that she would not be with me on my special day. I knew when I left it would be like saying goodbye to her all over again. Even after nine years, I missed her so much.

It was amazing how little I had to pack after living here for almost nineteen years. It was a true testimony of how sad and empty my life here had been. Over half of my life was going to fit into a couple of suitcases and a box. The apartment had been furnished right down to the dishes and cookware in our kitchen when Mom rented it; and not much of anything had been replaced over the years. What little belonged to me, I left for the next person to use if they needed it. All I really wanted, other than my clothes, was my camera and my pictures, which I always kept in an album, and the one thing my dad had given me when I was little: a small jewelry box with a ballerina that danced when the top was opened. Inside the jewelry box was a heart-shaped locket my parents gave me when I was nine. There was a picture of Mom in one half and Dad in the other half. I thought to myself, *What a perfect gift they gave me without knowing it.* I would forever hold them both in my heart. "I may be leaving but I'm taking you both with me," I declared out loud to them while holding the locket close. I felt as if they were watching over me on this new journey, along with Grandma Ruth.

❧ Chapter Three ☙

Making Friends

I arrived at the airport extra early on February fourth. The day my life would change forever. My flight was scheduled to depart at 6 a.m. with a short layover in Chicago. Once I reached Anchorage, a small bush plane was supposed to take me on to Old Harbor. This would be a long day, but with time changes I should be in Old Harbor around 1:30 p.m. despite the ten and a half hours I would spend getting there. I sat by the window so I could get one last look at the lights of New York as we departed. I was an emotional basket case. I was both excited and scared to death about the future I had agreed to. I was sad to be leaving New York with the memories of my mom and the security of familiarity, but I was glad to be leaving a city where I had felt so small and alone for most of my life.

I could not wait to meet William Hickman. He sounded so nice when we talked on the phone. He had continued to call me every day, including this morning when he wished me a safe trip. He again told me how happy I had made him and how he could not wait to see me. He had also continued sending pictures and information about Old Harbor in emails. His emails were long and informative, full of details about the small town I was going to live in, but most of all he talked about the job he loved.

He was a guide for the many tourists who came there to hunt and fish. He had a boat to take people out fishing and sightseeing, an ATV, and a truck for going deeper into the woods with those who wanted to hunt. Apparently this area was home to bears and moose, along with a lot of other wildlife that people wanted to hunt. I had always loved being outdoors, but I hardly think spending time in the park or the zoo or walking to work on crowded sidewalks prepared me for what sounded like rugged territory. In his picture, he appeared to be nice looking. It was not a formal pose like mine. He was standing in the river, fishing. He had on a pair of those rubber waders people wore when fly fishing, and also a hat and sunglasses, so I couldn't really see his eyes. His hair was about chin length and appeared to be curly. He looked tall and slim as far as I could tell in the waders, but of course standing in water made it hard to judge his height. The one feature that did stand out was his smile. He had a wonderful smile. He looked very happy in the picture and I couldn't help but wonder who had taken it. Could it have been his wife who took this before she passed away? *Okay Allie,* I thought to myself. *Stop stressing about the dead wife. Don't let your need to over-analyze things ruin this chance for you.* Not knowing much about his appearance would have normally made me cautious, but I remembered his kind voice and his laugh when we talked. Our conversations were easy and relaxed, as if we had known each other a long time. He was funny and interesting, and I realized it didn't really matter anymore how he looked. I was looking for someone who would be good to me, someone who would love me and I could build a future with. Possibly someone I could have a family with, and I believed that is exactly what I found with William.

I was looking at his profile and picture when someone sat down in the seat beside me. I barely glanced her way and gave her one of those courtesy smiles, and then I went back to the paperwork on my lap.

"Oh hell, you've got to be kidding me!"

I looked at the woman who had joined me to see what caused her reaction. She smiled as if she had made a fantastic discovery and pointed at my papers. The words across the top read: *Old Harbor, Alaska.*

"So, I guess we're going to be sisters. You know, sisters of circumstance?" she said, and pointed at my papers.

I must have looked totally confused, so she pulled out a packet from her purse that had the same heading as mine. In a city the size of New York, could there really be another person who read the exact same article from the exact same magazine, filled out the application, and was chosen? I suddenly felt like I should run for it; get off the plane before it was too late. I stared into the eyes of this stranger, and she seemed giddy with her discovery. My first concern was that I had been the victim of some scam. I wasn't sure if she was part of the scam or another victim of the same one. If it were a scam and William really had been too good to be true, I knew I would never survive the heartbreak. *OK, Allie, stop already with the crazy thoughts.*

"My name is Roxy, I mean Rachel." She chuckled at her mistake. "I have got to get used to using my real name again. So, who are you?"

She was an attractive woman, and if I were guessing I would say from parents of two different races. Her skin was the color of the perfect tan and her eyes, which supported a lot of makeup, were wide and the color of dark honey. Her hair was shoulder length and fell in soft ringlets that showed highlights from being in the sun. Her vibrantly red dress was very tight and very short, clinging to every curve of her body and leaving very little to the imagination. My grandmother Ruth would have said her neckline was way too close to her hemline. I realized I had been staring at her for several moments, so I turned to look at the lights from my window. I felt panic, not sure what to say. I considered running off the plane but I couldn't move. I turned again to face her curious eyes.

"Damn girl, you got a name?" Several of our fellow passengers turned and looked at her with disapproval. "Oops, sorry, that's something else I've gotta work on. Been on the streets so long, I guess my language needs a little toning down. After all, if I'm gonna to be a wife and maybe even a mama someday, I need to learn to be more respectable!" She laughed as if she had told a funny joke. "Well, your name?" she asked again.

"Oh, I'm Allie Davis. Did you respond to the ad in the travel magazine, too?"

"Yeah, I figured it was my chance for a do-over. I'm thirty years old and not gettin' any younger."

To my surprise, Rachel proceeded to tell me all about her life. I assumed one reason for her burst of information was probably nerves. If she was as full of nervous excitement as I was, it was

Old Harbor - Sisters of Circumstance ~ P.J. Rhea

understandable. But I also got the feeling she desperately needed to tell me everything about her journey up until this point. There was such urgency in her words. I had never met anyone so open about their past. And I had never met anyone with such a colorful and complicated past.

Rachel continued to use what she called "street words," but would apologize every time she caught herself.

"I have just got to break that habit," she said.

As she talked, I realized my life had been wonderful compared to hers. It seemed her life was a tragedy from the minute she was born. She started life as a safe haven baby. Someone left her at a fire station when she was no more than a day old. There was no note from a parent saying they couldn't care for their child, but simply a tiny baby left in a box, naked except for an old blanket. All they knew for sure about her mom was that she was on drugs, because Rachel was born addicted to crack. She was in the hospital for several weeks and then released to child welfare.

"The nurses named me Rachel, and when you are a foundling your last name is the name of the county you are left in, so my last name was Franklin. I guess they figured I didn't need a middle name. My caseworker once told me I was lucky because I was born pretty healthy, all things considered. Funny thing is, I don't feel so lucky," she said in a whispered voice that seemed to trail off for just a minute.

She continued to tell her life story, explaining everything in great detail. I had to admit I was clinging to every word. Her story seemed to pull you in, as if listening to a book on tape. I felt as if we were alone on this plane and all other sounds were drowned out by her eager voice.

"I went from one foster home to another 'til I was a teen. Some of 'em were okay, but some were real bad. There always seemed to be at least one male in every foster home who wanted to touch me in a 'wrong way.'" She said this while making quotation marks with her fingers in the air. "I was so desperate for affection, for someone to love me, I took it as love at first, but I knew it didn't feel right. The worst was when I was around fifteen. I was put in the home

20

Old Harbor - Sisters of Circumstance ~ P.J. Rhea

of an older couple. The husband was obsessed with me and caught on fast to my need for a father figure. I realize now that he groomed me for months, so the night he came to my room to be with me I actually thought it was love. I enjoyed the way it made me feel."

She looked down and seemed ashamed to admit to that.

"I know now it wasn't love, just lust. He had no intention of leaving his wife for a kid. Then one night his wife walked in on us. Let's just say I left there pretty quickly that night. I should have told the police about the sorry bast...ah, man, but I guess I felt sorry for his wife. Up until that night she had been really nice to me. I was placed in other homes, but I finally couldn't take it anymore and ran away at sixteen. I went to New York City and lived on the streets at first. It was scary as hell, but I was free.

"I made myself one promise. I would stay away from drugs. The social worker and some of my foster parents had been more than glad to fill me in on my mom and her likely addictions. Most told me more than once what they expected of me. According to some of 'em, I was doomed from birth to be an addict living in an abandoned building somewhere by the time I was grown, and I should be grateful they bothered with me at all. I knew how I was born, and I would most likely be an addict if I ever started taking anything. I stayed away from drugs if for no other reason to prove 'em all wrong."

She had survived for a long time on the streets just asking for change from strangers. In the park it was easy to make them believe she had lost her money and just wanted something out of a vending machine while waiting on her mom.

"Finding a safe place to sleep was the hardest part. Shelters would notice how young I was and call the cops. I'd get placed back in a foster home, but after a few days of rest I'd run away again. I learned not to go to shelters alone after that. Sometimes I'd make friends with an older lady on the streets and she'd let me go to the shelter with her, like I was her daughter or sister or something. I found a few churches that left the doors unlocked all night and I'd find the darkest corner and get under the seat to sleep. Nobody ever found me. I'd lock myself in a bathroom some nights and sleep in the floor. Eating was a little easier."

21

Old Harbor - Sisters of Circumstance ~ P.J. Rhea

She said there were times she would see someone toss half a sandwich in the trash and walk away.

"I'd get to it fast before someone tossed something else on top of it. I always watched for somebody who looked clean. It just seemed less gross that way," she admitted. "I realized right away that if I could keep myself and my clothes fairly clean, people would believe my story. But as I got a little older, it got harder to use the excuse of waiting on a parent. I was approached many times about sex for money or food, but I managed not to go down that road until I was eighteen. Some of the more aggressive pimps started to really harass me. They noticed me on the streets long enough to know I was a runaway and a target. One day a man sat down beside me on the park bench. He was well dressed and polite, nothing like the men who had started asking me to be their 'girl'."

I had a feeling she was putting it in less offensive words for my sake.

"He had noticed," she continued, "I was different from the other girls who worked the area. I had made a choice not to do drugs, which believe me, made me a rare find. I tried to stay clean. I kept a little bag with me that had a bar of soap, shampoo, a toothbrush, toothpaste, and a hair brush. I had a backpack with two changes of clothes in it and I'd bum enough coins to wash 'em sometimes. A few times, if I noticed someone put clothes in the washer at the laundromat and leave to run an errand, I'd put my clothes in and try to dig 'em out before they got back. I could always find enough change for at least the dryer. Most of the women who worked the streets were looking to score their next fix. They'd do anything for enough money to make it through the night. Most of 'em were showing signs of their habit: bad teeth, sores all over, not keeping up their appearance at all. And their 'clients' weren't any better.

"The man told me he ran a business that provided companionship for visiting businessmen. They were often fond of younger women, but insisted on their dates being attractive and healthy. I knew what he meant: no drugs and no STD's. He could provide an apartment I'd share with a couple of his other employees and a salary big enough to provide me with what I needed to stay in working order. It was funny how careful he was when wording his offer. I was also told I could keep any gifts the client offered as gratitude for my attention while they were in my company. You know, like a tip," she explained, in case I wasn't sure what she was implying. "He never gave me his name. He gave me a business card with the name of an attorney on it...'If you need help, or need to contact me, call this man. My clients will be given a number to call, that is, if you are interested in the opportunity.' He looked straight ahead and waited for my answer. I took him up on it. What other options did I have?"

Rachel looked in my eyes as if checking to see if I understood why she would make such a choice. I gave her a slight smile to assure her, because I really did understand. She seemed relieved by my smile and continued.

"He asked me my name and I told him Rachel, but never offered a last name. 'From now on, you are Roxy,' was his reply, and he handed me a cell phone. For the first time since he sat down he looked me in the eyes for just a couple of seconds then he just got up and walked away. Two minutes after he walked away the cell phone rang and a woman told me the address of where I would be staying. When I got there the other women showed me my room and a closet that already had clothes in it for me. It wasn't so bad. I was a favorite among his clients and they gave me a lot of nice things."

She pointed to diamond stud earrings, and I had already noticed an expensive-looking watch.

"I made good money for a while, but soon got too old for his client base. Staying fit isn't enough in this line of work. You have to be young. By the time I was twenty-nine years old I found myself without a job or a home. I tried to waitress and work retail to survive, but with no education or references it's really hard to find work. I was about to get desperate enough to take a really bad path working for less desirable 'bosses' when I saw that ad. It was the chance I'd been looking for. For the first time in my adult life I let myself feel hopeful. I mean, this Kevin guy can't be all that bad, and it's better than dying on the streets, right?"

Old Harbor - Sisters of Circumstance ~ P.J. Rhea

I wasn't sure if she expected me to answer her. I guess anything sounded better than where she had been. She hated what she did to live, but she had dreams, just like I did. She had dreams of being someone's wife. She also dreamed of being a mom someday, and she would never leave her child the way her mom left her. I was mesmerized by her story. It read like a trashy novel. It was like one of those talk show stories that let people know just how lucky they are. Could it really be true? Were some people just born for tragedy to follow them their entire life? When she finished talking, she was quiet for the first time since she sat down, and her expression changed from descriptive story teller to embarrassed and sad. She looked at me, waiting for my response. Her eyes were wet with tears that desperately wanted to fall, but she was trying to hold them back. She also seemed to be holding her breath, and I felt as if she couldn't make a move until I did. I placed my hand over her hand and gently patted it without saying a word. What could I possible say?

After a few minutes, she looked at me with pleading eyes.

"Allie," she said, "I just had to tell someone. Someone needed to know…me, know the truth of how I got to this place in my life, you know?"

She put her head back down and placed her other hand on top of our two hands. I saw a tear hit her dress near our cupped hands. She didn't look up when she spoke again.

"Allie, please don't tell the others. This is my new start. I really want to be a new person. I am ready to put Roxy behind me and be Rachel again for the first time since I was a young girl. But I need someone to know my past, in case I need a friend. You should always be true to your friends."

Friend—the word made my heart leap. She was the first person who ever asked me to be her friend. I placed my other hand on the stack and waited for her to look up.

"Rachel, I would be glad to be your friend and your sister."

She hugged me and cried for just a minute. Then, as if all was right again, she wiped her face, blew her nose, and smiled a smile that was pure relief.

Old Harbor - Sisters of Circumstance ~ P.J. Rhea

"I knew I could tell you, Allie. The minute I saw those papers in your hands I just knew you would understand. I knew I could trust you."

She was right. I would keep her secret; after all, that's what friends do.

I filled her in on my life up to this point and why I made the decision to leave New York for something so unreal. It sounded straight out of a made-for-TV movie. My life sounded wonderful compared to hers. We both agreed it was fate that brought us together, because in New York we would have never met and would certainly never have been friends.

The rest of our flight, we talked about less serious things. No mention of painful memories or feeling alone. We were two giddy girls talking about the guys we were about to meet. Talking about what we would wear on that first date. I must admit I was relieved when she said she had brought more conservative clothes for Old Harbor.

"I just figured I would get one more wear out of my favorite dress," she laughed.

We talked about what we liked about the men we were matched with. How strange to feel like good friends with this unlikely stranger. I had to leave town to make a new friend. Maybe this was a sign that I had made a good choice.

We arrived in Old Harbor around 1:45 and it was a beautiful, sunny day, but I knew it would soon be dark outside. This time of year Alaska had short daylight hours. William had already prepared me for that in one of our many talks. Brother Bible was standing near the airport entrance with a sign reading "Brides." We approached him smiling and excited.

"Rachel and Allison, I presume?"

"Yes sir," we both answered together.

"How wonderful to finally meet you both," he continued.

Old Harbor - Sisters of Circumstance ~ P.J. Rhea

Just as the words came out of his mouth he noticed Rachel's "little" dress, and for a few seconds he just stopped talking and stared in disbelief. I wasn't sure whose face turned the brighter shade of red: his, mine, or Rachel's. It was nice to know Rachel wasn't so hardened by her past that she couldn't be embarrassed. It made me hopeful that she could be the wife and mother she dreamed of becoming. Brother Bible gathered his thoughts and cleared his throat about the same time Rachel pulled her coat together and tied the belt. He smiled in appreciation and continued his greeting.

"The other two ladies arrived this morning and are already settled in. We have a fifth lady who will join you later today. Believe it or not, she's from Kodiak, Alaska. Kodiak Island is the borough we're in. Kodiak is a town about forty miles away, and that's where our residents do their shopping, for the most part. Old Harbor is like the little community on the edge of town, I guess. She saw the ad and was the first to answer it. Because she was nearby, she's already met her match and they've been seeing a lot of each other."

Carl was beaming with pride over the success of at least one match. And you could tell he was hopeful for the rest of us.

"Please follow me."

As we stepped out of the airport I felt like Dorothy from the *Wizard of Oz* when she first steps out of the house. The airport was at the edge of this tiny town and beyond its gate it was like walking into a postcard. The mountains were majestic bald peaks capped with snow, and most had clouds that encircled them just below the tops as if God himself had placed a halo on them. I was not expecting so much green, however. Despite all the snow I could see that there were a lot of evergreen trees. The amount of land that stretched out before me was massive. It all seemed so rugged and unspoiled; unlike anything I had ever seen. The sky was a beautiful blue, but clouds seemed to be gathering for more snow. The town spread out before us seemed like the little towns you saw captured in the snow globes from the department store. Tiny buildings with smoke coming from chimneys and everything covered in a blanket of white. It was so perfect you felt wrapped up in it. Rachel appeared to be as amazed as I, because we both just stood there with our mouths hanging open.

Old Harbor - Sisters of Circumstance ~ P.J. Rhea

Brother Bible had to chuckle at our reaction and mumbled something about city girls under his breath.

"Are you ladies coming?"

He led us to a minivan parked in front of the airport. It was bright blue and had the name of the church on the side. Brother Bible explained to us that this area only had about thirty miles of road leading from the small airport to the end of Old Harbor.

"There is a ferry crossing to get you to Kodiak, but other than that the roads do not go anywhere inland, so you have to depend on seaplane or boat. Almost everyone has a small seaplane," he added. "Having a plane here is like having a car most other places. People like me who don't know how to fly depend on an occasional ride from a neighbor."

Brother Bible was a constant flow of information as he drove the short distance through the town. You could not help but like him instantly. He was friendly and talkative and smiled constantly. His smile was contagious. I noticed Rachel smiling as well. It was as if being around him gave you no choice but to smile. You couldn't help yourself.

"Brother Bible, when will we meet the grooms?" I had to ask. I was so eager to meet William Hickman. He seemed so wonderful in our communications; I needed proof he really existed.

"Not until tomorrow night, Allison," he explained.

"Just call me Allie. I go by Allie."

"Sure thing, Allie it is. And please call me Carl. My wife, Gwen, and I want to give you girls the chance to get to know each other tonight and tomorrow. There will be a meal at my house tonight, prepared by my lovely bride."

He smiled with pride. We somehow knew he wanted to do this so these men would have the chance to be as blissfully happy as he was. I was wishing for the same thing.

He continued, "Then she's taking all of you to town tomorrow to allow you to purchase any supplies or clothes you might

Old Harbor - Sisters of Circumstance ~ P.J. Rhea

need. Tomorrow evening there's a dinner planned at the church, where you will all be formally introduced and share a first meal with your future husbands. After that, we pretty much have something planned every day for three weeks. The fourth week, if everyone is still on board, you can have more time together, but just not arranged. Get to know each other on your own terms. Also, we'll have a night of joint marriage counseling, and I'll meet with each couple alone, as well. Then the wedding rehearsal will be on Friday evening, March 4, followed by a celebration meal. On Saturday, March 5, we'll have a day of weddings at different times throughout the day. Some of our couples may want a formal wedding, with the white dress and family in attendance. Others may just want a small ceremony with only the other couples in attendance. So in other words, if all goes as planned, you will both be married women in about four weeks, praise God!"

Under her breath Rachel said, "Amen," and I couldn't help but laugh.

When we arrived at the house Carl and Gwen shared, the other three ladies were already there. We were introduced to each other and did the normal polite things. "Nice to meet you," "What a pretty dress," "Can't believe we're all here doing this." But we were all sizing each other up. Wondering what story was behind the others' decision to be a bride to a stranger.

Gwen was very pretty, and very pregnant. I had to wonder if that had been another reason for his effort to find a wife for the single men of this little town. He wanted playmates for their child. She beamed with excitement over meeting us. She hugged each of us like we were family. She and Carl were a good match, it seemed; both smiling a constant, contagious smile.

She gave Rachel and me a chance to freshen up before dinner, and Rachel used the opportunity to change her clothes. She didn't want a repeat reaction from Gwen or the other ladies. I noticed the relief on Carl's face right away. Gwen led us into the dining room and told us dinner would be buffet style; we could help ourselves as soon as Carl said grace. We all bowed our heads, feeling a little awkward it seemed, except for Corinna Herring. She was obviously accustomed to this formality and reached out to take the hands of the

Old Harbor - Sisters of Circumstance ~ P.J. Rhea

lady to either side of her. Gwen was to her right and gladly took her hand, which caused a chain reaction when Gwen reached for Rachel's hand on her other side. Rachel took my hand and gave me a look that showed she was feeling out of place. The gesture made its way around the group and Carl led a prayer, thanking God for us, for our safe arrival, and for the food. I had to admit I was touched by his kind words. Gwen, who was just overwhelmed by our presence, had tears in her eyes when he finished, but managed to choke out a whispered, "Help yourselves, ladies."

Gwen had really gone all out for us. We ate in silence for a few minutes, and finally the one among us who actually lived in Alaska opened the conversation by complimenting Gwen on the delicious food. Her name was Trudy Crockett. Trudy was a large girl with a very pretty face. I couldn't help but wonder if people who are so overweight resent it when people tell them that. I mean, no one walks up to a thin person and says, "You have a pretty face," in such a way that they're waiting for them to finish the statement.

The other lady was Lynn Frost. She was tall and thin. She loved to talk and kept us entertained during our meal with her stories of all the things she wanted to do in life. I found it odd that she would come here. She was young and full of future plans. I couldn't understand what would have made her want to do this. Did she even realize what this was all about? That she would be getting married to the man she had been matched with? Trudy and Lynn seemed to become instant friends, just like Rachel and I had.

It seemed to leave Corinna with no one to talk to. Rachel and I noticed it at the same time and tried to make conversation with her. She was the most fragile looking girl I had ever seen, as if we could break her by touching her too hard. She was very quiet and unwilling to share much about herself at dinner. She seemed really shy and almost afraid, as if she wasn't very trusting of people. You just felt protective of her from the start. I knew we would be spending a lot of time together the next few days, so maybe we could get her to open up.

Once we finished our meal, Carl announced that he would clean up and Gwen would take us to where we would sleep. He also said Gwen had some icebreakers planned. Maybe I could find out more about these women who were, after all, supposed to be like sisters. Gwen told us to take our luggage from the entrance and follow her. She led us to the basement of their house, which had been converted into a kind of dorm. They had set up four cots and a twin bed for us. There were shelves made by placing planks across plastic crates about three high so we could use them for our clothes and toiletries. There was also a full-sized bathroom in the basement with a shower and a vanity that had two sinks and two mirrors. This will be fun, I thought. I felt like a kid, in a way. This was as close to going to camp as I had ever gotten, and I hoped we would have fun bonding as friends in this basement dorm.

There was also a circle of six chairs, and I instantly assumed they were for the icebreaker Carl spoke of. Gwen told us she would give us an hour to unpack and refresh ourselves and then she wanted us to get to know each other a little better. Trudy spoke up first and requested the twin bed. We could tell she was a little embarrassed to ask for it, but we all knew the cots were just too small for her large frame. No one had a problem with her taking the only bed. Lynn took the cot next to Trudy's bed and Rachel, Corinna, and I took the three cots on the other side of the room.

Once we were all settled and comfortable, Gwen asked us to sit in one of the chairs in the circle. She told us more about herself; the story of how she and Carl had met in college and fell in love. How they both loved God and wanted to help people. She shared with us that her baby was a boy and they planned to name him John, after their favorite Bible character. She told us she had suffered three miscarriages over the past eight years and this was the first one she had carried to term. She didn't seem at all bitter about the babies she had lost, but was thanking God over and over for the son he was going to bless them with. She was the church's secretary, but without pay. It was her job to keep up with the people in this small community who needed cards or visits. The little church tried to work as a welcoming committee if anyone new moved in. Gwen admitted that was not very often. She also kept the books and filed the taxes for the congregation. As a sideline she also helped many of the locals with filing their taxes. It not only gave her and Carl a little extra

Old Harbor - Sisters of Circumstance ~ P.J. Rhea

income at least for a couple of months out of the year, but was a way to reach out, to get know her neighbors a little better. She explained to us that in a town this small you really become one big family. Everyone looks out for each other, especially in the winter months when the snow can be crippling at times.

"People check on each other and share if one person is a little better prepared than another for the long winter."

That could have made me a little apprehensive if I had not been used to the New York winters. Gwen had a way of making things sound positive. She made us all feel very welcome and at ease. She said she felt we all needed to share our story of the journey that had led us to this place with each other. I could see the panic on Rachel's face as she searched her mind for a story that was nothing like the real one she had confided to me. Trudy was sitting to the right of Gwen, so she asked her to go first. I had to admit I wanted to know more about these women. We all seemed so different from each other, but there was one thing we had in common. We all had felt the need to mail off an application to try to meet and marry a man from Alaska.

Trudy lived in Kodiak, just a few miles away. She was the oldest of six children. She was thirty years old, just like Rachel, and the only one of her siblings who remained unmarried. She had always been very different from her siblings, and it wasn't until she was a teen that she found out the reason why. She was not the biological child of her parents. She was the child of a girl named Gail who got pregnant too young. The girl was not married and Trudy's father left town shortly after the pregnancy was discovered. Trudy's mother didn't want the responsibility of a baby. The Crocketts ran a little markct whcrc Gail worked and they befriended her. Gail asked the Crocketts if they would watch after Trudy for a while, until she could get on her feet. Gail had been in foster care until she turned eighteen and convinced the Crocketts she needed time to establish herself in a warmer place before coming back for the baby. The Crocketts were newly married and not really prepared for a baby, but agreed to help. She left Trudy with them and never returned. She mailed them a package a few months later with the baby's birth certificate and a notarized letter giving up all parental rights. I couldn't help but glance

31

at Rachel, to see her reaction to Trudy's rejection as a baby. She was deep in thought and her face looked so sad. I wasn't sure if it was sympathy for Trudy or for herself. Trudy went on to explain she made the discovery of her parentage accidently when searching for something in the attic of her parent's house.

"In the bottom of an old trunk I found the envelope my mother had sent them when I was a baby." Her face gave away the hurt she must have felt at that moment. "By the time they received the package, they had fallen in love with me and so they raised me as one of their own. I knew I was loved, but still I became so depressed when I found out my mother had never wanted me. When I felt sad I would eat; for comfort I suppose, trying to fill the emptiness in me. That's how I got this big. I ate because I needed to fill a void. The bigger I got, the unhappier I became; and the more unhappy I became, the more I would eat. Needless to say, there were no men asking me out. I was ready to accept my life and never fall in love, until I saw the ad. It sparked hope in me that I had never felt and I answered it within minutes of reading it. Samuel Carter responded within a few days after the deadline and he is wonderful!"

Tears were filling her eyes and her voice gave away the pure joy she felt while telling this part of her story. She looked at all of us as if making sure we heard her next statement.

"And he loves me just the way I am." She gasped at her own statement. "He loves me," she repeated, "and I love him! We like all the same things and he is funny and sweet!" She stopped for a minute and examined our faces to see how we were reacting to her enthusiasm. "He hasn't said a thing about my weight. He tells me all the time that I'm beautiful, and I believe him. I actually feel pretty."

She looked at us and then at Gwen with an expression of pure happiness as if her face might erupt from total bliss, but then she burst into sobs. Gwen hugged her and, one by one, we all went over to share words of comfort or encouragement. I could tell this was going to be a long and emotional night.

I went next with my introduction. I told them about my dad, who had loved me and my mother, but had a sickness called alcoholism that took him from us way too young. I explained about

Old Harbor - Sisters of Circumstance ~ P.J. Rhea

my wonderful mom, my best friend, who had been stolen from me by cancer. I told them of my poor skills at building friendships and at finding someone to share my life with, and that the ad sparked excitement, and maybe even a sense of adventure I knew my mom would appreciate. I told them about William Hickman, who had responded on my birthday, and how we had talked by email and phone every day since. How kind and gentle he seemed to be and how romantic his proposal had been. There were no tears for my story and it occurred to me how truly lucky I was. How loved I had been. I felt a little guilty for putting myself in a category with Rachel and Trudy. Rachel gave me a hug when I was done and the others just told me how happy they were I had found William. They all sounded very sincere and truly happy for me, but it made me even more curious about what brought the others to this place.

Lynn Frost went after me and it made me feel a little better. Her story was not one of hurt and tragedy, but more of curiosity. Her jobs had all been retail; mostly in small clothing stores. She was all about fashion. She was attractive but not really pretty, and could have been the poster child for blonde jokes. She was from California and said the word "like" often when explaining herself.

"I'm twenty-two years old and, like, I know I'm younger than the rest of you, but it's like this was meant to be."

She had been matched up with Luke Fowler, and the only thing she had to say about him was that their initials were the same so she would not have to change hers. That made her happy. We all smiled while she spoke, but we almost felt sorry for Luke.

"Three down and two to go," Gwen said with nervous effort to end Lynn's chatter. "Would you please share with us next, Rachel?" Gwen asked.

I knew Rachel was worried about what she could say that would not be a total lie, but also not the complete truth. Rachel looked at me with frantic eyes, as if she wanted me to help her or maybe to be sure I wouldn't betray her with my reaction to what she said. Her voice seemed almost robotic when she started.

Old Harbor - Sisters of Circumstance ~ P.J. Rhea

"My name is Rachel Franklin and I was an orphan. I was never adopted and was very unhappy at the orphanage, so as soon as I turned eighteen, I left and worked in customer service jobs for many years."

She looked at me when she said it and I had to cover my mouth to hide a wide smile. I actually thought it was a clever way to put it. She did have customers and she did provide them with a service.

"I could see my life was going nowhere" she continued, "and at age thirty I had no boyfriend to speak of, so when I saw the ad, I figured, why the hell not?" Everyone's eyes grew big, including Rachel's, as she realized what she had just said. "Oh Gwen, I'm so sorry! That just kind of slipped out."

Gwen and the other ladies looked a little shocked. Rachel looked embarrassed and I was about to pop; I had to fake a cough to cover the laugh that tried to escape. Rachel rushed through the rest of her story while the other ladies watched Gwen for her reaction.

"Anyway, here I am and I've been matched with Kevin Marshall. We've talked several times and he seems nice enough."

When Rachel finished she just sat there for several minutes looking at the floor. She did not want to see the possible looks of disgust on the faces of these ladies who were supposed to become her family. I could tell the others were offended by her crudeness, but I knew she was just trying to get it over with as quickly as possible. She took in a deep breath and looked up at me. I could see in her expression that she was relieved to have her turn over with. No one had words of congratulations for Rachel when she was finished. No one rushed over to give her a hug or a pat on the back. There were just a few awkward moments of quiet before Gwen spoke up again.

"All right Corinna dear, it's your turn. Tell us what brought you to this place," Gwen prompted.

We all turned to Corinna for her story. She was a beautiful girl, with long brown hair and the biggest brown eyes you would ever find. Her features were delicate and soft and she held herself with the control of a ballerina. Her figure was one we all would have liked to

Old Harbor - Sisters of Circumstance ~ P.J. Rhea

have. It was perfectly proportioned. She looked pale and scared to death to open her mouth, and tears had already filled her eyes. We looked at each other, wondering what was coming. Then after a few uneasy minutes she began.

"My name is Corinna Herring, and I'm twenty-three years old. I live...well, lived in Wilmington, North Carolina. I worked in a bookstore as a clerk."

Up until this point her voice was shaking and she looked like she wanted to bolt out of the room, but all at once there was a stern defensive tone and she spoke as if she wanted to be sure we would not judge too harshly.

"I was raised by my mama. My daddy left a few weeks after I was born, and my mama would tell me all the time about how evil men were. How they only wanted to use me and toss me aside. We went to church all the time and she would read to me from the Bible every night and we would pray. I was never allowed to watch a lot of television or go out with friends because Mama felt I would be tempted to do evil things. It wasn't so bad until I became an adult and I wanted some freedom to make my own choices, you know."

When explaining how she had been raised by her mother she looked out as if not really seeing us. But then her expression and her voice both softened and she looked at all of us as if she wanted us to approve of her need to make choices for herself. I could tell that approval was something she had never been given and desperately desired. As she continued to speak it was obvious that she was growing more nervous about what our reaction to her story might be.

"She'd get real mad at me every time I would talk about going out with friends. One weekend, I went to a club with the people I worked with. They were all on the dance floor so I was sitting in a corner booth by myself and feeling a little silly for even being there. I knew I was out of place and was about to leave and go home when two men sat down across from me and started talking. They bought me a drink, as a gesture of good will, they said." She let out a quick nervous laugh as if amused at her own naivety. "It made me a little nervous, but I admit I was enjoying the attention. After a few sips of my drink, I started feeling strange. I was dizzy and felt like I might

35

Old Harbor - Sisters of Circumstance ~ P.J. Rhea

pass out. They told me they would help me outside for some fresh air, that I was probably overcome by all the noise or something. That's the last thing I remember clearly."

Corinna put her head down as if she were afraid she couldn't tell us what happened next if she looked into our eyes. The tears were streaming down her cheeks as she continued to relate her story. We all held our breath for what we knew must have happened.

"When I came to, I was in a motel room, alone." She put her face in her hands to finish the sentence, I suppose out of embarrassment. "I was naked and there was blood between my legs and on the sheets. When I got home, Mama was so angry. I told her I fell asleep at a friend's house, but she knew I wasn't being honest. I had never lied to her and I wasn't good at it. She called me a whore!" It was the only statement she had made where she sounded angry. "My mama had no idea what had happened to me. She assumed since I had gone out without letting her know, and had stayed out all night, the logical conclusion was that I had met a man and willingly slept with him. I was hurt by her low opinion of me, almost as much as I was sick at the idea of what had just happened to me. All I wanted to do, all I needed to do, was take a hot shower. I wanted the water as hot as I could tolerate for as long as the hot water would last. To scrub my body to remove what had happened to it."

Again she stopped and it seemed as if she were going back to the memory of that event; that horrible frightening event that had changed her forever.

"I heard some noise when I was..." She struggled for the right word, but could not find it. "Asleep...but I have no idea how many men there were. I'm sure there were more than two, because I felt the weight of them on top of me and heard them encourage each other as they took turns on me."

Her voice trailed off with the words as if she couldn't believe them. For a few seconds she just stared out with tears so large you could measure the hurt running down her cheeks and landing on her folded hands in her lap. We all just sat and waited until she could continue.

Old Harbor - Sisters of Circumstance ~ P.J. Rhea

"I wanted to fight. To push them off of me, but I couldn't make my body move. I remember the pain, a burning ache down there, you know?"

She was humiliated, and her innocence prior to this tragedy was becoming more obvious as she told us her story. We all had tears on our cheeks by now. Rachel was sobbing, almost uncontrollably. She, more than any of the others, knew some of the pain Corinna had endured. The others seemed to resent Rachel's reaction, as if they felt she was trying to take the spotlight off Corinna and put it on herself. I knew better and my heart was breaking for them both. I felt so ashamed of the self-pity that led me here. I had been so blessed and never stopped to be happy for it. I also felt honored to be among these women, to be trusted with these inner secrets and stories. I was starting to feel as if we sisters of circumstance may be closer than family.

Once we were able to calm ourselves and Corinna felt ready, she continued.

"Mama made me stay on my knees and pray with her for two days, with almost no rest. When we finally stopped, my knees were bruised and I rushed to clean my soiled body. I scrubbed until my skin was raw!" She almost vomited the words out as proof that the memory sickened her still to this day. "I never told her the truth and did not report it to the police. I couldn't stand to look at myself in the mirror. Maybe I deserved it for deceiving Mama."

All of us at the same time practically screamed "No, you did not!" Even Gwen insisted, "No!" which seemed to make Corinna feel a little more at ease.

"After a few weeks passed, I started feeling sick and my period didn't come. I knew I couldn't tell Mama, so I planned to run away somewhere to have my baby in secret. I was looking at a travel magazine while working in the bookstore when I saw the ad. I figured God was giving me the help I prayed for. Jay Ellis answered my application just a few days after I sent it in. We had to talk by way of email at the bookstore. Mama never allowed a computer in our house and I knew she would be furious if he called me at home. He did call me once at work and he sounded so wonderful. It was during that call that Jay invited me to come to Old Harbor and be his bride. And, well, here I am."

She searched our eyes, trying to read our thoughts. We didn't know what to say. Gwen looked like she had been punched in the stomach. I knew she was thinking about Jay. He didn't know about the baby and that wasn't acceptable.

Gwen stood up and gave us all a quick, almost frantic, goodnight. She looked at Corinna with great sadness and fled from the room with such an urgent sense of escape that we were all certain this was not the end of the session for Corinna. She would have to tell Jay before this went further. Once Gwen was gone, the room fell silent for several minutes. Suddenly, Corinna fled to the bathroom. We all just stared at each other as we heard her being sick. I wasn't really sure if the sudden need to vomit was from the pregnancy, or from the fact that she had to tell and relive the most horrific time of her young life.

We all pretended to get busy preparing for sleep, feeling too awkward at first to speak. Rachel waited near the bathroom door, and as soon as Corinna stepped out Rachel embraced her and they both cried on each other for a while. It was a cleansing cry for them both. As they ended their embrace, we made our way to them and hugged them both, and the silence was broken. We all tried to say something positive to Corinna. I told her how brave she was for telling her story. Rachel assured her none of it was her fault, and Trudy told her she would be an awesome mother. Poor Lynn, who still seemed a little confused as to why Gwen left so quickly, just smiled and said congratulations; but again her comment broke the tension and made Corinna smile, so we were able to relax. We all got into bed and turned out the lights. It seemed easier to talk there in the dark of our makeshift dorm room. We talked most of the night, asking questions of each other, telling things we wanted to share, and even laughing at some of the experiences we shared. We laughed a lot at Lynn, even when she wasn't trying to be funny. My grandmother would have said that Lynn had plenty of book smarts, but not enough common sense to fill a spoon. We all shared a story of a time when we had gotten hurt or in an accident. Lynn told us of the time she fell down the stairs at her home while on the phone with her mom, but that it was okay because she didn't drop the phone. We all started to laugh and she was clueless as to what was funny.

We had only been asleep for a couple of hours when Gwen came to the door. We heard her go to Corinna and whisper to her, "Dear, I need you to dress and come upstairs. We have to talk."

Corinna quietly dressed, and after washing up and combing her hair she climbed the stairs to the main part of the house. When the door shut we all sat up, as if the beds were spring-loaded, and looked at each other. It was on all our faces. Would we see Corinna again? Were they sending her home because she hadn't been truthful with Jay? Maybe they had told Jay last night after realizing what she had kept from him and he told them to send her back home. In less than twenty-four hours we had formed a bond. And we were all worried for our new sister.

One by one we showered, dressed, and waited for our signal to join Carl and Gwen upstairs. It seemed like a long time, but it had only been a couple of hours. Finally, Gwen came downstairs. She was trying to act happy and cheerful, but her eyes showed the same worry we all shared.

"Will Corinna be coming to town with us?" Rachel asked.

"No dear, perhaps she'll join us later today." It was a question Gwen was asking herself. "Carl will bring her to town later if..." The word trailed off but she didn't finish her thought. She wasn't willing to give away too much information. We had breakfast and loaded into the blue church van. At one point we had to drive onto a ferry and cross the water to reach Kodiak. Old Harbor was truly a world of its own, separated from all others by either mountains or water. Kodiak wasn't a large city by any means, but it was much bigger than Old Harbor and had several stores on the main strip through town.

"You all have appointments at the beauty salon in Kodiak," Gwen said excitedly. "My cousin is the owner and she agreed to set aside the day to pamper you and make you even more beautiful than you already are before meeting your grooms tonight...hair, nails, makeup, whatever you want."

Old Harbor - Sisters of Circumstance ~ P.J. Rhea

We were all grateful and would have been very excited any other time, but all we could think about was Corinna. What would Jay do? If he rejected her, where would she go? The remainder of our trip was quiet as each of us feared the worst for our new friend. Gwen pulled up in front of her cousin's salon then turned toward us and chirped, "Here we are!" in an effort to build our excitement, but we knew she was as worried as we were.

It was small but very nicely decorated. Each station had sheer white curtains pulled back by thick gold cord dividing it from the next. It had a station toward the back for pedicures and manicures. There was even a room with a tanning bed if anyone had wanted to use it, but none of us wanted to risk a burn so close to our first meeting. We were all introduced to Gwen's cousin Elizabeth, who owned the salon, and her two employees, Marie and Sarah. They were very nice to us and tried hard to make us feel special. They had even prepared coffee, juice, and pastries for us as a special welcome gesture. We were all very grateful and tried to be enthusiastic, but all we could think about was Corinna and what she must be going through right now. We were all placed at different stations to begin our makeovers. I doubt there had ever been a beauty salon full of women so quiet, but we just couldn't help it. Corinna just had to stay…she just had to.

Old Harbor - Sisters of Circumstance ~ P.J. Rhea

❧ Chapter Four ❧

Jay Ellis

Carl called Jay and asked him to please come to the church office as soon as possible.

"Is everything all right, Brother Bible? I mean, we are coming to meet our brides tonight, right?"

"Yes, Jay," Carl stammered. "We just have a little business to finish before tonight. Can you come now, please?"

When he hung up the phone, Carl turned to Corinna.

"I know this will be very difficult for you, but you simply must tell Jay the story of what happened to you. If you are to marry, he has to know the truth."

Corinna was softly crying, her face wet with shame and fear. "I know you're right, Brother Carl. I should have been honest with him from the start. I should have told him about the baby."

Corinna said these things as if scolding herself in a frustrated voice. Then, looking up and meeting Carl Bible's worried gaze, she told him her biggest fear.

"He will not want to marry me, Brother Carl, not if he knows I'm pregnant with a child and I can't even tell him who the father is. I won't even know 'til the child is born what race it is. How can I expect a man to raise another man's child and know so little of what to expect that child to be like? I haven't even been to a doctor yet. There could be something wrong with the baby, or there could even be more than one."

Her eyes grew big at her own revelation, and she became frightened at the possibility. She had not allowed herself to think about all these things until now. The sudden reality made her almost hysterical.

Old Harbor - Sisters of Circumstance ~ P.J. Rhea

"Brother Carl, what will I do? Where could I go if Jay sends me away? I can't go home to my mother."

Carl tried to soothe Corinna. "Please, Corinna, don't underestimate Jay. He's a good man. He's been so excited about meeting you. I think you may be surprised by his understanding. When I was matching names for these men, you were the only one I considered for Jay. You both seem to be such gentle, godly souls. Jay will listen to the entire story and I promise you, he will not judge you harshly. But he does need to know."

Corinna nodded shamefully. "I know you're right, and I'll be completely honest with him. I should have been from the start, and I can only hope he will forgive me for not telling him, even if he asks me to leave."

There was a knock at the door. "Brother Carl, it's me, Jay Ellis. May I come in?"

Corinna looked at Carl with panic and fear in her large brown eyes as she grabbed his hand for some sense of security. Carl patted her shoulder gently and gave her a look that was meant to comfort her fear as he replied to Jay's question.

"Yes, Jay, please come in."

Jay walked in and instantly spotted Corinna. He knew her from her picture. A big smile came across his face and he started toward her, but stopped suddenly when he noticed the tears.

"Are you okay, Corinna? You haven't changed your mind have you? Oh, please give me a chance before you leave. I'm not such a bad guy and we've had some nice talks on the computer, haven't we?"

Jay was looking at her, then back at Carl, desperately searching for an answer.

"Please sit down, Jay. Corinna has to talk to you about something. You need to know a few details before we plan a marriage."

Old Harbor - Sisters of Circumstance ~ P.J. Rhea

Jay eased into the chair next to Corinna and took her hand in his. "I'm listening, dear Corinna," Jay said softly.

She took a deep breath and began. She told him everything, every detail she remembered. She wasn't able to look at him when she talked and the tears streamed down her cheeks the entire time. When she finished, she sat quietly for a while and slowly looked up to meet Jay's eyes. Brother Carl was satisfied that Jay knew what he needed to know, and got up from his chair and left the room. He closed the door gently and left them alone. It was up to them now and, like the rest of us, he would have to wait for the answer.

∿

We were trying to enjoy our day at the salon. They were certainly pampering us. We all had facials, had our nails done, and were given pedicures. All of us had our hair washed and dried.

Lynn and Trudy also had their hair trimmed and styled. Lynn was even having her makeup done. It was wonderful and we should have been enjoying every minute of it, but we were so worried about Corinna we just couldn't be happy. Was she on a plane? Going back to the mother who would make her feel shame for being raped, as if it had been her fault? Had Jay been cruel and spiteful in his rejection of her? Had he called her names the way Corinna's mother had, and possibly yelled at her for lying to him? Rachel and I kept looking at the clock, then at each other. Both of us were almost sick from the wait. Gwen filled her cousin in on the situation, in an effort to explain our mood. She didn't want her to think we were not grateful for this welcoming gesture.

The little bell above the door made a tinkling sound and we all looked to see who it was. "Corinna!" we all screamed in one voice. We darted toward her in different stages of progress. Rachel, who had been soaking her feet for her pedicure, almost fell trying to reach Corinna with wet feet. Trudy's hair was crazy from the blow dryer in mid-style. Lynn left the chair so quickly it smeared eyeliner across her cheek. I had been drying my nails and waddled across the floor with toes extended and fingers spread apart in an effort to keep the polish intact. Corinna was sobbing as we approached her, and we feared the worst. Had she come to tell us goodbye? As we surrounded her, she almost seemed to be laughing along with the sobs. There were tears completely wetting her face, but at the same time she had a big smile. Had she just lost her mind from the stress? We all held our breath waiting for her to speak. Finally, Rachel couldn't take it.

"Well?" she loudly inquired.

"He wants me to stay," Corinna finally blurted out.

We all exhaled together and relaxed for the first time that day.

"He is so kind and sweet and forgiving. He said what happened to me was terrible and if he could change it he would, but this baby will be a welcome blessing. He said as horrible as it is that this happened to me, it led me to him and God turned this tragedy into a miracle."

She held out her hand to show a ring with a small diamond. Her excitement and enthusiasm overflowed, and we all bounced around holding hands and squealing like a room full of preteens talking about the cute boy in class who asked our friend to be his girlfriend. I am sure it was a funny sight to see, but we couldn't help ourselves. We were as happy for Corinna as she was for herself.

"He got down on one knee and asked me to please let him be my husband and the father of my baby."

She started to cry again. That happy cry only a woman would understand. We were all blubbering. Even the ladies who worked at the salon were becoming emotional and teary-eyed. We all loved Jay Ellis. He had just made us some very happy sisters-in-law, whether he knew it or not. We were all so relieved it made us tired. It felt like we had been holding our breath since Gwen came in to get Corinna this morning, and now we could finally exhale.

We returned to our appropriate stations and continued the pampering. Corinna gladly joined us, and we enjoyed the rest of our time there. Next we had a nice lunch with lots of girl talk. We talked and laughed, making plans for the future we all hoped was awaiting us. Then we purchased new clothes for the evening. All of us had

Old Harbor - Sisters of Circumstance ~ P.J. Rhea

packed up our lives in a bit of a hurry, so buying a new outfit for meeting our groom had not really occurred to us until today. Lynn was in her element now. This was her expertise, so she helped each of us find something that would complement our figure and coloring. I had to give her credit. She might be a little—shall we say, flakey— but she knew clothes. We tried not to dwell on it, but as the day passed we were getting really anxious. It made me think of how it must feel to get ready for prom with your friends. The only one of us who had ever gone to a prom was Lynn. She agreed the feeling was similar. There was so much excitement in the air we could barely breathe. We loaded into the van and headed back to Old Harbor. Two of us had met our grooms. Three of us would meet ours in only a few more hours. I wanted to believe our stories would end as happily as it seemed Trudy and Corinna's would. At least we were hopeful after hearing about Jay and Samuel. Those two men were genuine and good, so maybe the other three men would be as well. I had developed strong feelings for William Hickman before actually meeting him. If he was anything like the man I had talked to for the last several weeks, I knew my story would also have a happy ending.

We were all excited while we helped each other get ready for our first official meeting. Once we were dressed for our dinner, Gwen had us climb into the van and she drove us to the church building. It was only about a block away, but we didn't want to risk getting our new selves messed up walking in the slush and snow. The church was a beautiful old building, its domed rooftop revealing its Russian architectural heritage. It was at the center of town, and behind it was a landscape so rugged and unspoiled it was as if two separate worlds lived beside each other. Having come from a city like New York, as large and modern as they come, Old Harbor was like going back in time to a world I never dreamed still existed. We were told that the basement of the building was used for many things. Family gatherings and town meetings were held there. The congregation that met there would often have meals together after worship on Sunday morning.

"It makes us feel like those of us who worship here are family," Carl explained.

Gwen had really outdone herself preparing for our first official meeting. They had transformed the fellowship hall in the church basement to a formal dining room. Six tables with white linen tablecloths were placed as far apart as possible for privacy. Gwen and Carl had a table placed for them as well, so as not to just stand around watching. Each table had a centerpiece, with a candle covered with a globe in the middle of the floral arrangement. The candles were lit, but the room was too bright for the full effect. There was no way to change that because the candles did not give off enough light on their own, and since the fellowship hall was in the basement of the church there were no windows. The lighting consisted of a long row of florescent tube lights in the middle of the ceiling. There was one switch and it gave only two options, on or off, but I still thought it was perfect. Gwen asked each of us to sit at a table and wait for our gentlemen to arrive. We were all so nervous we just sat quietly, watching each other and touching things on the table as if we were correcting the placement or something.

Carl stood up and cleared his throat. "Ladies, I would like to point out to you that the restrooms are located in the back, just behind the kitchen."

He look like the host of an airline telling the people on the flight where the exits were located in case of an emergency.

"Tonight's menu will consist of baked salmon, asparagus spears with a butter sauce, smashed potatoes and rolls, and for dessert a wonderful spice cake with a caramel glaze, prepared by my lovely wife."

Gwen couldn't keep quiet. "For Pete's sake, Carl, these ladies have waited long enough and the food's going to be cold. Please get on with it."

Carl laughed and gave away that he was torturing us on purpose. He was as excited as we were.

"Okay, you're right, dear. Sorry, ladies," he grinned, and bowed his apology. "I will introduce the gentlemen one at a time and they will take their seats with their brides-to-be."

He was almost giddy when he spoke, and I thought for a minute he was going to cry. I, on the other hand, felt like running out the door and finding William myself if Carl didn't get on with it.

Old Harbor - Sisters of Circumstance ~ P.J. Rhea

"If you remember, one of the questions asked on your application was your favorite flower. I have, shall we say, suggested strongly that it would be nice of them to present you with a floral gift. We'll see how they do. Since Trudy has already met her groom, I will begin with Samuel Carter."

Samuel walked through the door and—well—we all looked at each other with shock clearly on our faces as he made his way to Trudy with a big smile and a bouquet of yellow roses. We had assumed that since Trudy was so heavy, the man who chose her would also be on the plump side. But Samuel was her total opposite. He was very tall and—well—just plain skinny. It was almost funny to see the contrast, and at first we almost wondered if it was a joke on us. But when he reached their table and gave her the flowers, his face was alive with the love he felt for her. He gave her a hug and she beamed with pride.

"Welcome, Samuel. And now, would you please join us, Jay Ellis."

We were all anxious to see Jay and we all stood to see him enter the room. Even Trudy took her attention from Samuel for a few seconds to see Jay walk in. It was tempting to applaud when he came in, but we restrained ourselves, not wanting to embarrass Corinna. She stood by her chair, looking so proud. The look on her face was total serenity. Jay was a nice-looking man, not exceptional by any means, average size and build. He had short brown hair and pleasant features, but to this group of women who knew what he had done for our sister, he was a prince. He carried a circle of daisies accented by wildflowers and placed them on her head, like a crown. He said he wanted his angel to have her halo. Of course, the men would think that was corny or silly and I guess it was, but all of the females in the room were very impressed, which was obvious by the sounds heard from each table. We all sighed and smiled with such delight for her. He took her hand and kissed it before pulling her chair out for her. Oh, man, if someone boxed him up and marketed him, they would make millions. Could the other men even hope to compare to this fairy tale?

Old Harbor - Sisters of Circumstance ~ P.J. Rhea

I started to analyze it, because that's what I always do. I could never just accept things at face value and go with it, I had to analyze it and be sure it made sense. This time I concluded it would be unlikely that all five couples would be perfect matches. It just wasn't realistic. Who would be the one to stop the winning streak? I hoped it wouldn't be me. But I didn't want it to be any of us. I was bonding with these women. We were truly starting to feel like a family. Like the sisters we joked about.

Carl interrupted my thoughts. "Okay, now may I welcome Luke Fowler to our happy group?"

Luke walked in with a nice bouquet of red roses. He seemed uncomfortable with his bouquet, but we knew Lynn had not filled out all of the questions because she wasn't really sure what to put. We concluded that he wasn't really sure what she would like. They shook hands and Luke made his way over to pull her chair out for her, but she sat down before he could. Lynn seemed bored, and Luke looked preoccupied and more than a little uncomfortable. He was a nice looking man, but appeared much older than Lynn, maybe in his mid-thirties. I was thinking maybe this would be the bad luck couple. They both looked uncertain of their choice.

"Next we have William Hickman."

I heard Carl call his name and a jolt went through me, followed by sudden panic. My heart was pounding in my chest and I realized I was holding my breath. There he was in the doorway. My first thought was that he was a very good-looking man. He had wavy brown hair and beautiful brown eyes that were looking right at me. He was smiling, and as he got closer I noticed he had a deep dimple in one cheek. He wasn't a lot taller than me, maybe five-ten or so. I was glad because I always hated to look up the entire time I talked to someone. He looked slim but muscular. Not big and bulky like the guys in the fitness magazines or at the gym, but just healthy looking. He was tan from all the time outdoors fishing, I guessed. His smile was kind of crooked. It leaned to the same side as the dimple and it was enough to melt me. I could not have been happier with my choice. He had been kind and interesting in the conversations we had before my coming here, and now he was just knock-out gorgeous to

48

boot. I guess I was staring at him because when I noticed he was calling my name and handing me tulips, my favorite flower, the others were laughing.

"Oh, thank you so much. I'm so glad to finally meet you, William," I managed to say.

"I'm very happy to meet you too, Allie. Your picture doesn't do you justice."

"We had makeovers today," I replied.

Oh good grief Allie, how could you say something so stupid? I thought to myself. He grinned and pulled out my chair for me. I could hardly breathe, and I was so nervous you would think I never met a man before. Well, it was true, I had never met one this wonderful, of that I was certain. I noticed Rachel grinning at me and when our eyes met she gave me two thumbs up. I couldn't help but laugh. William smiled back at me, not really knowing what was so funny. I noticed he had also placed two roses aside on the table. I wondered what they were for. Were they for me?

"Thank you for the tulips," I said, "they're beautiful."

"You're welcome, Allie. I can't begin to tell you how happy I am that you're finally here."

Under the table, I pinched myself hard. *I have got to be dreaming,* I thought, *but what a wonderful dream it is.*

Carl cleared his throat to get our attention. I looked quickly in Rachel's direction. She took a deep breath, smoothed her dress and checked her hair. She was bracing herself.

"Welcome Kevin Marshall, our final groom."

When Kevin Marshall entered the room, there was nothing really wrong with him physically. He was attractive. He had dark hair and his eyes were almost black. He was tall and his arms seemed as big around as tree trunks. His smile showed his perfect white teeth. I should be happy for Rachel because he looked really nice. I could not explain it, but I had an uneasy feeling go through me. He made me uncomfortable from the second he entered the room.

Old Harbor - Sisters of Circumstance ~ P.J. Rhea

A quick glance around the room made me think I wasn't the only one getting a bad signal from this man. The other women in the room were not smiling. Rachel seemed to be trying to smile, but I could tell it was a polite smile and not one of happiness. What was it about this man I didn't like? After all, I had never met him, had never talked to him and knew nothing about him. But my gut was telling me to beware and I was concerned for my friend. I glanced at William and was surprised to see a look of disapproval on his face, too, as he watched the man approach his table.

Kevin gave Rachel a single, long, peach-colored rose. I knew from the many talks we had that her favorite flower was the sunflower, but I guess in all fairness, a sunflower may have been harder to find and would not have been the most romantic of choices. Rachel smiled at Kevin and took the flower. He helped her with her chair and sat down. There was just something about the way he looked at her. It bothered me and I could tell it bothered William. Maybe later I could ask him about it.

Once we were seated Carl said the blessing for the food and asked God to bless the couples and their future lives together, and then our meal was served. Two very sweet older ladies from the church were our waitresses. They were glad to see new faces in this tiny church. Of course, they knew the men, and one of them pinched William's cheek and told me what a sweetheart he was. He blushed and smiled at her.

"Aw, Mrs. Whitmore, you know the only reason I had to do this is because you were taken."

She giggled with delight at his comment and hugged his shoulders. I could tell these women of the church were very fond of him, which I took as a good sign that he was as wonderful as he seemed to be. He teased them every time they came to our table, and when we finished the meal he gave them each one of the roses and kissed their cheek before they left. I had a feeling I had better be good to him, or I would have to answer to them. He must be a good guy to have made such an impression on these two. They also praised Samuel, Luke, and Jay as they waited on their tables. It didn't escape my notice that they too seemed uneasy around Kevin Marshall. They

50

Old Harbor - Sisters of Circumstance ~ P.J. Rhea

would smile at Rachel as if they felt pity for her and seemed almost nervous when serving Kevin. Both ladies stood at each table and talked to us in an effort to get to know the new ladies in town. But they seemed to spend very little time at Rachel and Kevin's table.

During our meal we were given the opportunity for our first face-to-face conversation. William was not shy and made it so easy to talk while we ate. He told me more about Old Harbor. He also talked about the majestic mountains just behind his house and how he could teach me to fly fish, if I was willing. He told me he had supplied the salmon for our dinner tonight. He had caught it from a stream near his home in late summer and stored it in his freezer, a common habit of all the Old Harbor residents. "An eagle tried to steal it from me but I put up a good fight and won out over the bird in the end." He smiled and pointed to several large scars that decorated his fingers. Without thinking, I took his hand and kissed the fingers like a mom would kiss a child's boo-boo. He grinned at me, making his dimple go deep into his cheek, and I felt my face burn with embarrassment. It was one characteristic of my red hair and pale complexion that I truly hated. The least thing would turn my cheeks a bright red. It was proof that vampires did not exist because the way the blood was always rushing to my face, if they were real they would be lined up for me like I was an all-you-can-eat buffet.

William didn't make me suffer the awkwardness for long. He continued to explain that there are a lot of eagles in the area and they are known to attack fisherman in certain areas. They were especially aggressive around the harbor where the commercial fisherman brought in their catch. He laughed and remarked that it must look like a big buffet to the eagles. He also told me how he had seen bear and moose walk across his yard on several occasions.

My mom would have hated this wilderness I had moved to, I had no doubt of that, but I was falling in love with this beautiful land as quickly as I was falling for this man who brought me here. He asked me questions about New York, which I answered with far less enthusiasm than he had displayed when describing Old Harbor. He explained that he had not always lived here. He was born in Texas and that was where his mom, dad, and sister lived. I wondered if he had told them about me and about our getting married, but I didn't ask him and he didn't volunteer that information. Eventually all the couples started to walk around the room, introducing themselves to each other. Every woman in the room would shake hands with the other men, except when it came to Jay. All of us, including Gwen, felt we just had to give Jay a hug. We knew the other men were confused by it, and even Jay seemed unaware of his hero status among the other brides. Corinna beamed with pride. She knew exactly why we all felt so proud of her Jay.

I kept an eye on Rachel and Kevin as much as I could without neglecting William. I guess he noticed my preoccupation with them and finally leaned in to speak in my ear.

"There's something about the guy I just don't trust. He doesn't usually come around much and he has been known to step on a few toes around here."

I had to agree. "I know, he gives me a bad feeling. I'm worried for my friend."

He tried to reassure me, "I'm sure she'll be fine. After all, Carl matched them together from their applications, so as long as they were both honest with their information, they should get along just fine."

I had a sick feeling. I knew that Rachel had not been completely honest on her application. There were so many things she was trying to hide. I hoped she wasn't going to be with someone who would make her unhappy.

We were all enjoying our visit and getting to know each other. To help us out, Carl and Gwen had come up with a few games to play. We laughed until our sides were sore and it was the best time I had ever had in my life. Finally, about one a.m., Gwen said it was time to call it a night.

"My feet are swollen and the baby says we need some sleep, so say your goodnights; and ladies, if you will follow me back to the van I will escort you home."

We had been informed in the beginning that we would not be left alone the first week and we respected that. William kissed my

Old Harbor - Sisters of Circumstance ~ P.J. Rhea

cheek and told me he would see me tomorrow. I noticed Jay do the same to Corinna. Trudy and Samuel were more comfortable with each other and had an official goodnight kiss. As a matter of fact, Carl finally got behind them and coughed to let them know it had been long enough. We laughed at their sheepish grins when they parted ways. Lynn and Luke just said goodnight and went their separate ways. I could tell it wasn't working too well for them and hoped it would get better as the week went on. Kevin pulled Rachel to him and kissed her hard and quick on the mouth. It was almost a gesture of ownership he was presenting to the others. I could tell Rachel didn't like it. I couldn't wait to get back to the room and talk to her about this man who seemed to make everyone a little uncomfortable. We stood and watched as our future grooms left the room, most of us completely thrilled with the outcome. It was obvious that Lynn was less than thrilled. I didn't understand why because Luke seemed very nice.

Gwen followed us to the van. She was exhausted and I realized this was too much for her right now.

"Gwen, you have got to slow down and get some rest. What's planned for tomorrow? You're not going to overdo it again tomorrow, are you?"

"No dear," she sighed, "we're going ice fishing. We arranged to have three shanties placed on a lake near here. There will be two couples per shanty with the sixth couple being Carl and myself. Each group will share a picnic basket filled with goodies and a thermos of hot chocolate and one of coffee."

It wasn't exactly the romantic day we had imagined. Most of us had never done fishing of any kind and ice fishing sounded a little intimidating, but no one complained. After all, it could be fun, and as long as I was spending time with William I didn't care what we did. Gwen seemed concerned by the lack of excitement shown, so almost all of us started telling her what a good idea it was at the same time. No one wanted to hurt Gwen's feelings and we knew she had been the one to plan most of the dates.

53

Old Harbor - Sisters of Circumstance ~ P.J. Rhea

"Later in the evening you'll enjoy a movie night here at the church. We even have one of those big popcorn machines. It will be so much fun."

Poor Gwen yawned three times while telling me about the plans for the next day. She and Carl were working so hard to make this work for us.

"Well, I insist you let us help tomorrow. We can pack the picnic lunches and make the popcorn. And we can certainly clean up."

The other ladies were all nodding in agreement. We had to take some of the load off poor Gwen.

"Oh, thank you girls. That's so nice of you. Well, goodnight."

"Goodnight," we all called back.

I had a feeling she would be asleep before her head hit the pillow. I tried to talk to Rachel, but with everyone milling around the room I couldn't get a minute alone to talk. Next thing I knew, she was asleep. Maybe tomorrow we would get a chance to talk alone before we reunited with our grooms.

When I woke up, Rachel was already upstairs helping Gwen with breakfast. I showered and dressed so I could also help out. The day was full of activity. I tried to talk to Rachel about Kevin several times, but someone always walked up and I would change the subject.

It was wonderful to see William again. The fishing was a lot of fun. I'm sure all the laughter coming from the shanties scared the fish away, but no one seemed to mind. We all had a sack lunch that contained a sandwich, chips, and one of Gwen's delicious brownies.

Staying warm wasn't as difficult as I thought it would be. We had dressed as warmly as we could and the body heat from the four people in each shanty helped make it a little more comfortable. Gwen stayed home to rest, but Carl came along as our chaperone. He fished with William and me, and Rachel and Kevin were teamed up with Corinna and Jay. That left Luke and Lynn together with Trudy and Samuel. Lynn was the only one who complained. She was also the only one to scream when a fish was caught. We could hear her

Old Harbor - Sisters of Circumstance ~ P.J. Rhea

protest across the ice. "Poor Luke," I heard Carl say under his breath. William and I had to grin at each other over Carl's sympathy for Luke and not for Lynn when she whined about the cold.

When we finished fishing the van took us back to Carl and Gwen's house to freshen up before the movie. The closer we got to town the closer the ocean seemed. In the distance we could see a glacier, and William explained that the minerals from the melting glaciers as they scrape across the bottom is what gives the water that beautiful, almost milky turquoise color. How magnificent it was here. The mountains and the water took my breath away. I wished I had my camera with me. Everywhere I looked was a beautiful picture waiting to be captured.

Later, we gathered in the church basement once more, but it had been transformed for our movie. There were two couches and a loveseat that had been covered with sheets the night before. Trudy and Samuel took the loveseat and the rest of us sat on the two couches. Rachel, Kevin, Lynn, and Luke were on one couch; Corinna, Jay, William, and myself on the other. It was a snug fit, but we didn't mind. Gwen provided a table of pizza and snacks, including the popcorn popper she had promised. It was full of wonderful-smelling popcorn. The movie was "You've Got Mail," which happened to be one of my favorite movies. It was so nice to just sit and cuddle with each other. In this short time, I had grown very fond of William Hickman. I knew I was falling in love with him and I hoped he was feeling the same way. Of course, Trudy and Samuel were crazy about each other and Corinna and Jay were growing closer.

I wasn't sure about Rachel and Kevin. They both seemed to be acting the part. I think that was what concerned me. They seemed to be pretending. Their smiles seemed phony and their actions forced, and I knew Rachel had spent much of her adult life playing a role in order to please a man. I was worried about my new friend. Yes, she knew how to act interested and pretend affection in order to survive, but I hoped she wasn't doing that now. Lynn and Luke had us all concerned. Lynn wasn't happy and she wasn't even trying to pretend she was. Poor Luke seemed lost. I think he wanted it to work, but he just could not seem to do anything right. He also seemed very concerned with Kevin and Rachel. He watched them as much as I did

55

and I wondered if he knew something about Kevin that caused him concern.

The rest of the week went by so fast. We were kept active with one thing after another. Monday would be Valentine's Day and we were supposed to have dancing and a romantic dinner at The Lodge. It was the closest thing to a nice restaurant that Old Harbor had to offer. It would also give us a chance to meet a few of the townspeople. The Lodge offered this dinner and dance special every year on Valentine's Day. Our plans were suddenly changed when, bright and early Monday morning, Carl was banging on our door in a panic.

"It's time, Gwen says it's time, we're on our way to the hospital! I'm afraid you ladies are on your own today." Poor Carl was a wreck.

"We'll be fine, Carl, you take care of Gwen and we'll see you at the hospital later," we assured him.

We informed our grooms-to-be as soon as they arrived for the day's activities, and we all headed to the hospital in Luke's boat. We were too excited to wait for the ferry to take us across. We arrived about noon and walked the floor like a room full of expectant fathers. Carl would come out often to keep us updated. Finally at five p.m., exactly twelve hours from when her labor began, Carl came out holding a six-pound, eight-ounce John Carl Bible. He was a beautiful baby with a perfect little round head. After we all took turns holding him and wished Gwen a speedy recovery, we left the couple alone to enjoy their new son. We decided we would all go back to the Lodge for the Valentine special. It was actually very nice. The food was good and the fire that roared in the large fireplace made everyone feel warm and, dare I say, a little romantic. After a couple of dances we all agreed to go our separate ways. After all, what could be better than Valentine's Day for our first alone time?

William and I went for a walk. It was too cold to be outdoors for long, but the Bible's house was not far away. As we walked, William talked about this place he loved, how much he loved to fish and to share it with others. It made his job perfect for him. He asked me lots of questions about New York and Tennessee, and I answered

Old Harbor - Sisters of Circumstance ~ P.J. Rhea

as best I could. He talked some about his family in Texas and his childhood and how much he loved his family. We covered it all. All, that is, except his wife, who had died somehow and left him a widower. Not one word about her. I wanted to ask him, but I just couldn't work up the nerve. Maybe it was too painful to talk about it. Maybe he just wasn't ready to share that part of his life. I told him all about the painful death of my mother. How I had walked the streets weeping and people would comfort me, thinking I was upset over the towers and all those lives lost, not knowing that I had lost my best friend and my only remaining family on that same day. He was very sympathetic and tried to comfort me when I relayed my story, but never mentioned his loss. Why?

I did ask him about Kevin Marshall.

"I don't know why, but I just don't like the guy. He's usually a loner. He works from home making fly fishing lures, and he sells fishing bait. I've bought lures and bait from him a few times and have also taken tourists to his little shop before. He's friendly enough when conducting business, but not so friendly the rest of the time. He hasn't lived here all that long, just a little more than a year. When he arrived here, he had a female companion. Don't think they were married, but she lived with him. She would come into town some at first, but only with him, and then she stopped coming completely. One day he showed up at church for the first time, but without her. He told us she had run home to mama and had left in the night. None of us saw her leave, but we had no reason to think she hadn't. He just gives me an uneasy feeling."

A shiver ran down my spine. I had already felt alarmed by Kevin, but after what William said, I was very afraid for Rachel. What might she be getting herself into? I would have to find time to talk to her, to warn her. But warn her of what? Was I supposed to tell her that my gut feeling said that he was no good? Should I tell her he once had a girlfriend who left him, but no one saw her leave? Rachel was very street smart. Surely she would notice if there was a reason to worry. She had dealt with a lot of men, some I'm sure who were not the safest to be associated with, and had kept safe. I was probably just overreacting. Brother Bible would never have allowed someone to participate in his project if his character was in question, at least not

57

knowingly. *Okay Allie, once again you are over-analyzing.* It was the one thing about me that drove my mother crazy. Just let it go and let everyone be happy. That is all any of us wanted. We just wanted to be happy.

"Penny for your thoughts," William said, while looking a little worried.

"I was just thinking about how happy I am." I wasn't lying. I was so happy I wanted to shout it for all to hear.

"Allie, I am so glad you're happy. I want to spend the rest of my life making you happy and I want to thank you, Miss Davis, for becoming my Valentine." William smiled and bowed at his waist, making a gesture as if he were tipping his hat at me. "I haven't been this happy in a long time."

He kissed me—our first real kiss—and I realized that nothing else mattered. Finally, standing in the cold brisk air in front of Carl and Gwen's house, I felt the warm glow of my perfect summer starting to bloom.

Chapter Five

Weddings

The remaining time before the weddings was a little slower pace. The counseling sessions that had been planned had to be canceled, which concerned Carl, but he was too busy with his own situation to fit it in. Gwen came home on Wednesday with the new baby and we were all trying to make it easy on her. We did all the cooking and kept her home and the church building clean. That was usually a job she shared with Carl. She tried to help us all plan our weddings as best as she could. We tried to stick to the scheduled events the Bibles had arranged so lovingly for us. We knew they were both concerned that their absence might be a problem, but when they realized we were sticking to the plan they seemed very relieved and appreciative. Time went by quickly and here it was. The day before our weddings.

Most of us had no family to attend. Trudy, Samuel, and Jay had family who would attend all of our marriages. We knew Lynn had family, but when asked if any would attend the wedding she would just say no and change the subject. I had the feeling she had not said anything to her parents about what she was about to do. She had mentioned her parents in past conversations, but we never sensed closeness. We had all concluded that Lynn did things very spur-of-the-moment and with little thought of long term effects in order to gain the attention she missed from them. Our suspicions were proven on the Friday before we were to marry. Just minutes before the rehearsals were to start Lynn announced that she just couldn't do this. It simply wasn't for her. She assured Luke it wasn't anything to do with him.

"You are so nice and a great guy, really, but I'm young and just not ready to settle down. I don't know what made me think I was ready. I mean, I didn't want to go to college, so I thought this would be fun, but it's not as much fun as I thought it would be."

Old Harbor - Sisters of Circumstance ~ P.J. Rhea

We all just looked at each other, not really that shocked. She had never seemed ready for this, and I thought back to my concern that it was unlikely all five couples would be a perfect match. Maybe Rachel and Kevin would be okay, because somehow the odds seemed more in their favor now. I had to laugh at my own messed-up way of looking at the situation. We felt sorry for Luke, but to be honest, he looked relieved. He told her it was okay and wished her the best of luck in the future. He told her she should stay and see her friends' weddings, and he would gladly drive her to the airport afterward.

After the rehearsals were over, we had a celebration meal hosted by the parents of those who had family here. Some of the townspeople helped. Everyone in this tiny town was excited about these weddings. I couldn't believe it; in less than twenty-four hours I would be Mrs. William Hickman. All the brides were wearing dresses, but only Corinna and I were wearing actual wedding gowns. We found them at a second-hand store in Kodiak. They weren't expensive or fancy, but they were very pretty dresses and made us feel beautiful. I only planned on doing this once and I wanted the dress my mother had always talked about me wearing. We decided that William and I would go first, followed by Rachel and Kevin. Since the others had family in attendance, they would go later to allow more time to take pictures.

When we returned to our room for the last night we would spend together, the excitement was electric. We were all talking and jetting around the room like crazy, doing last minute preparations for the big day, packing up anything we wouldn't need for the next day, and saying goodbye to each other, knowing the next day would be too busy for long goodbyes. We told Lynn how much we would miss her, that we were glad to have met her and hoped she would stay in contact with us. She let out a sigh of relief.

"I was so afraid you would all hate me for backing out."

"No," I told her, "better now than after you married Luke. If it doesn't feel right, you shouldn't do it. My grandmother always told me to listen to my gut: 'If it's telling you not to do something, listen to it.' People who don't listen to their inner voice sometimes live to regret it."

Old Harbor - Sisters of Circumstance ~ P.J. Rhea

I looked at Rachel as I said the words, hoping it would make her consider her own inner warnings, if she had in fact felt them.

Gwen came in to visit us. She was apologizing because she would not be at the weddings. "I'm so sorry, but I just can't get the baby out among all those people when he's only three weeks old. It would just be too great a risk that he might catch something. Please tell me you understand!"

We assured her we did understand, and it was fine. "We love little John, we don't want him to get sick any more than you do. Really, it's okay," we all agreed.

"Well, I do have something for all of you...a blue garter, which will take care of something new and something blue. And Carl and I chose a piece of jewelry from things that belonged to our mothers for you to wear and then return—something borrowed and old. We picked necklaces for Allie and Rachel, and we have earrings for Trudy and Corinna. I hope you girls like them."

Poor Gwen was starting to tear up. She had grown to care for all of us and we loved her and Carl. As far as we were concerned, they were part of our family.

"We love them Gwen, they're perfect," we assured her.

"Thank you, Gwen, for everything," I said.

We all gathered together for hugs and tears about the time Carl came in to check on Gwen. He looked completely overwhelmed at what he saw.

"Oh, dear, is everything all right?"

I smiled at him and said, "Yes, we're all just very happy."

We had to laugh; could there be anything more emotional than a room full of brides the night before the wedding? Carl smiled, still not too sure what to make of it all, and retreated up the stairs. Gwen said her final goodnight and followed him. It wasn't long until the room grew quit and the sounds of sleeping filled the room. I knew this would be my last chance.

"Rachel, are you asleep?" I whispered.

"No, not yet," she said.

"I need to talk to you about something…"

I hoped she wouldn't be insulted by my concern or mad at me for implying something might be wrong with Kevin, but I knew this was my last chance before the weddings to share my concern with my new friend.

"You know what I was saying to Lynn earlier, about listening to your gut? What did you think about that? Are you feeling okay with your decision?"

"Allie, are you thinking of backing out? I thought you really cared for William!"

"Oh, I do! No, I wasn't talking about me. I was just wondering how you feel about Kevin. I mean, are you sure this is what you want to do, Rachel?"

She thought about this for a few seconds.

"I won't pretend I love him, and I know he doesn't love me, but this is my chance, Allie. I'm not a kid like Lynn, with lots of time to wait. If I want a family of my own, I got to give this a try. Kevin seems like an okay guy. Maybe with time, we can grow to care for each other."

I didn't exactly take comfort in what she said, but I could tell her mind was made up and I didn't say any more.

Earlier that day, the four of us had made an agreement to meet for lunch in one month to see how each of us was doing. It was Corinna who made the initial suggestion.

"We can meet every month for a girls' outing. After all, we're sisters, right?"

Everyone liked the idea. In one month, we would meet for lunch and see how things were with each other. Then I would at least be able to check on Rachel. In such a small town we were likely to see each other every few days, but it just made us feel more like family to have this standing date each month to meet as a group.

62

Old Harbor - Sisters of Circumstance ~ P.J. Rhea

"And we sisters have to stick together," I added. Just thinking of them as my sisters brought me such joy.

It had been a long day, and after our little talk both Rachel and I fell asleep very quickly. When the alarm went off, we bolted up at the same time.

"Well ladies, our big day has arrived."

And the madness began as we all rushed around getting ready to begin a new chapter in our lives.

It was Saturday, March fifth, my wedding day. The day was perfect despite the short daytime hours this time of the year in Alaska. The hours we did have were sunny, and the sky was blue. The weddings went off without a hitch—well—except that poor Samuel almost passed out. He was so nervous he started going to his knees at the altar. Carl had someone bring him a glass of water and made him just sit and calm down for a few minutes. He told Trudy he was so happy he had found her, he was overcome with emotion. I noticed Kevin made a face and laughed under his breath. He seemed to think men should not show emotion of any kind, and he certainly never did.

Jay and Trudy both came from large families, so the little church was packed with people. Even though I knew none of them were my family, it made it nicer. When the music started and I walked down the aisle in my long dress everyone stood up and smiled. I even noticed some of the ladies from the church had tears in their eyes, probably because they were so happy for William. I saw William waiting for me at the altar, and he looked so happy. People always say the bride is beautiful, but to me there was nothing more beautiful than the sight of William Hickman standing there waiting for me to become his wife. He wore a simple black suit with a white shirt and sky blue tie. His hair, which had been a little messy and curly before, had been trimmed just a little and he had put something in it to make it lay in place. It almost reminded me of a little boy who had tried to fix his own hair for the first time. His smile was wide and the dimple on his cheek was so deep you could get lost in it. I looked into his eyes and knew this was the right thing to do. All doubt was gone and I floated up to him and placed my hand in his. *Oh, mama I wish you were here. If you could have been here, it would be so*

63

perfect. I couldn't help but hope that somehow she knew how happy I was at this moment.

For those brief moments, as Carl Bible spoke to us about love and commitment and William and I repeated our vows to each other, it was as if we were the only people in the room. But suddenly reality hit me when I heard him say, "You may kiss your bride," and William's lips again met mine with tender acceptance.

"I now present to you Mr. and Mrs. William Hickman."

As we walked down the aisle as man and wife I imagined my mother, my father, and my grandmother Ruth sitting in one of the pews smiling at me. I knew they were not really there physically but I believe with all my heart—they were there.

Chapter Six

Ghosts

It was really late when we finally arrived at William's house. It would take time for me to feel like it was my house, too.

"I can't believe this is the first time I'm seeing your house. I don't know why I didn't get the tour during these past two weeks," I teased.

"Well, Mrs. Hickman, let me give you the royal tour."

He picked me up and carried me in over the threshold. I couldn't help but blush and he laughed at me as he put me down just inside the first room of his house.

"This is our living room, kitchen, and dining room, all conveniently located in the same area. There's a bedroom down the hall to your right and a bathroom to your left. Feel free to look around and become familiar with the surroundings. Try not to get lost when venturing around without a guide."

William laughed and gave me a gentle hug and a long kiss. He was being way too modest. He had a beautiful home. It was actually a log cabin and it was perfect. The living room area had a large stone fireplace with an overstuffed leather couch and chair. There was an antique rocking chair near the fireplace as well. In front of the fireplace lay a rug that, to my shock, was the hide of a real bear—minus the head, thank goodness. The ceiling was very high and made the room seem large. The kitchen area was small and practical. The dining area was a sort of thick, lumberjack picnic table, with benches on each side and a chair at each end. The only other door leading outside led to an enclosed porch just off the kitchen. That was where the washer and dryer were kept, and it also served as a mud room for boots and coats. The front of the house had a porch the

Old Harbor - Sisters of Circumstance ~ P.J. Rhea

length of the cabin, with two large rockers on one end and a swing at the other end.

The house had a woman's touch, despite the rustic decor. I could only assume his late wife had decorated it. Little touches, like lace curtains and doilies under flower pots, just didn't seem like something William would have chosen. I made my way down the hall to check out the other rooms. The bathroom was like something from a magazine. There was one of those oversized tubs with the claw feet. I couldn't wait to soak in it. The bedroom was also wonderful. The bed looked like it had been carved from a massive tree and formed a canopy, where long decorative blankets draped loosely over the top and hung down at each bed post. They looked like something made by the natives of this area. So many earth-tone colors, it was very impressive. The down comforter was so thick it made the bed look almost too high to climb into. There was also a fireplace in the bedroom, and the flames from the fire made the room warm and inviting. William walked up behind me and placed his hands on my shoulders. I had noticed a door at the end of the hall.

"Does that door lead outside?" I asked.

He suddenly tensed up and turned away. "No, that's just a room for storage. I always keep it closed. I don't bother to heat it, so please just keep the door closed."

It almost sounded like an order. I think he realized he had been a little defensive.

"I need to check a few things, so I'll give you some privacy and you can get settled in. I put your suitcases there in the corner. There's a walk-in closet beside them. You can have all of one side and probably half of the other."

He put his hands up to his cheeks and pretended to be excited at all that closet space. He obviously found humor in the importance placed by women on their closet needs, but I admit I was thrilled to have that much space.

"I also cleared the left side of the dresser for you. If you need more space, let me know."

66

Old Harbor - Sisters of Circumstance ~ P.J. Rhea

"Thank you, William. I'm sure that's plenty."

"Oh, and the towels are under the sink in the bathroom, if you need one."

He must have noticed my enthusiasm over the old-fashioned tub. He left the house to do some things outside. When we pulled up I had noticed a building that looked like a barn down a long path to the side of the house. Perhaps he was tending to some animals. He hadn't mentioned them if he had them, but he hadn't really said much at all about his home or what he had. He had told me he had a little cabin, but this was such a beautiful place. I was impressed and thrilled that I would be living here. This was a far cry from the tiny apartment in New York that had been home for so long.

I put my things away quickly and retreated to the bathroom. I needed a little time to myself to prepare for our first night together, and I thought a warm bath would relax me. There was a bottle of scented bath oil under the sink, which was kind of hidden by the towels. It was in a decorative bottle something like a small-scale version of the clay pots made by the natives and sold in the shops in Kodiak. The stopper was a cork and the label looked homemade. I suspected that someone made these oils in their home or something. It read "MARY." I wondered if this was his late wife. He had never mentioned her, so I was unsure of her name. The scent was wonderful, like nothing I had ever smelled before, so I put a little in my bath water. I soaked for a while and soon heard him come back in the house.

Well Allie, this is your wedding night, so guess it's time to get out of this tub and into that little white nightie you purchased for the occasion; time to get on with your wifely duties, I laughed to myself. William had kissed me several times in the past two weeks, and let me just say, the man knows how to kiss. We had not had a lot of time alone, but when we were, he had been a perfect gentleman. I had to admit, I was ready for this night. He was an attractive and sexy man and he was my husband now, so let the honeymoon begin.

When I walked from the bathroom into the bedroom, he was already in the big bed waiting for me. His eyes widened when he saw the little silky gown.

Old Harbor - Sisters of Circumstance ~ P.J. Rhea

"You look so beautiful, Allie, you're breathtaking!"

I felt beautiful tonight. I had worn my hair up or pulled back every time he had seen me, but it was down tonight and the long locks shimmered like gold in the glow of the fire. My strawberry blonde hair was my most attractive feature, I thought. William pulled back the cover on my side of the bed in a gesture to invite me in and I gladly climbed in next to him. He just looked at me for a moment, as if he were soaking me in. He gently stroked my hair away from my face and neck and smiled. I reached up and touched his face and he kissed me softly. His face was near my neck and he inhaled, as if to take in my fragrance.

For just a second, he seemed to freeze, as if something had stopped him. Suddenly his kisses became harder and almost frantic. His lovemaking was still wonderful, but it was more intense than I had expected it to be and it had a sense of urgency. Was this because it had been a long while, I wondered? Each time I looked at his face, his eyes were closed tightly and his face almost seemed sad. Suddenly, he was finished and he buried his face again in my neck. I could feel his breath, warm and quick. He was out of breath from pleasure, I assumed. I was surprised by his urgency, but still satisfied. I kissed his head and held on to him in a loving embrace, thinking how wonderful this was, how happy I would be as his wife.

Then he whispered the words in my ear that brought my world tumbling down. My heart felt pain, as if a knife had cut through it.

"I love you, Mary!"

The second the words left his lips, he realized what he had done. My body released his and I slowly dropped my arms to my sides. He looked at me with horrified shock at what he had said to me.

"Allie, I'm so sorry! I'm so sorr…"

He started to repeat it and just got up, totally dazed. He sat at the side of the bed for a moment, then dressed and left the room. I heard the front door open and close quietly. I lay there in this magnificent bed, having just made love to my new husband for the first time, feeling more alone than I had ever felt in New York. I wasn't sure what to do. Should I go after him, or just wait to see when or if he would come back?

It was around four in the morning and I had waited in that big bed for a long while. I heard his truck engine start and drive away. He wasn't ready to face me, so I would get up and gather my things. I could get a flight out today if I could if I could find someone to take me to the airport. I was packing, when I started crying. I had tried hard not to, but the overwhelming sadness on top of the exhaustion were just too much to bear. I cried so hard, my whole body shook.

"It just isn't fair," I shouted. "This was my chance to finally be happy! I was happy!"

There was no one to hear my cries, but I needed to yell at something. I was angry and hurt that my happiness had been pulled out of my arms so suddenly and without warning. The tears were flowing so heavily down my cheeks that the front of my new white gown was now wet and clinging to me like a sad hug. Once I had cried all I needed to, I sat there staring at my things, half of which were back in my suitcase, and thought, *No! I promised I would give this at least a year and I'm not leaving. William is worth it. There is a ghost in this house and I'm going to fight her for him. She had her time and now it's my turn.*

I put the suitcase in the closet and went to the bathroom to clean myself up. After getting dressed, I poured the oil down the toilet and flushed it away. I wrapped the bottle in an old newspaper I found and was prepared to put it in the storage room. I didn't feel I should throw the bottle away. I wasn't sure how he might react to that. I opened the door at the end of the hall. It was very cold in there and completely dark. I felt for the light switch.

When I flipped the light on, I couldn't believe my eyes. I was prepared to see boxes stacked on top of each other and maybe some old furniture in need of repair. I stood in the cold room and saw more unanswered questions than I already had. In the small bedroom was a baby crib and changing table. There was a dresser, painted to match the crib, and the room was decorated in blue, with little boats everywhere. There were boats on the border around the top of the walls, and in pictures on the wall. Everything was covered in dust and

Old Harbor - Sisters of Circumstance ~ P.J. Rhea

it was obvious no one had been in this room for a long while, but everything was neatly preserved, I'm sure just as Mary had left it. Not one item seemed out of place or appeared to have been moved from where she had carefully placed it. On the dresser were two pictures: one was William and Mary working together on this room. He had his hand on her very pregnant belly as they looked at each other with big smiles on their faces. They both seemed so happy. The other was a framed picture of an ultrasound with the words "It's a Boy" across the bottom of the frame. In the rocking chair in the corner was a homemade quilt with a boat in each square. I wondered if Mary had made it for her baby.

What had happened to Mary and where was the baby? I just couldn't ask William and I didn't want him to know I had looked in this room. I closed the door, leaving everything untouched and placed the empty oil bottle back under the sink behind the towels. Gwen might know. I would go back to the house I had moved out of yesterday and ask Gwen what happened to Mary and the baby. I needed to know if I was going to win out over the ghost in this sad house. Like my mom would always say, "Allie, sometimes you have to fight for what you want. Sometimes destiny depends on how badly to want it. If you don't fight for it no one else will."

It was still very early in the morning when I knocked on the door of Carl and Gwen's house. William's cabin was at the far edge of town and off the path, but in this small town it was still not a long walk to where the Bibles lived. I knocked softly, not wanting to wake the baby, and when Gwen opened the door her expression admitted that she was very surprised to see me.

"Allie, what are you doing here? You're supposed to be on your honeymoon. Oh dear, what's wrong?"

"Gwen, did you know William's wife?" I blurted out.

Suddenly she understood, and the saddest look came across her face. Her voice became almost a whisper and I could tell this was a conversation she would rather not have.

"Come in Allie, I'll make us some coffee."

Old Harbor - Sisters of Circumstance ~ P.J. Rhea

I held baby John while Gwen made us both a cup of coffee and placed a plate of muffins she had made for their breakfast on the table. Carl was next door conducting worship at the little church, which gave us the privacy I had hoped for. She took John and laid him in his bassinet.

"You're so lucky, Gwen. He's such a beautiful little boy."

She smiled down at him in complete agreement and took her seat across from me. I could see she was trying to pick her words before she started. There was such sadness in her face, and I wondered if I really wanted to know the truth. I concluded that if I was to make it work with William, I had to know what I was up against. I took a sip of coffee in an effort to brace myself.

"Please, Gwen, can you tell me about her?"

She took a deep breath and began, "Mary was my dear friend, and I miss her very much."

For a few seconds I thought she might start to cry. Her eyes were wet with tears near the edge of falling and her voice was low and uncertain, but she took a deep, cleansing breath in an effort to pull herself together. I could tell she was determined to tell me what I needed to hear.

"William and Mary came to us from Texas. They grew up together. Their families knew each other and they were great friends first. As they reached adulthood, they realized they felt more than friendship for each other, and of course both families were thrilled. They came to Old Harbor for their honeymoon, if you can believe that."

I let out a breathy laugh, as if to agree with the unusual choice.

She continued, "Carl and I had only moved here a few months prior to that and were trying to establish a relationship with this little church that had hired him. We were also newlyweds, having only been married for a little over a year, so we had a lot in common. They picked this place for the fishing they both loved to do. They were staying in The Lodge in one of the little cabin rooms. Mary fell in love with this town. William had been working in an office job and hated it, so Mary suggested they should move here. She told William it was perfect for them, and she was right. Their parents were not at all happy about the move, but could not argue the fact that they thrived here. William worked as a fishing guide in the beginning, and later added hunting to his talents. Mary was teaching at our tiny school and loving it. She could devote so much one-on-one time with each student because of the small number of children in this area, and the kids adored her. William and Mary would come over to our house often to visit, and we would go to their cabin. Carl even helped William build it.

"When Mary realized she was expecting a child, it was like the gold at the end of the rainbow. Could any two people have a more perfect life? Carl and I were also very happy, but envied the closeness they seemed to share. They were two halves that made a whole. It was as if one could not exist without the other. They stayed busy preparing for William Anthony Hickman Jr. Mary insisted on the name, saying it belonged to a perfect husband so of course, it made sense to name her son the same thing.

"She was about three weeks from delivery when William went on an overnight hunting trip with some tourists. They always paid well when it was overnight and he was already building a savings account for his son, so any extra money was welcomed. While he was gone, it started to snow. It was one of those storms that comes quickly and takes you by surprise. In this area, that often means no phone service for several hours or even days. The only way to call out was by two-way radio. Mary had asked William to move their two-way from the house to the barn because it was noisy and kept her awake with its sounds of static. We assume she started having pain and began bleeding. She tried to make her way to the barn to call for help, and we know that because of the trail of blood in the snow. The doctors determined that she had placental abruption, where the placenta tears away from the uterus, usually in the last weeks of a pregnancy. If she could have received help right away, they probably could have saved her and the baby, but she never made it to the barn. When William returned the next day, he found her. Oh Allie, he was so pitiful."

Old Harbor - Sisters of Circumstance ~ P.J. Rhea

Gwen was starting to tear up by now, but tried to keep it together enough to finish her story. I, on the other hand, had tears streaming down my face and could hardly take a breath from the sorrow welling up in me from the very pit of my stomach. Gwen took a ragged breath and continued, while trying not to look at me for fear my crying would cause her to lose control of her own emotions.

"We all thought he would lose his mind with grief and the guilt he felt for leaving her alone. We tried to comfort him, but he would not be comforted. His parents begged him to come back to Texas, but he wouldn't even talk about it. They came to see him several times, but he was so angry and bitter, he wouldn't even visit with them. Mary's parents were furious that he wouldn't return her to Texas to bury her. He insisted she belonged here with him, so he buried her in the little flower garden she had made on their property. They blamed him for taking her away from them and they have never forgiven him. That was six years ago and he only started to be around other people, aside from work, in the last two years. The ladies of the church have all taken him under their wing, which I am sure you noticed that first night."

We both smiled at the memory.

"You can't imagine how happy and relieved Carl and I were when William came to the first meeting about finding a bride. It meant he was finally trying to move on with his life. Allie, I know this is a lot to take in all at once, and I assume something happened last night to make you come to me this morning. I hope you'll give him a chance. I've watched him these last few weeks and I know he cares for you. He would never have married you if he didn't have feelings for you. He isn't that kind of man. Please don't leave, Allie."

I was so deep into her telling of his story, that I didn't realize I had been clutching my coat for the last several minutes. The collar was damp from my tears. *Oh William, how could anyone have gone through something so horrible and remained such a wonderful, caring man?* I felt numb and my heart ached for him, so much so I was afraid I would burst into tears the minute I saw him again. I would have to get myself under control. I didn't want him to think I was staying out of pity or obligation. I truly loved him and I wanted

73

more than anything for him to love me even half as much as he had loved his Mary. Gwen brought me out of my thoughts.

"Are you going to stay Allie? Please say you'll give him a chance."

"Yes, Gwen, I'm going to stay, and I'm going to be a good wife to him. Thank you so much for telling me what happened. It will make it so much easier to understand him."

I hugged her tightly and left for home. Not just William's house, but my home. I would stay there unless he asked me to leave, and I would be patient and loving to this man who deserved so much to be happy again. I prayed he would find that happiness with me.

∽ Chapter Seven ∽

Meeting Mama

It was getting late when William finally came home. When he walked in, he seemed shocked to see me sitting there. I waited to see what he would say. I was trying to control the urge to run up and hug him and tell him how sorry I was about Mary and the baby and that I just wanted to make things right again for him. *Oh, William, please let me help you,* was what I wanted to say. I had been drinking coffee, and I was gripping my cup so tightly I was afraid it might burst into pieces from the pressure. He just stood there and looked at me for several minutes, as if trying to believe what he was seeing.

"You're still here? I thought you would have taken the first plane back to New York after what I did. Well, after what I said, at least."

"Is that what you wanted me to do, William?"

"No. God, no! Allie, I'm so glad you stayed…just surprised, I guess. I'm so sorry Allie, about what I said. I want you to understand what happened."

I didn't tell him that I understood very well why he said it. He was still grieving over the tragic loss of his first true love and their child. And like an idiot, I had put on her fragrance and lay half-naked next to him in their bed in a dimly lit room, and made him think of her. It was my fault and I wanted to tell him that, tell him I knew the whole story, but I just waited to see what he would say.

"Allie, my first wife died here…at this house…several years ago. She was pregnant with our child and they both died."

He seemed to be struggling with the words and stopped for a minute to gather his thoughts, and then he swallowed hard and continued.

75

Old Harbor - Sisters of Circumstance ~ P.J. Rhea

"I really miss her and I haven't been with anyone since she left. Since she died, I mean," he regretfully corrected himself. "I guess it was stupid of me to bring you here our first night together. I should have taken you somewhere new to both of us and I'm sorry for my mistake. When you came into the bedroom, Allie, you were so beautiful and I had no thoughts of her, believe me. But when I took you in my arms it was as if her memory flooded back and I could actually smell her. At that moment she wasn't gone. It was as if she had come back to me or something. I can't explain it Allie, but it was Mary in my bed with me and it was as if it had all just been a long, horrible dream and she had never died."

I didn't tell him it was because I put her bath oil all over me. I was glad he hadn't made the connection. How could I have been so stupid?

"I know I hurt you, Allie, and I promise I'll make it up to you. Please say you'll forgive me and you'll give me a chance to prove myself. Prove that I care for you very much. I think this can work if you'll give me time."

"Of course I forgive you, William. I'm so sorry you had such sorrow in your past, and I understand how last night brought back memories that were overwhelming. I want this to work too, William. I came here to build a life with you."

He seemed relieved, but he thought for several minutes before commenting on what I had said.

"I don't ever want to hurt you like that again, so I think the smart thing would be to not make love to you again, until I know in my heart it is you I love and not a memory. Can you give me more time to grow to love you, Allie?"

His eyes were pleading with me. I would have given him a lifetime for the chance to have him love me.

"Yes, William, I'm here for you as long as you want me."

He looked so happy at my willingness to give him a chance. *I love you enough for both of us,* I thought. *I'm not going anywhere.*

Old Harbor - Sisters of Circumstance ~ P.J. Rhea

The next few weeks went smoothly. Things seemed awkward for a couple of days, but then we relaxed and formed a routine. He had to go back to work because he had taken so much time off those first four weeks prior to the wedding. Of course, being self-employed helped. He was with me as much as he possibly could be. I had not really toured my new home town in those four weeks. We had designated places to be and I was too involved in getting to know everyone to pay much attention to the little town of Old Harbor. William took me somewhere every day.

Since I had enjoyed the ice fishing so much a few weeks ago, William informed me he was going to teach me to fish in the stream that ran behind his house as soon as it was warm enough. We went to the stream for a practice session to prepare for summer fishing. He was explaining his secrets to the perfect cast and I was trying to copy his every move as we pretended to cast our invisible rods. I guess I tried a little too hard because I lost my balance and tripped, sitting down in the icy cold stream. Lucky for me, the water where I fell wasn't deep and with all the layers I had on very little water soaked through, but what did was freezing cold and I screamed like a child on a roller coaster when it reached my skin. William laughed so hard he could hardly help me back up and out of the water. He wrapped me in a blanket he kept in the truck and took me home to get dry and warm. Every evening we would sit on the front porch and drink coffee or hot cocoa and watch the ocean waves. The ocean was no more than a hundred yards away. Even with the cold snow that covered the beach and the sometimes bitter-cold breeze it was still calming and beautiful. We kept a pair of binoculars nearby to see if we could see ships. When it wasn't too cold out, we would sit in the rockers, but when it was too chilly, we would both sit on the swing wrapped up in a blanket together. William would put his strong arms around me to keep me warm.

It was so perfect it almost scared me. I knew if this didn't work out for some reason, if he tried to love me enough and just could not, I would never survive the heartache it would bring. I knew he wanted to wait until his feelings were sure before we made love again, but I wanted him so badly. He would often wait until he thought I was asleep before coming to bed. I could tell he was laying there looking at me, often so close I could almost feel his heart beating hard in his chest. He was struggling with desire too, but he was the kind of man who wanted to give himself completely to a woman. Not just for his physical need, but to actually give his whole heart to her. Some nights, when he assumed I was sleeping and thought I wouldn't know, he would run his fingers through my hair. Get close enough to smell the floral shampoo I used. I would feel his breath on my cheek and neck, and his lips would touch my skin very faintly, as if he were trying to get as close as possible without waking me. My body would tense from the desire to be with him. I wanted nothing more than to turn toward him at those times and plead with him to make love to me. I knew if I asked he would take me in his arms and we would make love, but I wanted it to be on his terms and not just an uncontrolled physical need.

There were times when he was away from the house; I would look at the picture of William and Mary that still sat as a reminder in that tiny, back bedroom. Now that I knew the story of what happened to her and to the baby whose image was forever captured in that framed ultrasound on the little blue and white dresser, the room was like a shrine. A tomb within the walls of my home that kept my happiness buried along with a past life. The smile on his face in that picture was different than any smile I had seen from him. He had smiled at me hundreds of times since our meeting and it showed off his cute dimple. It was a perfect smile, but the smile in the picture was different. As a photographer, I had studied smiles, eyes, and expressions, and I knew when a smile was out of politeness or satisfaction. I could tell when a smile was phony or even if it was flirty. The smile in the picture, when he looked at Mary, was none of those. It was a smile of completeness. When he looked at her, he was complete. He wanted for nothing else in this world but to be right there with her. I wanted him to look at me like that someday. I would wait as long as I had to in hopes of seeing that smile.

One day, near the end of our third week together, William and I went to see the few businesses in Old Harbor. He joked that I better not blink or I would miss the tour. Old Harbor was a tourist attraction and every business in it was to accommodate the tourists. The truth was that this small town could not support the few

Old Harbor - Sisters of Circumstance ~ P.J. Rhea

businesses it did have were it not for the tourists who came here year-round to hunt and fish.

The town consisted of a building that held the bank on one side and the post office on the other. From outward appearances, it looked like a duplex. The biggest building was The Lodge. It was a big two-story log building with about twelve little one-room cabins lined up in rows of six behind it. There were some rooms in The Lodge itself, but most tourists loved the little cabins, which were the size of an average motel room. Each was heated by gas logs in what looked like a fireplace and really added to the rustic ambiance. There was a restaurant in The Lodge, along with a gift store, both located downstairs on one side. On the other side was a larger room used for the few events or meetings the town might conduct. There was a sign above the room that read "The Midnight Sun." William explained that because so many of the social events held here took place in the summer months when Old Harbor could have up to twenty hours of sunlight, it sometimes felt like daytime late at night. There was also an office space and two larger suites upstairs. It was obvious that The Lodge was the hub of the little town.

When we left The Lodge we walked past the little school. It was a beautiful old building and reminded me of pictures I had seen in history books of the little one-room schools of the frontier—well, with a little modern flair. It did have a play area in back with swings and slides. There were windows along the side of the building and I could see children of different ages seated in sections as the one teacher lectured from the chalk board at the front. William had nothing to say as we passed the Old Harbor Academy, but almost seemed to hurry his pace and turn his head so not to look at it. I remembered Gwen telling me that Mary was the schoolteacher for the few children who lived in this town, so I didn't comment on the school at all. I think William was relieved to have the tour extend past The Lodge and the school. Those two buildings held too many strong memories of Mary. I wanted to break the spell, so I pointed out a little store near the middle of the one street that ran through the town. It looked like the kind of store you might see in a very old western on late-night television. The sign above it read "Trading Post," and there was a tall totem pole on one side of the steps leading to a long porch.

79

Old Harbor - Sisters of Circumstance ~ P.J. Rhea

On the other side was an even taller statue of a wooden bear. William's smile returned as we approached the store.

"Now that is the true character of this little town. It's run by the large family of Alaska Natives who live here. Their ancestors really discovered and established Old Harbor a few hundred years ago. The lady who owns it will insist you call her Mama."

I looked at him, confused as to why she would request such a thing. He chuckled at the look I gave him and explained.

"She's about a hundred years old as far as we can tell, and has been almost blind the last ten years. No one knows her real name except her family, and they aren't allowed to tell. She says she is the mother of this town and all who live here should call her Mama. She has about sixteen children of her own, and you can tell that those left of her tribe consider her like a chief or something. They always show her reverence and respect. It's kind of strange the way she talks to some people. She will sense that they're in the store and call them to her. She whispers things to them and they always leave looking amazed. It's as if she can read their thoughts or their future. She's actually responsible for our meeting."

I looked up at him with questioning eyes. "How could she possibly have anything to do with our meeting when I've never met her?"

"Well, I went into the store for a few supplies about a week before the deadline on the applications. I had been to the meeting at the church, but just hadn't been willing to apply. Mama called me over to her and told me to lean in close. She placed her hand on my chest over my heart and said, 'It's time William, she is near.'"

At first, I figured he was teasing me, but I looked in his eyes and there was no joke behind them. I had goose bumps and wasn't really sure what to say.

"I'm glad you listened," I finally managed.

William took my hand and we walked into the store. The store was as rustic on the inside as was implied on the outside. Several animal heads were mounted on the walls along with a few very large fish. The creaky, wooden floor was covered in wood

Old Harbor - Sisters of Circumstance ~ P.J. Rhea

shavings, and there was a very old-looking soda machine to the left that must have been one of the first ever made. The store seemed to be divided into four sections. Near the entrance were grocery items: just the basic things people might need between shopping trips, like milk, bread, soft drinks, coffee, tobacco, a few snack foods, and a small selection of canned goods. Then there was a section of clothing: things used by fishermen and hunters mostly, plus a few items a tourist might have forgotten such as socks, underwear, toiletry items, film, and batteries. Another corner was filled with things like fishing poles, gun supplies, knives, a few sets of waders, and fishing nets. The largest area was for souvenirs to tempt the tourists, such as blankets, jewelry, and moccasins. In the middle of the store there were a couple of small tables with chairs for old men to play checkers or sit and carve the little animals they sold in the store.

Mama's children ran the store. Some of the older members wore clothing you would expect to see on an Alaska Native—I figured mostly to attract the tourists—but the younger adults were in jeans and shirts with a picture of the Trading Post on the front. Of course they could be found in the store to purchase. At the end of the counter in an old rocking chair sat Mama. Her hair was snow white and braided. The long braids looked like rope as they piled up next to her in her chair. Her face was well worn, with deep lines to confirm her many years, but her expression was still soft and comforting. She had a lot of beads around her neck and wore moccasins on her feet. I could tell her eyes did not focus on anything and they seemed to have a film or callus over them that hid their former color. They were dull and had no light in them, but when she turned her head toward me I felt as if she saw me.

In a soft, raspy voice, she said, "Come to me child, come close and let me talk to you."

I looked at William for instructions. "Is she talking to me?"

William nodded without speaking and motioned toward her to encourage me to go to her. He looked a little frightened at what she might say, too. I slowly walked toward her.

"Well, come on child, I won't hurt you. Good morning William," she added.

81

Old Harbor - Sisters of Circumstance ~ P.J. Rhea

How did she know he was with me, or even that I was there? We had not made a sound when we entered the store. I went to her and leaned in close. She placed her hand on my stomach, not exactly what I was expecting to happen, so I jumped. She smiled and made a motion with her hand for me to come close again. She placed her hand back on my stomach and leaned as if to whisper to me.

"William loves you child, I have heard it. And this child you carry will be his healing."

I backed away from her. *What was she talking about? What child?* I was backing toward William, shocked and speechless. William placed his hands on my shoulders to stop me from backing right into him.

"What did she say?"

I couldn't speak for a minute but finally replied, "She's crazy."

He shrugged his shoulders, but I could tell he was very curious about what she had told me. I was too. *What did she mean? Does she really know something I don't know?* I had better find out. Could the one time William and I made love really have resulted in a pregnancy? I couldn't help but smile at the possibility, but I didn't want him to question me as to why I was so happy so I struggled not to give it away. I didn't dare tell him now. Not until I was sure and not until he was sure he loved me.

We finished our tour of Old Harbor. William took me to lunch at the little restaurant owned by Jay's family. Jay and Corinna were both working there and seemed blissfully happy. Seeing Corinna and her growing pregnant belly just made me more curious about what Mama had said. I wasn't going to say anything to William about it just yet, but I could not wait to talk to Rachel. I had so much to tell her. Trudy and Samuel were in town at The Lodge. Trudy had started working there behind the desk and Samuel came to visit her on his lunch break. Rachel, however, had not been seen by anyone since the weddings. I tried to call her a few times, but she never answered her cell and never called back. I had an uneasy feeling about her. The four of us had planned on meeting next Saturday for lunch. One month from our wedding day was the time we choose to reunite and catch

82

Old Harbor - Sisters of Circumstance ~ P.J. Rhea

up. Maybe then I could see my friend and tell her how crazy my world had been since we last talked.

After we finished our lunch, we continued our tour. William kept looking at me and smiling as if he had some secret. My mind was so preoccupied I had not really paid attention to where we were going. I realized we had stopped walking and we were standing in front of an empty little house with a sold sign on it. It was in the middle of the tiny town so I assumed it had been a business at some point. William seemed to just be waiting for me to ask him what this was. He was grinning ear to ear.

"Well, what do you think?" he finally asked.

"It's very sweet, what kind of business is it?"

"It's the newest business in Old Harbor, a photography studio," he answered.

"Oh, how nice."

Just as I was about to see if we could go in, I realized what William was trying to tell me. It was for me? I looked at him for conformation and he put his hand forward as if to invite me to go in. I went crazy with excitement. I ran into the little building and squealed like a child on Christmas morning.

"Really, William, it's for me?"

I couldn't control my happiness. I hugged him and rushed around, looking at everything it contained: a wonderful camera, with a tripod and extensions to get close-ups. There was a room that seemed like a bedroom to the left. It contained a walk-in closet that led into a bathroom. It had been equipped with everything needed to develop my own pictures, and tons of film. I mostly used a digital camera, but I had told William I also loved to develop pictures. It was a relaxing hobby, I guess. I knew I wouldn't use it much in my business but it was sweet of him to remember and I loved him for thinking of it. William explained it was the only room with running water but without a window, so it would have to serve double duty.

This room would be my office, I quickly decided. I mentally placed a desk and file cabinet—oh, and a table and chairs to sit down

Old Harbor - Sisters of Circumstance ~ P.J. Rhea

and look at proofs with my clients. The tiny kitchen had a pantry perfect for supplies, and the other small room was the right size to set up for the photo sessions. There was a half-bath just off the kitchen I could use as a dressing room for people who wanted their picture made in more than one outfit, and the front room would need a couch and a couple of chairs for people to sit while they waited. My active imagination was in overdrive and in a matter of seconds I had mentally decorated the entire studio and had customers lined up. Once I had looked it over from one end to the other I hugged him again.

"Oh, William, thank you so much, this is fantastic!"

I could tell it made him happy to see me so thrilled with his gift. He was beaming with pride.

"I just figured you needed something other than taking care of the big mansion and cooking my meals to take up your time. Plus, don't women like having their own money for all that shopping you like to do?"

"You're exactly right!" I smiled a little sarcastically. "As much fun as I have cooking and cleaning, this will be a nice change. I think my first shopping trip will be tomorrow, if that's okay. I have supplies to purchase if I'm going to start a business. I'm sure I'll need a permit, too, so I can take care of that as well."

I didn't add this, but I was thinking a trip to a doctor might not be a bad idea. My mind had been reeling since our visit with the old woman who called herself Mama. It occurred to me that my period was late, which had never happened before. I felt a little foolish for not noticing it, but I had been a little busy trying to win my husband's affections from the ghost of his dead wife, after all. I remembered some of the other signs of pregnancy Corinna had talked about during our four weeks in our basement dorm. Always tired: I had blamed that one on not having enough to keep me occupied, and of course, not resting well due to sexual frustration. I had also been sick to my stomach a couple of times, but had assumed that was from eating my own cooking. I was learning to cook for William. All the years in New York, it was just so easy to get fast food or things I could just pop in the microwave.

Old Harbor - Sisters of Circumstance ~ P.J. Rhea

How would he react if I were pregnant? I wanted to think he would be happy. That it would be the thing we needed to cement us as a couple, but after hearing what happened with Mary and his son, I couldn't be sure of his reaction.

The next morning, I was up early and ready to go to Kodiak. William was enjoying my enthusiasm for the photography studio. I had talked his ear off the night before as we sat on the porch. I decided since the town was so small and would probably not have a lot of business for family portraits and there are not a lot of weddings, as we well know, I would make it mostly a tourist thing. I'd offer to take pictures of people with the fish they caught or the animal they had killed. I would get what I needed to make rustic frames for them. I would have to get Gwen to bring little John in for a picture. It was going to be wonderful, and I would be my own boss for a change and could be as creative as I wanted to.

I found all I needed to get started at a place in Kodiak that catered to hobbies. I had noticed a clinic when I first arrived in town and went in to see if I could see a doctor. They gave me an appointment for later in the day, so I decided to do a little shopping and grab some lunch, then head back to the clinic. When I entered the clinic I saw Corinna going through the door toward the exam rooms. I hoped she didn't notice me enter, and chances were I would be in a room by the time she left. I wasn't ready to explain any of this to my friends, except for Rachel. I knew she would keep it secret until I could tell William. I sat on the exam table waiting for the doctor to come in and tell me the results of my blood work. I wasn't really sure what I wanted the results to be. I had always wanted to be a mother. It was one of the reasons for my filling out the application that brought me here. But knowing what William had been through changed things. The doctor entered the room and extended his hand to shake mine. He was a very tall man with dark features and very dark hair both on his arms and sticking up from the neck line of his scrubs, implying he had a very hairy chest.

"Hello Mrs. Hickman, I'm Dr. Harry Bear."

Old Harbor - Sisters of Circumstance ~ P.J. Rhea

I guess it was partly nerves, but I laughed out loud and then felt my face heat up with embarrassment from my reaction. I shook his hand.

"Glad to meet you doctor, and I'm so sorry for laughing. That was very rude of me but I guess I'm a little nervous."

"That's fine, and believe me, you're not the first. Well, I looked at your test results and I have great news. You are definitely expecting."

I couldn't help it, I was so happy. I was crying and laughing at the same time. It was the best news I could have received. I looked at the doctor and chocked out a "thank you so much." He did a pelvic exam and wrote me a prescription for prenatal vitamins. I got a list of do's and don'ts and made an appointment for the next month. I dropped by the studio and put away all I had purchased, and worked on a sign to post in the frame built into the outside of the building. I had decided to take some pictures of the beautiful landscape of this town and sell them to tourists and maybe to local businesses to hang on their walls. Life was perfect for me right now. I couldn't think of anything more I could want—well, except for William to love me enough to want to be my husband in every way. I wanted to wait to tell him about the baby because I wanted him to love me just for me, and not because I was pregnant with his child. I hoped it would happen before it became too obvious that I was expecting. Tomorrow would be my luncheon with my new sisters. I wouldn't tell Trudy or Corinna just yet, but I could not wait to tell Rachel. She would gladly keep my secret just as I had kept hers, and I just had to tell someone. *Rachel, I hope you are at least half as happy as I am,* I wished. It would be so good to see her and compare things. I was ready to catch up with my sisters. They felt like family to me now, and it had been so long since I had a feeling of family.

I had to admit I felt closer to Rachel than the other ladies. We had a connection I could not explain. It made no sense that two people from such different backgrounds, total strangers, could feel so close in only a matter of weeks. I don't think I could have felt closer to Rachel if we had been actual sisters. Maybe it was because of our closeness that I could not shake my feeling of dread. I had an almost

Old Harbor - Sisters of Circumstance ~ P.J. Rhea

instant dislike for Kevin Marshall and my gut told me Rachel was not in a good place. I had tried since the weddings to not dwell on it. I wanted to give William my attention and work on my own happiness, but there was always the thought of Rachel in the back of my mind. What had things been like for her these past few weeks? Had Kevin made her feel welcome in his house? No matter how hard I tried to push the thoughts from my mind, I wanted to hear from Rachel. I wanted to know how her first few weeks as a wife had been.

ᴓ Chapter Eight ᴕ

Through Rachel's Eyes: My Personal Hell

The weddings were beautiful and I can't believe I am a married woman, Rachel thought. Allie made such a beautiful bride and I believe with all my heart she will be happy with William.

It was easy for me to be happy for Allie. After all, we are best friends, practically sisters, and I have never felt so close to another person. I realized I actually felt happier for Allie than for myself. I was trying to be realistic about it. I didn't love Kevin and had no misplaced notions that he loved me, but I had hope. I was going to do whatever I had to do to make him happy. After all, he had no idea about my past, and this was my perfect opportunity to have the life I dreamed of. Kevin seemed oddly preoccupied as he drove to his house at the very end of the town that was Old Harbor. He almost seemed smug in his silence, as if he had done exactly what he had set out to do, and it was making me very uncomfortable. I finally saw a house through the trees and couldn't help but think about the life I had lived prior to this. The many nights I had slept in foster homes, in shelters, and in the beds of strangers. Despite my lack of romantic feelings for Kevin, I was still excited about the idea of a life as someone's wife and the fairy tale ending.

His house was on the line that divided Old Harbor from the rest of Kodiak Island. Just down the road from his driveway was the ferry that carried us to Kodiak a few days ago. It was a good location to attract business for his bait shop. The shop was an A-frame building with a tank outside filled with small fish used for angling for larger fish. It was beside the main road that ran through Old Harbor and faced the ferry landing. The house was at the end of the drive and hidden in the woods, almost out of sight from the road.

Old Harbor - Sisters of Circumstance ~ P.J. Rhea

Kevin showed no excitement as he led me into my new home, but I thought maybe he was nervous too. It was a nice house with a screened-in mud room in front, with a large freezer on one end. Inside, it was extremely clean, almost to the point that you wondered if anyone actually lived in it. Everything was perfectly in place and as clean as a picture in a magazine. *Maybe Kevin went through a lot of effort to impress me,* I thought. It wasn't a large house, but the layout made it appear roomy. I could be happy here. I could picture myself cooking in the little kitchen and sitting in front of the fireplace cuddled up together talking about our day. I hated to jump too far ahead, but I could almost picture a small child playing at my feet. It was finally becoming a possibility for me. The past could die now and I could just be a normal wife; the dream of being a mother might be close enough to touch.

I turned to face Kevin, thinking he would be smiling at me and waiting for my reaction to his home, to our home, but when I met his gaze I felt a shiver go down my back and felt almost sick. I saw something in his eyes: coldness, and an evil that made me afraid. He turned and locked the door behind us and looked at me with a grin on his face that was sinister, not the flirty grin expected of a groom toward his bride on the wedding night; a smile that said he had won and he was in control. I was frozen where I stood, not sure what to do. This was not the first time I had found myself in a room with a man I was afraid of, but it was the first time I felt helpless. I knew there was no one who would be checking on me in a few hours to be sure I was okay. There was no one in a hotel room next to me to hear if I screamed for help. The other ladies were with their new husbands and we weren't planning on meeting again for a month. He had me trapped in a place I knew nothing about. Not even where I might run.

Rachel, you are acting like Allie. Letting your imagination run wild and over-analyzing this, I thought. *This is your husband, I told myself. He picked you out of several applicants as the woman he wanted to be with. Sure he's way too quiet, and not exactly the romantic type, but you wanted a home and a family and this is your new beginning.*

My mind was racing as I tried to put logic to the panic I was feeling. I remembered what Allie had said to me last night about

Old Harbor - Sisters of Circumstance ~ P.J. Rhea

listening to my gut. I was beginning to wish now that I had admitted to her and to myself that red flags had been popping up since the first night we met. I had just finished my thought when he reached for something from behind a cushion on the couch. He held up an outfit he wanted me to put on; something very trashy and revealing. I had owned things that were even more revealing, but something about the way he looked when he pushed it toward me…I felt embarrassed.

"Put this on, whore!" he ordered.

"What did you call me?"

I cringed, not sure where this was coming from, and my body tensed from the complete shock of his statement. I had to be dreaming and I wanted to wake from this nightmare before it got any worse. He had been nice to me for the past two weeks, polite and considerate. Sure, we had never been as close as most of the other couples, but we had a nice time and I had been hopeful that we would grow closer and maybe find love with time.

"Come now, Roxy, this can't be the first time you've been called a whore."

"Why would you call me Roxy?"

I felt dizzy and I could tell my face was flushed. I couldn't believe what was happening. *How could he know?*

"You don't think I'd bring someone here without checking her out first, do you? Once I picked a name, I had you followed and had a private detective find out what he could about you. Turns out you've been arrested a few times, Roxy, and had a long career in…what was it you put in your application? Oh yes, customer service."

He laughed in a way that made me feel foolish. It was an insulting kind of laugh.

"That was very clever of you. Now put it on."

He barked his order at me and tossed the teddy hard into my face. Maybe it wasn't the smart thing to do, but I decided to take a stand.

90

Old Harbor - Sisters of Circumstance ~ P.J. Rhea

"I will not put that on and I think maybe it would be best if I leave. This wasn't a good idea and I think I'll just go back home to New York."

He laughed at me and I knew by his expression that things were not going to end well. I braced myself for whatever was about to happen. Kevin drew his hand back and hit me hard across the face. I felt blood run down my chin and I could tell my lip was quickly swelling. I think he may have caused a tooth to become loose. I guess from years of having to be so strong and taking care of myself, years of living in a world of people who forced me to be defensive at times and to put my foot down at some request, I stood my ground and looked at him with defiance. He grabbed my hair and pulled me down to the floor hard, and I knew there was no possible way I would ever win over this man. As I struggled, desperate to free myself from his grip, he dragged me to a door at the end of the hall. He opened the door and continued to drag me down the stairs to the cellar of his house. With each step I felt sharp pain shoot through my body, but the pain from having my hair pulled was the worst. It was excruciating. When we reached the bottom I lay on the dirt floor, bleeding and crying. I looked up at him and with the breath I could collect I tried to reason with him.

"Please, Kevin, let me go."

With that he lifted me and threw me toward a wall. Kevin was a big man with large, muscular arms and he was able to pitch me around like a toy. It was all so unreal. Even as the pain throbbed in my body and the blood ran from my busted lip I kept thinking this could not really be happening to me. I tried to take in my surroundings, looking for a possible escape. This was one of those underground rooms most would use for storing foods they had canned. I remembered one of my foster homes having a room like this full of jar after jar of vegetables and fruit on shelves built into the wall. But Kevin used this room for something else. I wondered at that moment if I would ever leave this dark, damp hole under his house, or would this be my first view of my own grave? The only thing I saw was an old trunk in the corner. He had a firm grip on my arm and he pulled me along as he went over and moved the trunk from its place. He took his hand and moved a thin layer of dirt off a hard surface and

Old Harbor - Sisters of Circumstance ~ P.J. Rhea

pulled open the lid of something he had buried in the dirt. Then Kevin grabbed me and pushed my face in the opening of the dirt.

"You look in there, whore, what do you see?"

He reached up and pointed the one dangling light toward the opening. I couldn't believe it. I wanted to scream but nothing would come out. I tried to push myself away from what was in that box, but he wouldn't let me move. I was face-to-face with a human skull. He had a skeleton in a box buried in the dirt. Draped on the bones was what looked like an outfit similar to the one he had told me to put on.

"You see her? Unless you want to join her, you'll do as you're told. That's why I picked you. You have no one who cares; no one will ever come looking for you. I told the people of this stupid little town that she got mad and went back home to her mama. No one even questioned the fact that they didn't see her leave. You think anyone will miss you?"

He was so smug and so proud of what he had gotten away with. This poor girl had been here long enough to be nothing but bones and no one questioned where she was. His words were cruel and I knew then that he had planned this for a while. I was the perfect "bride" for him. Someone with no family to check up on them and no one to bother looking if he told them I went back to New York.

"Why, Kevin? It doesn't have to be this way. I can be a good wife to you. I just wanted to be a wife. I can make you happy; maybe we could even have a family."

I was lying, of course. I would never stay here another minute if I could escape. I would run straight to the police and report this poor girl in the cellar if given the chance, but I knew it was hopeless. I would never leave Kevin's house unless it was in a body bag.

"You seriously think I would have kids with a nasty bitch who slept with who knows how many men? You're here because of what you are. I can do as I want with you and when I'm done, well, I can make room for you with her."

Then Kevin started ripping my clothes off. He kept slapping me, even though I was no longer resisting him. I had no fight left in me. No strength left to struggle or attempt to resist. I simply laid there

Old Harbor - Sisters of Circumstance ~ P.J. Rhea

defeated and accepting of my fate, but he still continued to hit me as if I needed to be subdued. He seemed to be aroused by causing me pain. He would smile when hitting me, and at times even bite me. The more I screamed the more excited he became. When he was on top of me, he would thrust himself hard in me with more effort than needed, just to cause pain. It was the pain he liked. It didn't matter how I looked or what sexual skills I may have mastered in my former line of work, he got off on my pain and the more he caused, the more he enjoyed it. I had been used by hundreds of men since I was a young girl. I had been made to feel cheap before, made to feel dirty and worthless before, but this was the first time I had ever felt like I was being raped.

When it was finally over and he had spent all the time torturing me he wanted, he left me on the dirt floor of the dark, cold cellar and went upstairs. I laid there and cried for a long time from the intense pain he had caused physically, but also from the things he had said and the heartbreak I felt because my dream of a new start was gone. I was desperately afraid, and felt so hopeless I almost wished for death. I will die in this cellar grave and no one will ever know. As I laid there in the mud formed by my tears and blood thinking my life was over, something clicked inside me and a glimmer of hope started to build in my broken heart. He had said no one would care, no one would notice if I went missing. A few weeks ago I would have agreed with him, but I knew that was no longer true. Allie would miss me, she would look for me. *Oh Allie, please come for me, and save me from this hell.* It was the glimmer of hope that would help me survive.

Kevin continued his daily routine and I stayed in the cellar for what seemed like several days. I really wasn't sure how long I was down there because there was no way for me to know if it was day or night. Finally Kevin brought me upstairs to bathe. He also wanted me to clean and cook for him. Every day was filled with new torture. When the physical abuse would lessen, the verbal abuse worsened. He reminded me every day of how worthless a person I was; how no one would care if I died. I heard my cell phone ring a few times, but was not allowed to answer it. I hoped it was Allie. Who else could it be? Maybe she would wonder why she hadn't seen me since the weddings. I was having trouble keeping up with just how many weeks had passed, but I was sure it had to be close to time for our scheduled luncheon. When I didn't show up, would someone come to find me? It was the only glimmer of hope I had and I was holding close to it.

Kevin started letting me sleep upstairs, but would remind me of what he could do to me if I even thought of trying to leave him. Kevin would go to his shop during the day, but would give me my list of things I had better have done when he returned. The doors and windows were locked using padlocks from the outside, so even when I was free from that horrible cellar I was still a prisoner with no hope of escape. If he needed to go to town, he would lock me in the cellar, but if he was going to be gone very long, he would drug me to keep me quiet. The first time he came at me with a syringe, I pleaded with him not to give me anything.

"I'll be quiet, Kevin!" I assured him, but he just laughed and sat on my arm to hold it still. I had no idea what he was giving me. It made me sleep for long periods of time and I would feel hungover for most of the day once it wore off. I also realized my body was craving whatever it was. I would want it so badly I would plead with him at times, telling him I needed to sleep. He would just laugh at my ramblings and tell me I would get it when he needed me to get it and not before. I was ashamed of the fact that I had started asking for the drug, but it was my only relief from the pain my body was in and the only time I could escape from my hell.

Then one morning he came running through the door, yelling for me.

"Those crazy women who came here with you are on their way to the house. I saw them coming down the drive."

He pointed his finger at my chest and with his demands he would hit me hard with that finger following every word spoken.

"You will go to our room and stay there!" he ordered. "I'm telling them you have the flu and can't be around people. You will not do anything to make them think otherwise, will you, Roxy? I'd hate to see something happen to your friend, Allie. William has to leave Allie alone a lot, and accidents happen."

"I do promise, Kevin, please don't hurt Allie."

Old Harbor - Sisters of Circumstance ~ P.J. Rhea

I knew all too well what he was capable of doing to Allie or any of the other women who were my friends. The look in his eyes left me with no doubt at all that he would kill them before he allowed his secret to be discovered. I listened from my prison, as he answered the knock at the door. Allie, Trudy, and Corinna stood only a few feet away from me on the mud porch. I held on to the bedpost trying to keep myself from running to them and pleading to go with them. I wanted to beg them to save me from this monster but I couldn't put them in danger too. I loved them and would not put them at risk of losing their lives at the hands of this madman. He could kill us all and be gone before anyone knew what happened.

I heard Kevin as he lied to them, acting so concerned about me and pointing out that they wouldn't want to catch it.

"Especially you, Corinna, you have to be really careful in your condition. You need anything, sweetie?" he called out to me to be more convincing, and I knew I had better answer, or he would be even more cruel to me when they left. I would be punished if I didn't obey. I took in a deep breath and with a shaky voice that probably made me sound like I was really sick with the flu I answered him so my sisters would be safe.

"No, Kevin dear, I'm just going to lie down. Tell the girls I'm sorry, I just don't feel up to a visit."

I heard him say goodbye and softly close the door behind them. When I knew they were gone, I collapsed to the floor and cried until my body was too weak to stand back up. I wanted desperately to run after them, to escape this place, but I knew I had no chance. I think after their visit Kevin realized he would have to allow me to be seen occasionally by others. He was more careful after that. He no longer hit me in the face and he made sure I kept my appearance up, so as not to draw too much attention or cause others to question why I looked so different. To anyone who saw me, I would appear fine. Maybe a little thinner—and they might suspect I wasn't sleeping well because of the dark circles under my eyes; but if they could see the part of me that my clothes covered, they would see my body was covered in bruises, some old and some new. They would see scars from bites so hard they broke the skin and welts from being punched

95

Old Harbor - Sisters of Circumstance ~ P.J. Rhea

for no reason but the pleasure brought on by my pain. He no longer gave me the injections for fear it would be noticed I had glazed-over eyes or something, so if he left for a long while he would just chain me up in the cellar with my mouth taped shut. I tried to be good and do what he wanted. I would never give him an excuse to not trust me. I knew my only hope was that I could somehow let someone know I needed to be rescued. My first test was when he let me sit in the shop with him and see people from town as they came by for bait. I would run the cash register and talk to the tourists. I was careful not to give anything away. I had to earn his trust if I ever hoped to see my sisters again. William came by one day, and Kevin shot me a look I knew was meant to remind me of what could happen if I gave William any reason for concern. William told me all about a photography studio he had surprised Allie with, and how her business was growing.

"Things are going great, Rachel, but I know she misses you so much. Can't you come by for a visit?"

Kevin interrupted. "She's been really busy helping me work in the shop, but we'll try to make it into town soon. Maybe we can stop by the studio for a quick visit."

William left, and again my hope of a savior was gone. Kevin was especially angry after William's visit. He didn't like being pushed into a corner and he hated the fact that he was wrong about no one missing me if I was gone. It limited what he could do to me, and the tension was building. I could tell he wasn't far from a breakdown of sorts, and when it happened I didn't expect to live through it. He had been more aggressive and more threatening since the girls came and I knew my time was growing shorter. He was waiting until he could come up with a story they would believe as to why I left suddenly without saying goodbye.

He started preparing me for a visit to town; giving me long detailed warnings of what was going to take place if I didn't do exactly what I was told. He told me he would be by my side every minute we were in town, and if Allie or anyone else tried to get me to leave I had better make them believe I was so blissfully happy that I didn't want to be away from him for even a second.

Old Harbor - Sisters of Circumstance ~ P.J. Rhea

The day we went to town, he put on his holster and pistol under his coat. When we got out of the car, he took my hand and held it tight against the gun as if to remind me to watch my step. We were going to the Trading Post first. It was a little store where he shopped for supplies, and how well I behaved there would determine if he would let me see Allie. We walked in and I was surprised to see Allie and William in the back of the store. William was helping Allie hang some pictures in the store in an area that looked to be meant for souvenirs. She looked so happy there with her new husband, and I was glad to see her dreams had apparently come true. But then she looked in my direction and when our eyes met, I saw the shock as it covered her face. She knew something was very wrong and I knew she would not stop until she found out what it was. If she confronted Kevin he might panic. He might decide to shoot anyone who was in his way and run for it. I knew that look on Allie's face, and she was not going to keep her distance. I would not let my friend get hurt trying to help me. I couldn't let things keep going on this way. Everyone would be better off if I was gone. Something inside me snapped. I could not keep living in this nightmare. It took everyone, including Kevin, by surprise when I reached in his coat with my free hand and grabbed the pistol. In the same movement, I pushed myself away from him and put the gun to my head. I heard Allie screaming.

"I'm sorry, Allie, but this has to end!" I began to sob as I explained to my friends the reason I had to do this. "He tortures me, Allie; he beats me and locks me in the cellar. I've been living in hell and I just can't go back!"

Kevin started yelling back, "She's lying! I bet you didn't know she was a prostitute before she came here! She slept with men for money in New York! She's a drug addict and a whore. You can see the needle marks on her arm. I've been trying to help her get off of the drugs since the wedding, but she's having a breakdown, as you can plainly see!"

They all just stood there in disbelief as he screamed out his accusations. Then I started shouting too, hoping desperately that no one would believe what he had just said.

Old Harbor - Sisters of Circumstance ~ P.J. Rhea

"He has a skeleton in the cellar!" I added and scanned the faces for their reaction. "The woman who came here with him never left!"

Kevin was furious I was telling them and he lunged at me. I turned the gun toward him for a second. The barrel of the gun was pressed right between his eyes on his forehead, and for the first time ever I saw fear in his cold, dark eyes. He put his hands up as if letting me know he got the message and he slowly backed away. As soon as he was a reasonable distance from me I put the gun back to my head. Everyone remained frozen in their tracks, all afraid to make a move for fear of what I might do.

The only law enforcement in town was a middle-aged man named Mark Sims. Kevin made fun of the lack of protection in this town.

"Makes it a perfect location for my little hobby, don't you think?" he would say when reminding me of how no one would ever look for me.

Mark Sims was a member of the Alaska Department of Public Safety and was used to enforcing fish and wildlife law. Police departments existed only in those communities with the resources to support one. Old Harbor was not one of those communities. He had come in just after I grabbed the gun from Kevin. He had his gun drawn and was holding it on me, trying to persuade me to put my gun down, but he seemed more nervous about what was happening than anyone else. The room was noisy. There were so many people screaming at me to stop, except for Kevin, who was encouraging me to pull the trigger in a very low voice so the others wouldn't hear him. It felt like the room was spinning and I was so confused. Allie, Trudy, and Corinna were crying and trying to talk to me, reminding me how much they loved me and that we were sisters.

"We're here for you, Rachel!" "We can help you, please don't leave us!" I heard coming from various individuals in the crowd.

Suddenly, all the noise was muffled and I felt as if something was pulling at me. I focused on an old woman sitting in a rocking chair at the end of the counter. She was an Indian, I think, and had

98

Old Harbor - Sisters of Circumstance ~ P.J. Rhea

very long, gray hair that touched the floor beside her chair. She was wearing lots of beads and charms around her neck and a dress that appeared to be made from some animal hide or something. She was sitting there calmly, with her eyes closed, and she was gripping some kind of small animal figure at the end of the necklace that hung around her neck. I could see that her lips were moving, as if she was speaking, but I could not tell if any words were coming out.

With all the frantic people in the store pleading with me, I couldn't think. I screamed loudly for everyone to be quiet! Everyone in the little store stopped. They were standing motionless like children playing freeze tag and looked at each other for a clue as to what should happen next. There was no sound except for the sound of my heart pounding in my chest, and a sarcastic breathy laugh Kevin let out at my display. This was a joke to him, and a way to get rid of me without having to answer for it, I was guessing. As I held the gun's barrel tight against my temple, I could feel my pulse beating against it. Every breath sounded so loud to me I wondered if all these people could hear each breath as it traveled into my lungs and then back out.

The old woman opened her eyes and turned toward me, but her eyes looked dead. There was no light in them and they seemed almost milky, as if there was no pupil in the center. She must be blind, I thought, but I feel as if she is looking right inside me. I couldn't take my eyes off her. It felt like the native woman and I were the only two people in the room for a few seconds. The rest of the people almost seemed blurred around me and every movement was now in slow motion. She was no longer moving her lips, but I could hear what I assumed was her voice in my head. It was like she was assuring me that what I was about to do was the right thing.

"It will set you free, my child, your sisters will understand. Feel the courage that lies deep inside you. Listen to your spirit, sweet girl. You know what must be done."

It was like a whisper, but it was putting a picture in my mind that would end all of this. I could picture the end results. I could feel the peace enter my body. The voice was giving me my answer, encouraging me to do what had to be done. I pulled back on the hammer of the pistol that I held so tightly against my temple. I looked

99

toward Kevin and he had that same evil smirk across his lips that always meant he had won. Allie could no longer be silent. I could hear her pleading, begging, crying for me to not leave her, and then there was the loud pop of the gun as it fired.

∽ Chapter Nine ∾

Life Takes a Turn

I *hope I can arrive at The Lodge before the others,* I thought. I was hoping Rachel would get there before Trudy or Corinna so we could talk alone. Corinna asked that we eat here to give her a break from the Ellis Café. She loved it there and loved Jay's family. She had never in her life felt more loved and happy than she did right now, but she just wanted some time away. She arrived just after me and I noticed right away that her pregnant belly had grown more than I had imagined it would in such a short time. She was behind the counter most of the time when William and I were in the café two days ago, but now, with a snug-fitting maternity top on, it was certainly out there.

"You look adorable, Corinna!" I told her.

"Thank you, Allie. I went to the doctor yesterday and we now know it's a boy and there's only one, thank the Lord! I thought I saw you come in the office as I was called back for my exam. Were you at the doctor in Kodiak yesterday?"

"Oh, no, that wasn't me," I lied. "I was in town to get supplies, but not at the doctor's office. Maybe you just saw me in town. Oh look, there's Trudy. We're over here Trudy!" I yelled, and waved my hands in the air in order to change the subject.

Trudy was looking wonderful. She and Samuel were happy and were so good for each other. He had gained weight from her fantastic cooking, and Trudy was so happy she was no longer looking to food for comfort. She had actually lost around thirty pounds since we first met. We were having a great visit, catching up on all that had happened in the four weeks since we had seen each other. I didn't want to tell them everything—that William and I had not made love since our wedding night when he called me by his dead wife's name, but that the one and only time we had been together had resulted in a

101

Old Harbor - Sisters of Circumstance ~ P.J. Rhea

pregnancy William didn't know about. So far, my marriage was reading like a soap opera. But despite it all, I was so happy I kept thinking I should pinch myself. It had to be a dream. I told them about the portrait studio and all my plans for it. Corinna agreed to let me take a picture of the baby when he was a few weeks old and pretty much a picture of him every few months until he was grown. We were having a wonderful visit, but I kept watching the door, waiting for Rachel. She couldn't have forgotten. After all, she was the one to suggest we meet exactly four weeks from our weddings. If she had gone to the Ellis Café by mistake, Jay would have told her where to find us. Neither Corinna nor Trudy had seen her at all since the weddings.

After our meal, the three of us went to see Gwen and check on little John. Carl was changing a diaper when we arrived and I must admit it was entertaining. Little John had dirtied his diaper and Carl was acting like it was going to eat his skin off if it touched him at all. He gagged and complained through the entire process, and we all just stood back and laughed at him.

"You ladies owe me; I would think at least one of you would help me out here."

Corinna started to go take over for him, but Gwen stopped her.

"Oh, no, Carl Bible, you are not getting out of this again. We agreed on equal responsibility, and you haven't been doing your share."

We all enjoyed seeing them interact with their beautiful son. We had all grown to love this couple. Gwen had looked at me with questioning eyes when we first walked in and I smiled and nodded just to let her know all was going well with William and me. She looked pleased and asked us to have a seat, and offered refreshment.

"Actually Gwen, we were wondering if you or Carl had seen Rachel? She didn't show up for our scheduled luncheon and none of us have seen or heard from her in four weeks."

Carl and Gwen looked at each other with obvious concern on their faces.

Old Harbor - Sisters of Circumstance ~ P.J. Rhea

"I've seen Kevin in town a few times, but not Rachel," Carl admitted. "Perhaps you ladies should go by their place tomorrow and check in on her, but please go as a group."

Why would he insist we go as a group? I wondered. I was beginning to think everyone in this town had a bad feeling when it came to Kevin Marshall.

The next day, we met again in front of my studio and went together to the bait shop a little way down the road. When we got to the shop, it was locked up and no one was in sight. We parked the car in front of the bait shop and walked down the long drive to his house. Trudy knocked once on the door. Kevin opened the door the second she knocked, as if he had been expecting us. He placed himself in the doorway, blocking it in such a way that we knew we were not going to be invited in. He seemed cautious and rigid; nothing like he had been the four weeks we were around him before the weddings.

"Hello ladies. I'm assuming you're here to visit Rachel, but I'm afraid she's too sick for company."

He made his announcement so confidently, we felt like he expected us to just walk away with no further explanation. We all stood there baffled and not sure what to say. He was certainly prepared for what we were going to ask him before we had a chance to ask. When we stood our ground he looked frustrated and gave more detail to his excuse for not inviting us in.

"She has the flu and you don't need to be around her, especially you, Corinna, in your condition."

Then he called to Rachel in an affectionate voice, as if to reassure us of his concern. "You need anything, sweetie?"

I listened for her response, worried for my friend.

"No, Kevin dear, and tell the girls I'm sorry, but I'm just not up to a visit."

At least I heard her voice, knew she was still there, still alive. Her voice did sound weak and shaky, like someone who was very ill. It was just me letting my imagination go wild again, I concluded.

Old Harbor - Sisters of Circumstance ~ P.J. Rhea

"Please tell her to call me as soon as she feels better, Kevin; and the two of you need to come for a visit. I really miss her."

"I'll tell her, and you ladies have a safe trip back home now."

Kevin's voice sounded like he was holding down something sour. He was trying to act happy about our visit, but he was not. Maybe it wasn't my imagination after all. Something wasn't right, and I think Kevin could tell from the look on my face that I was not giving up on talking to my friend. I noticed several padlocks lying on a table in the mud room. Why would he need all those locks? Every nerve in my body screamed out that something wasn't right here. But I had heard Rachel and for now I would have to go on the assumption that she was sick but would get in touch with us soon. I would give Rachel a few days to feel better, but I was going to see her for myself soon. Trudy and Corinna seemed satisfied with Kevin's story, especially after hearing Rachel, but I was not going to stop until I could see for myself that she was okay.

In the meantime, I was working on getting the studio ready for its grand opening. I needed to get some nature pictures for the walls. I wanted something that would display my talent. William had gone on a fishing trip with some of his return patrons, a group of men who came every year and always insisted on William as their guide. He left in the early morning hours and didn't expect to return until very late. I decided it was time to venture out just a little beyond our yard. William told me not to go too far because there were bears. It was a rule in this town that you did not leave food in your trashcan or go into the woods with a lot of food on you, so I only took my camera and a bottle of water. I wouldn't stay out long.

As I reached the edge of the property, I stopped at the beautiful little garden Mary had created. I had noticed William sitting out here sometimes in the early hours when he thought I was still sleeping. There was a wooden bench that looked like it had been woven together using tree branches, and another bench on the opposite side made of concrete. There was an image of the mountains of Alaska carved into the backrest of the concrete bench. I had found a picture hanging in the living room of this garden in full bloom. Each section had a small marker telling what had been planted, and I could

104

Old Harbor - Sisters of Circumstance ~ P.J. Rhea

not wait for summer to bring it to life again. There would be roses called Rosa Rugosa. She had also planted snapdragons and Ligularia, a large orange daisy-like flower. The inner circle was reserved for a plant called Sweet William, which was ironic, but I could see where Mary did it as a way of honoring her husband and the son who would also share that name. She had wanted this to be a place for them to sit and admire the beauty of the flowers. It was never meant to be her tomb or the place where their child would forever rest when she planted those magnificent flowers. At the edge of the garden between the two benches was a birdbath with the statue of a small cherub. The little stone angel seemed to be keeping watch over this sanctuary. In between the flower beds was the grave of Mary and William Jr.

Gwen told me the baby had delivered as Mary struggled in the snow, and they laid his tiny body in the casket in Mary's arms. They were buried together in one grave so, as William had insisted, she could forever take care of their son. I sat there and cried for the heartbreak I knew haunted my William, and just from the pure sadness of the whole thing. I noticed I was holding my hands on my stomach, as if protecting this child that now grew inside me. I prayed that William would be happy about this baby and it would be like "Mama" had said—a healing for him.

I set out to find my perfect subjects for the pictures. I saw a moose in a field and it almost looked as if he were posing for me. The telephoto lens brought him close for me without risk, and I had several great shots. I saw other wildlife too, but it was the landscape that caught my attention the most. This place was a picture only God could paint, and I was taking picture after picture of the mountains and rivers and forests of this wonderful land using my wide angle lens. Each one was a portrait fit to be framed and enjoyed.

I didn't realize, in my obsessive hunt for another beautiful shot, just how far I had wandered.

I started getting very hungry and a little tired from all the walking. It was then I realized I wasn't really sure where I was or which direction I needed to go to get home. I knew a stream ran near the back of our house, so maybe if I found a stream and followed it, I could get home. As I walked through a field toward what sounded

105

Old Harbor - Sisters of Circumstance ~ P.J. Rhea

like water, I heard another sound. One that caused me to freeze in my tracks and made my heart feel like it was up in my throat. It was a low throaty growl which I knew was meant to be my warning. I looked to my side without making much movement and saw a large grizzly on the other side of the field. My mind started racing. *What's the right thing to do here? Should I run, fall down and play dead, or just stand here in hopes the bear will go off in the other direction?*

Suddenly the bear stood up on its hind feet and looked twice as big. I started to run, not knowing if it was the smart thing to do or not. The bear was coming toward me and I was desperately looking for a place to hide. There had to be somewhere a bear could not get into or climb up on. I could hear the pounding of the bear as its massive paws hit the ground not far behind me. This could not be happening to me. For years I walked the streets of New York alone, never once feeling threatened despite the crime I knew existed, and now I'm running for my life from a huge bear with claws and teeth that could easily rip me to shreds.

The bear was getting closer. I knew it was only a matter of time before the bear caught me and my dream of a new and wonderful life would be over. It was pure adrenalin that was pushing me forward, faster than I ever imagined I could run. My eyes were searching frantically for a safe haven and I could hear the heavy thud of the bear's paws as they hit the ground. I knew my time was running out, but then I saw my chance. There was a rock ledge sticking out from the hillside. There was very little room between the rock ledge and the ground, and I wasn't certain I would fit, but I had to try. I scrambled to the ground and wedged myself under the rock. I pushed myself as far back against the rocks as possible. If I had been even a pound heavier or an inch taller this would have not been enough to protect me. The bear was right behind me and made several attempts to reach me with its massive paw, missing me by only an inch at the most. My heart was pounding so hard in my chest it seemed to push the sound up into my brain. It seemed to be pounding on my eardrums from the inside so loudly that the growls of the bear were muffled. My legs were starting to cramp from the exertion I had put them through and I struggled to pull air into my lungs, my dry throat feeling as if it would close off the air's path at any moment. My

106

Old Harbor - Sisters of Circumstance ~ P.J. Rhea

mind was whirling. It was like people say all the time: my entire life was flashing before me as if I was trying to justify everything I had ever done. I was remembering all those I loved who had passed on and the new people in my life that I had grown to love. William's face was foremost in my thoughts and I had to do something. My life just couldn't end now. Not like this.

What I did next could only be classified as crazy. I had never let go of my camera and I started snapping the bear's picture. I knew the flash would go off in this dark hole and just maybe it would scare her away. The flash seemed to anger the bear the first time and she tried even harder to reach me with her long sharp claws. She would place her face in the opening of my sanctuary and growl a loud and frustrated warning to me. The size of her teeth and the hot breath should have made me retreat even further into the cliff if that were possible, but instead I took more pictures, and this time the flash seemed to scare her away. The bear only went a few feet away and it was then I realized why she was so aggressive: cubs came running up to her. She was protecting them. I snapped a few pictures of the happy family, but the noise caused her to look back at me so I pushed myself back in my hole as far as I could. That was when reality hit me.

I'm stuck here. Until that bear is long gone, I have to stay put, and even then I'm not sure how to get home. I would be too afraid I would run into the bear again. Would this be my grave, or would they find me? It would be dark soon, and I was beginning to feel the cold now that I had calmed down. I had dressed for the cold but not the extreme cold of the night. My feet and hands were already getting numb. I was also starting to realize just how miserably uncomfortable this retreat was. Jagged rock was poking me like small knives through my coveralls, and my legs were falling asleep from being where it was too cramped to move them. I was also starting to feel the symptoms of my pregnancy. I was feeling a little nauseated and I really needed to pee. It seemed like hours I lay there, but then exhaustion took over and despite how uncomfortable I was, I drifted off to sleep. When I woke up, I heard the roar of a motor and the sound of William calling my name.

"Allie, where are you?" He sounded so worried.

Old Harbor - Sisters of Circumstance ~ P.J. Rhea

"I'm here, William!" I yelled.

"Allie, is that you? Where are you? I don't see you!" he was hysterical.

I struggled to get out of my hiding place. I was so sore and stiff I could hardly move. The climbing out was much harder than pushing myself in this small crevice with a bear's growls of encouragement. I flashed my camera to give him an idea of where I was, and the motor roared as he got closer. When he reached me on his ATV, I was working my way out of the small shelter that had protected me. William raced to me and grabbed me up in his arms. He was kissing me and hugging me and had tears of relief on his cheeks.

"Allie, my sweet Allie, I thought I lost you! Why did you leave me? I've been searching for hours. Oh, Allie, I have you back, oh, thank you God, for giving her back to me!"

Others came up behind William. Apparently several men had been helping William search for me. Everyone seemed so happy and relieved I had been found alive and well. Everyone, that is, except for Kevin Marshall. He walked slowly toward the happy reunion and the look on his face surprised me. He almost looked disappointed that I wasn't dead. This man was evil; I knew it and I had to see if Rachel was okay. I was more convinced than ever that something was wrong with my friend. She would not go this long without talking to me unless someone was keeping her from it. She would have been in on the search for me if she could. But why couldn't she? *Something is wrong and I've got to find out what is keeping her away.*

William thanked all the men who had joined in the search and then he picked me up and placed me on his ATV.

"Really, William, I'm fine."

He didn't respond but softly kissed my forehead and placed a blanket around me. He seemed too upset to talk, so I started my usual chatter to fill the uncomfortable quiet. I told him all about the bear and how she was protecting her cubs. How I had become so involved in taking my pictures for my studio, I got lost.

"I'm sorry I worried you."

Old Harbor - Sisters of Circumstance ~ P.J. Rhea

He was very quiet on the way home. Only when we arrived home and he had helped me into the house, did he finally speak.

"Allie, I was so afraid something had happened, that I lost you just like I..."

He stopped himself before he finished the sentence. I knew he was thinking of Mary and how much it had hurt him to lose her. I was sure William had feelings for me. But did he love me? I wasn't sure. Maybe what happened with me just brought back the pain and his feelings for Mary.

William fixed us some soup and a sandwich. He drew a tub of warm water and suggested I should go soak in my beloved clawfoot tub. He smiled and kissed my cheek before clearing the table. I went to the bathroom and was putting out a few candles to light. I loved to soak in the tub by candlelight, with soft music playing. It was so relaxing and exactly what I needed. I went to the kitchen to find matches and noticed William was no longer in the house. I looked out the window and saw him sitting in the garden, Mary's garden. My heart sank. It was Mary he was thinking of today. He still loved her; the ghost who lived here was still in control. I went to my warm tub to soak my wounds and to think about when I should tell William about the baby. I still wanted him to love me before I told him, but would he ever be able to let her go?

I heard the door open and William came in the house. I leaned back and closed my eyes, letting the hot water and music embrace my tired body. I realized the bathroom door was starting to open. I looked toward the door and there stood William. He had a towel around his waist and he looked at me as if he were waiting to see if I would ask him to leave; if I would tell him I wasn't ready. When I didn't respond he came closer and eased his body into the water, while dropping his towel to the floor. I moved forward to give him room and sat there, my heart pounding. Was this another memory of Mary? Would he love me again, with her on his mind, in his heart? I noticed my pounding heart was causing tiny ripples in the water. He had to hear it, and as he leaned me back on his chest, he had to feel it because it was beating so hard my body seemed to shake with each pulse. William had not spoken a word, not uttered a sound. He took the washcloth and started to gently wash me, my arms, my back, my neck, but he refrained from touching areas that would assure me of his intentions. I think the fact that he wasn't touching those places made it more erotic. My entire body was begging for him, but I just leaned into him and waited. I would let him lead me to where this would go. If going to the garden had made him think of Mary, maybe he would realize she was not the one with him and stop before he called me by her name again, but I didn't want him to stop. Even if he was using my body to be with her, I didn't want him to stop. I wanted him desperately. He started to get out of the tub and I felt a wave of disappointment run through me. Was he leaving me like this, aroused and eager for his touch, just to be abandoned? Had he tried to love me but could not escape her memory?

He wrapped himself in the large towel he had left on the floor then reached out for me to take his hand. He helped me from the tub and pulled me into him and wrapped the towel around us both. Our wet bodies clinging together, he kissed me. It was not like any kiss he had given me before. It was a kiss so passionate it made my legs weak and I leaned into him not only from desire but for support, for fear I would fall. I wasn't sure if my legs would hold me up, but even if I found the strength I would still have melted into him. He lifted me up into his strong arms and carried me to our bed. The firelight, along with the candles he had placed all around the room, made both our bodies fully visible. William started at my feet and softly and slowly kissed me, working his way up my anxious frame. This time, he did not refrain from those areas he had in the bath. It was as if he was memorizing every inch of me. My body responded to his every kiss, every touch, as he worked his way back to my lips. I had never felt like this before, never so completely satisfied. Actually, I was satisfied more than once. He made sure of that. He was not a selfish lover and took time to be sure I was completely fulfilled. Suddenly, I realized he had not closed his eyes. He looked at me as he loved me, as if he wanted to be sure he stayed focused on who he was making love to. And then, as he reached his end, his face buried in my neck and breathing hard from the work of his lovemaking, he lifted his face and looked into my eyes and said the words that made my world wonderful and happy.

Old Harbor - Sisters of Circumstance ~ P.J. Rhea

"I love you, Allie, I love *you*, Allie."

He emphasized the word to be sure I understood what he was telling me. That he knew it was me and not Mary he had loved this way. And with that, he smiled and brought me close to him again. He held me for a long while, tenderly kissing me, touching my face and my hair, as if he was seeing me fully for the first time. We made love again and then we both fell into the most peaceful and perfect sleep.

Just before I woke up I dreamed I was being chased by that bear again. I was calling for William, but he would not come to me. In my dream, he had found Mary and she was alive, holding their sweet son. He was standing beside her, his arm around her back and smiling down at them with so much love. I called to him to help me, but he could not hear me because to him, I was not there; only Mary and their son. I bolted up from my sleep almost in tears. William wasn't next to me. I was alone in the bed. Had the love I experienced last night been a dream, too? I saw the towel lying on the floor near the bed. No, it had really happened. But where was William? Had he left for the day without a word? Was he regretting what happened? After all, I saw him at Mary's grave yesterday. I wanted to know why he felt the need to go there before coming in to me. I heard a noise from the kitchen and got up to see if William was there. I put on my robe and eased down the hall to watch him for a minute. I wanted to try to determine his mood before he noticed me there. To see if he was as happy as I was about what happened between us last night.

"Good morning, beautiful, breakfast is ready."

He smiled, flashing that dimple at me as he placed two plates on the table. He had prepared a huge breakfast for us and I was starving and grateful to see it, and to see him. He looked happy. He walked over to me and kissed me so passionately I almost suggested we skip breakfast despite my growling stomach, but I wanted to ask him about Mary. I hated to ruin his wonderful mood, but I needed to be sure. He pulled out my chair for me and poured my coffee. I could really get used to this treatment. We ate in silence for a few minutes and finally William broke it, speaking with a sound of concern in his voice.

"Allie, are you okay? I can tell you're deep in thought about something. Are you sorry about last night?"

Are you kidding, sorry for the best night I have had in my life? I almost said.

"No, William I enjoyed last night very much, especially what you said."

"You mean that I love you," he smiled a little sheepishly, "because I do, Allie, I love you with all my heart."

"William, I saw you in the garden last night."

There, I had said it and instantly felt regret for letting the words go. William seemed a little embarrassed by my declaration, but he had every intention of explaining. He pulled his chair closer to mine and took my hands in his. He kissed them both and then took a deep breath.

"I had to say goodbye. I told her all about you, Allie. How wonderful you are, and beautiful and loving, and that I knew I could never picture my life without you. Mary was my life for so long, and I just couldn't be with you again until I told her how much she had meant to me, but that I was ready to let her go. I won't lie, Allie, she'll be a part of me till the day I die, always live in a part of my heart, and I'll have my memories of her and what we had. But my heart has made room for another now, and I truly think if she could talk to me somehow, she'd tell me she was happy for me and that you're perfect for me. I told her she can rest now, knowing how happy I am."

Until this moment, I couldn't imagine loving this man more than I already did. I don't know if it was the crazy hormones from pregnancy or because I was so blissfully happy at this moment, but I burst into tears and no matter how hard I tried, I could not stop crying. William looked concerned at first and tried to comfort me. Finally, I was able to take in enough air to tell him I was okay.

"I'm just so happy!" I blurted out, and then started crying again.

Old Harbor - Sisters of Circumstance ~ P.J. Rhea

I was telling the truth; I was truly happy. William started to laugh and then gave me a hug.

"Well, I'm happy too, but maybe I'll leave the crying to you."

He continued to hold me and laugh under his breath, trying not to let me see his amusement until I was done.

"Okay, Mrs. Hickman, if you're finished being 'happy,' why don't you go get dressed while I wash these dishes and we'll go work some more on the studio. I'm your slave for the day," he proudly offered.

I stood up and took his hand.

"My slave, huh?"

I smiled an inviting smile while pulling him toward the hall and down to our room. I had a much better idea. The dishes and the studio could wait.

When we did arrive in town several hours later, I went to work editing the pictures from the day before. The pictures of the bear were amazing. One picture was so close to the bear you almost felt as if you were about to be swallowed by it. William was very impressed.

"I have to say, that is the best close-up of a grizzly I have ever seen!"

"I guess I had a unique vantage point. Not too many people get a close-up that good and live to tell about it."

He cringed at the thought of how close I came to being mauled by the giant animal. I had to admit it made me shudder. We spent the rest of the day working toward my open house. It was going to be so great. We had found a nice couch and loveseat at a thrift store in Kodiak for the front room, and I had purchased a new desk and file cabinet from the furniture store located just as you got off the ferry. Some of the talented locals were in the process of painting different backgrounds for me, and I was searching for props to use in the portraits. I refused, however, to buy a white wicker chair or a green carpet to use in any of them. I asked if he thought some of the local businesses would let me hang up a few samples of my work.

113

Old Harbor - Sisters of Circumstance - P.J. Rhea

"I don't see why not, let's go ask."

I picked out some of my favorites and framed them. I wanted to check The Lodge, the Ellises' restaurant, and of course the Trading Post. I was a little nervous about seeing Mama again. I hadn't told William about the baby and I hoped she would not mention it again within his hearing.

We went to The Lodge first, and they were more than happy to display the new pictures. I had a picture of William peacefully fishing, with a beautiful sunrise in the background. There was a mystical fog just above the water surrounding him. Was it just because I was so in love, or did he look like an angel? I laughed to myself when I hung it and he gave me a crooked grin, making his dimple deep, and he winked at our shared secret of a morning filled with lovemaking. While we were at The Lodge, Trudy and Samuel came over to admire the artwork. Trudy looked amazing. She continued to lose weight and glowed with happiness. They asked if they could follow along with us to the other shops just to say hi to everyone.

When we arrived at the Ellis Family Restaurant, they too were more than happy to display my work. They took the picture of a moose with her baby near a stream. I was saving the bear with her cubs for the Trading Post, simply because of the large wooden bear out front. And the close-up from under the ledge would go in my studio. Word would get around about that one, I thought, and it could draw potential customers. William said I had a very clever mind for business.

Corinna was doing well with her pregnancy and Jay's family seemed to love her; they were all very excited about the baby. It was hard to believe she was the same girl we met just ten weeks ago. Trudy and I were making small talk with Corinna about planning a baby shower, so they came along with us to the Trading Post. It was so wonderful to see my sisters and spend some time with them. We hadn't gotten around to our second girls' night out. I guess we were all just too busy having the best time of our life. Luke came into the little store while we were there and shared a letter he had received from Lynn. She was back in school and seemed very happy.

114

Old Harbor - Sisters of Circumstance ~ P.J. Rhea

"She may be growing up, finally," he laughed.

They were all impressed by the picture of the grizzly, and I told the story several times as people came up to admire it. It was a wonderful day and we were all having a great time. I couldn't help but think how perfect things could be if only Rachel would join us. I hadn't seen her in two months and I knew something was wrong. I had continued to attempt to visit and call with no luck. William had promised we would go by tomorrow. A surprise visit might bring us better success.

We were about to leave when I heard the people in the store gasp. I turned and saw Rachel and Kevin enter the store. My heart jumped, and I smiled for only a second. Then I realized something was very wrong. Rachel looked scared to death. She had deep, dark circles under her eyes and had lost weight. She was already slim, so she looked very frail and weak. Her eyes were lifeless and dull when she looked at me. She didn't smile. Her brilliant wide smile stayed hidden, and I knew this was not going to be a pleasant meeting. I started toward her, to hug my friend and say hello, despite the fact that Kevin was holding her tightly against him. I saw desperation in her face. She looked like a caged animal or something.

What's wrong? I wanted to ask. As I got closer a hundred questions were running through my mind, and the closer I got the more frightened she looked. When I was only a few feet away from her, she started to move quickly and with determination. She reached into Kevin's coat and pulled out something, then pushed away from him.

"Oh, God, no, Rachel, what are you doing! William, she has a gun!"

As the words left my mouth, my friend, my sister, placed the pistol against her temple. I could hear myself screaming at her, but at the same time, I must have been in shock. It seemed that everything was moving slower than normal. Everyone's movements were exaggerated.

"Oh please, Rachel, put the gun down," I pleaded. "Don't leave me; you're my sister, my friend. I need you to stay with me!"

Old Harbor - Sisters of Circumstance ~ P.J. Rhea

Trudy and Corinna were also begging Rachel to put the gun down and to come to them. I could hear William, Luke, Jay, Samuel, all begging; all of us desperate to help our friend; everyone except Kevin. The man who had asked her to come to this place to be his wife was just standing there with a smirk across his face. When we started to question him about his lack of action, he started shouting about her being a whore and a drug addict.

I wanted to scream at him, "You're a liar!" I knew one thing for certain: Rachel would not be on drugs, not without force. I didn't care if she had needle marks; I knew it was not true. Just as I was about to speak, Rachel yelled at Kevin about a skeleton in the cellar of his house. Everyone was stunned by the words, shocked at the implication behind them. Kevin started toward Rachel and she turned the gun toward him as a warning that he better not take another step. As soon as he backed off, she put it back to her temple and screamed for us to be quiet. She had the strangest look on her face. At first she appeared frantic and almost crazy but suddenly her expression changed to what looked to be calm and relaxed, as if her mind was made up and she was at peace with what she was about to do. She started looking toward the corner of the store, and I realized she was watching Mama. Mama was facing her as well, and seemed to be communicating with her in some way. With the gun still against her head, I heard the click of the hammer.

I couldn't help but cry out, "Oh, please, Rachel! I need you here to help with the baby, stay with me!"

Then I buried my head in William's chest, not wanting to witness my friend's end. I heard a loud pop, then the sound of one big gasp from all who witnessed her action. It was followed by silence, as if all who stood there could not believe what just happened.

I smelled the gunpowder; at the same time I heard a heavy thud on the floor. I looked up at William to confirm my fear and realized he was looking at me with a shocked expression on his face, and not at what had just happened. He had heard what I said to Rachel. We both turned to look toward Rachel and Kevin, and William rushed to them. There stood my friend with the gun still clenched in her hand, and Kevin Marshall lay at her feet with a large,

Old Harbor - Sisters of Circumstance ~ P.J. Rhea

bleeding hole in his chest. William approached Rachel and asked her to hand him the gun, which she did. It was obvious Rachel had been a victim of something horrible, but before any of us could get near her Mark Sims swiftly approached and led her away from us in handcuffs. Luke followed behind Rachel and the rest of my friends followed Luke. I tried to run after her, but William stopped me.

"We'll check on her back at the jail in a little while, but for now, is there something you need to tell me?"

I was still so rattled by what just happened I wasn't sure what he meant at first, but then it hit me.

"Oh, yeah, I guess we do need to talk."

We walked over to my studio so we would have privacy. I was so emotional about what happened with Rachel that as soon as I was alone with him I began to cry. William was patient, and seemed to understand that I had to cry first before I could talk to him. I laid my head on his strong shoulder and my body shook with grief and relief at the same time. Once I felt I had cried as long as I needed to, I moved to the edge of the small couch we had placed in my studio's front room and faced my new husband.

"I'm sorry I haven't told you about the baby, William, but I wanted to be sure you loved me and not just loved the fact that I was having your baby. Apparently I became pregnant on our wedding night."

I was expecting him to be overjoyed. I smiled, waiting for a hug and a returned smile with words of how wonderful the news was. I looked into his eyes and it was not joy that I saw.

"William, are you angry with me? I thought you would be happy when you found out."

William looked away from me for a few minutes and I could tell he was trying to decide what to say. He looked very unhappy. I started to feel as if I might start crying again, but for a different reason. William realized I was becoming upset and took me into his arms.

117

Old Harbor - Sisters of Circumstance ~ P.J. Rhea

"Oh, Allie my love, I am happy about the baby. But I'm also scared. I'm afraid I'll lose you; that something will happen to you and this baby like…well, like with Mary. I can't go through that again. If you die trying to give me a child, I'll die too. Losing Mary almost killed me, and I never dreamed I'd love anyone again. I could never have imagined this kind of love twice in a lifetime. Please don't leave me, Allie; I love you more than I have a right to."

He was upset and holding me so tightly I had to push hard to get free of his grip. Once he released me, I took his hands in mine.

"William, I'll never leave you. I know life is uncertain and I can't promise nothing will ever happen to me, but I can't imagine God letting such a terrible thing happen to such a wonderful, caring man twice in a lifetime. We're going to be so happy, and this baby will be such a blessing, maybe even a healing for us both."

I decided to use Mama's word. He seemed to feel a little reassured by my words and smiled that crooked smile I loved so much. The one that made his dimple look so deep. He placed his hand on my stomach for a few minutes.

"I love you, Allie."

After a long embrace and a cleansing breath or two, we were ready to go check on Rachel. We walked the short distance to the little jail where Mr. Sims' office was. It reminded me of an old T.V. show and I almost wanted to ask Officer Sims if he carried one bullet in his pocket and did he have an Aunt Bea at home, but I decided it would be impolite. Not everyone appreciated my sarcastic sense of humor. We asked if we could see Rachel.

"I'm afraid she isn't here, Mrs. Hickman. That poor girl has been to hell and back the last two months," he said, as he shook his head in a gesture of disbelief. "We had her transported to the hospital in Anchorage. I have a feeling she'll be there for a while. Luke Fowler rode along in the helicopter that brought the police from Anchorage. He agreed to represent her, so he'll know how to get her some help."

118

Old Harbor - Sisters of Circumstance ~ P.J. Rhea

It had never occurred to me before to ask what Luke did for a living. I guess I had assumed he was a guide or something in this small town. How lucky for Rachel he was an attorney.

"Poor Rachel," I said. "I hope I can talk to her soon."

William took my hand in his, as if to assure me he understood my disappointment in not making it to the jail in time. Mark Sims continued to explain to us that a doctor had also been flown down from Anchorage. He was their medical examiner, and first went to pronounce Kevin dead so the officers could start processing the scene. Then he was escorted to the jail to check on Rachel.

"Well," the officer continued, "she was in shock. Once we got her to the jail, she had a breakdown of sorts and had to be sedated. It was so sad; she got upset when the doctor tried to give her the shot to relax her. She started fighting us and yelling, 'please, Kevin don't, I'm begging you.' The doctor gave her a quick look-over before transport, and I swear the man broke down and cried when he saw what that animal did to the poor girl. He said he had never seen such abuse in all his years!"

I buried my face in William's arm and shuddered at the mention of what my friend had endured since the day of our weddings. While we were talking to Officer Sims, he got a call to confirm that a skeleton had been found in the cellar of the Marshall house. They also said Kevin Marshall had pictures of not only Rachel, but of the woman he had moved here, and of several other women in different stages of torture; many after he had killed them.

"The FBI will have to be called in on this, because it appears that our Mr. Marshall was a serial killer."

Oh, Rachel I am so sorry. I should have tried harder to get to you. My heart was sick with remorse to the point I felt like I might throw up.

"William, will she ever forgive me? Can I forgive myself for letting this happen to her?"

William reassured me, "Allie, she'll be okay; it's going to take time. You probably saved her life. She knew someone cared, and

119

Old Harbor - Sisters of Circumstance ~ P.J. Rhea

that gave her the will to stay alive. In the store, you let her know there were reasons to go on, to not end her life."

William took me back to our cabin and just held me all night. I spent most of the night asking myself all the questions that cause us to beat ourselves up, but eventually I realized I had to forgive myself and just be ready to help her when she came back.

Before my mother died, one night while she was still coherent she said to me, "Allie girl, I have not always been right and I've made my share of mistakes. I've hurt people without meaning to and I've disappointed people who loved me, but I'm at peace because I know I never did any of it on purpose. I've forgiven myself for being human and I've asked as many as I could to forgive me as well. Life is way too short for regret and guilt. Regrets are a waste of time, Allie, they're just your past crippling your future. Don't be too hard on yourself."

I knew I had to let go of the feeling that I had caused Rachel's pain. It happened, and I would be the friend she needed in order to get better. I fell asleep in William's arms and dreamed of a brighter future for Rachel. It was not too late for her to find happiness. And now she had family to lean on. She had three sisters who would give her strength. And she was going to be an aunt. Corinna and I would both make her realize that. She was no longer the foundling no one wanted; she had family.

∞ Chapter Ten ∞

Justice for All

Two weeks passed and I wanted desperately to go see Rachel, but Luke, who gave us daily updates, insisted she did not want visitors. She did not want to face us in her present situation.

It had never occurred to me that she would be charged with Kevin's murder. If anything, she should be given a medal, I protested.

"I agree with you, Allie, and I promise I'm doing everything possible to see that she's found not guilty."

Luke was working day and night for Rachel. He was able to convince the judge to leave her in the psychiatric wing of the hospital instead of jail because of all she had been put through. She was in a part of the hospital that had bars on the windows and a door that locked from the outside. It was hospital policy to have a security guard at the entrance of that particular wing of the hospital, so no extra security was ordered. Luke apologized to Rachel for not getting her released, but she told him she didn't mind.

"I know he's gone, but I still feel safer knowing he can't get to me. I know that sounds crazy, but I still have vivid nightmares and when I wake up and find myself in this room…I'm actually relieved," she explained.

Rachel was feeling stronger physically every day; however, the emotional wounds would not heal as quickly. Try as he might, Luke couldn't keep the reality of what was happening outside away from her. She watched the news religiously, hearing her life story told for all to hear, and there were always newspapers available in the room where the patients waited for their scheduled time with their counselor. The district attorney was using this case as a career stepping-stone and felt the need to share as much as he was allowed to with the media. Before finding out exactly what kind of monster

Old Harbor - Sisters of Circumstance ~ P.J. Rhea

Kevin Marshall was, they made Rachel the villain. *Man Shot in Cold Blood by His New Mail-order Bride,* was the headline the first morning after her arrest. It was full of information about her past profession and accused her of killing him because he was keeping her from the drugs she craved. Apparently there were a couple of tourists in the Trading Post that day, and they were very talkative when the reporters showed up. Rachel was becoming more and more depressed and ashamed of what the whole town now knew.

"How can I ever face my friends again? I can't imagine showing my face in Old Harbor after what Kevin told them and the newspapers have confirmed. They must all think of me as trash now."

Luke tried to convince Rachel that her friends still cared for her. That no one believed Kevin's accusation about the drugs, and she would be welcomed back with open arms once she was found not guilty.

"What if I'm found guilty, Luke? I don't want to go to prison. It's so unfair that I could go to jail for killing a killer."

"Rachel, please believe me. I will not let that happen."

Luke placed his hand over Rachel's hand but she quickly pulled hers away and they both blushed at the awkward moment between them.

Luke, how stupid can you be? he thought. *After what she's been through the last thing she wants is for any guy to touch her. If she only knew how I feel about her she would...she would...what, run into your arms? Get over yourself, Luke Fowler. This poor girl only sees her lawyer when she looks at you, and the last thing she needs right now is the added complication of knowing you have feelings for her.*

Rachel walked over toward the window and looked outside, almost afraid to make eye contact again with Luke.

"I know you're doing all you can and I do really appreciate it. I don't know how I'll ever pay you for all your help, but I'll figure something out."

Old Harbor - Sisters of Circumstance ~ P.J. Rhea

Luke almost seemed hurt by her concern about fees and left the room with a quick response of, "You don't worry about that. I'll be back tomorrow, Rachel...have a good night."

Oh Luke, it isn't going to prison that scares me...It's the idea of never seeing you again that I can't stand. Rachel, how stupid to even wish he could ever care for you. You're just a client. He'd never want to be with a woman who's done what you've done...a woman who has a body that's a constant reminder of what happened to her. He'd probably be repulsed by the thought of touching you.

But touching her was exactly what he wanted to do. He wanted to take her into his arms and hold her close and whisper to her that he would protect her. Tell her that no one could ever hurt her again and that to him she was the most beautiful and most desirable woman on the planet. But he would never do that. How could he, knowing what she had been through? Men had used her and treated her like property her entire life. He couldn't take a chance on hurting her again, even if it meant never telling her how he felt.

Rachel watched from the window as Luke made his way to his car in the hospital parking lot. He looked up at her window just before getting in and waved to her. Rachel knew men, and the sad truth was that she had been with hundreds in her lifetime. Most were nothing more than a job. She had felt absolutely nothing while she engaged in what should be an intimate act with them. She had become quite the little actress, always making them think they were pleasuring her. But the truth was she had never felt anything with most of them. She had never had a physical relationship with Luke Fowler, but every time they had touched since her arrival in Old Harbor it had been electric. The handshake in the basement of the church that first night, the hug to congratulate her on her marriage on the wedding day, and now when he placed his hand on her hand. She had to admit there was something between them. There was electricity that surged between them. But if he felt it too, he certainly wasn't letting her know it.

How can you even think about a relationship right now? You've been through hell and you're wondering if he likes you back. I must have lost my mind to even be considering any of this. You killed a man. You could be going to jail for the rest of your life. How can you possibly be thinking about love?

But she was.

While Rachel spent time getting stronger in the hospital, Luke was finding out more and more about Kevin Marshall. Once the skeleton was discovered in his cellar the Crime Scene Investigators had been called in from Anchorage. Kevin's house was searched from top to bottom, and so was his bait shop and property. The more they found, the more Luke realized just how lucky Rachel was to be alive.

It turned out Mr. Marshall had lived in several out-of-the-way places over the past twelve years. The skeletal remains of his victims had been recovered as a result of the evidence found in his Old Harbor home. Each one had been in a different town. He feared if he killed twice in the same area it would draw attention to him, but he liked Old Harbor and the fishing trade and wanted to stay there. When he heard about the mail-order bride idea the men were considering, he laughed at the idea of participating. He had highlighted in his writings that it was like ordering take-out. Luke shuddered when he saw it. To Kevin, she was an easy target and nothing more. To Luke she had become everything, and as he learned more details of Kevin's plans for Rachel he became so angry that if Kevin were not already dead it may have been Luke on trial for murder. Luke had no doubt he would have killed him himself if he had known.

It seemed that Kevin had started keeping a record of his quest just after his first victim and the journals, along with other pieces of evidence, were kept neatly in a box in the attic. He had kept souvenirs of his victims. Each was listed in the journal, telling who it belonged to and even in some cases what it had meant to the woman he had taken it from. One was a locket with a picture of a baby she had lost. There were rings and locks of hair; even a gold tooth. There was also a picture of each victim, possibly taken early in their time with him. All of them had on the exact same style of teddy, and all of them had the same expression of terror on their faces as if it was at this moment they knew what was going to happen to them—including Rachel.

Along with the pictures and property he also had a daily log of what he had done to them on any given day. Some were luckier

Old Harbor - Sisters of Circumstance ~ P.J. Rhea

than others, because their death had been quick. He had killed them after only days, or maybe weeks. Others were kept for months, and one poor woman had lived this hell for two years before she finally died, possibly from starvation. How long they lived depended a lot on his location and how easy it was to keep their existence a secret. To him they were like experiments to see how much they could endure. He even logged the food he had given them, how often he allowed them to bathe, and how often they had to relieve themselves in the toilet. As his interest in a victim started to lesson due to boredom or because she no longer excited him with her fear, he would kill them by hitting them in the head with something. In the case of one woman he just stopped feeding her until she died. The pictures of her were the hardest to look at. The last picture was taken as she lay dying. She looked like skin stretched tightly over bone, with her hair mostly gone. Her naked body was covered from the top of her face to her feet in scars showing the torture she had suffered for those two years. The section he wrote about her revealed she had not gone one day in those two years, including her last, without some pain being inflicted upon her.

As each woman's body was discovered and identified there was another sad discovery. None of them had ever been reported missing. He chose his victims carefully from people no one would miss, and had hidden their bodies so well that had it not been for Rachel he may have never been stopped.

He also wrote about his childhood almost as if trying to explain why he had to do this, as if any explanation would make it okay. He had come from a family with a very abusive father. Life had not been good to him and from what his journal seemed to imply, as he got older it got worse. Once he was away from home he really needed help dealing with a lot of bad memories. He was full of anger and hate toward his father and he didn't know how to deal with it. He was getting into fights almost daily and was told by many people— including the police—that he needed to get help dealing with his problem. Instead of getting the right kind of help he continued dealing with his own pain by inflicting pain on others. Soon he realized the pain he caused others somehow gave him pleasure, and when the pain

125

was inflicted on a woman it was arousing him sexually. It was something he had inherited from his father, apparently.

The first time he killed someone it had been a total accident—at least according to his own journal. But he liked the excitement and the thrill he got from getting away with it. The woman was a prostitute and had no family to speak of. He wrote of how he wanted to try to get away with it again, so he sought out someone who would not be missed if she vanished. When he got away with it a second time, he felt powerful. He was unstoppable. The book gave details about how he found his victims, and with each one he would try to make it more challenging. He recorded eight victims in all.

The last one was Rachel. He told about how he had played on Carl Bible's need to make all the men of Old Harbor as happy as he. He managed to sneak into the church office when Carl and Gwen were gone to Kodiak and looked over all the applicants. He said when he saw Rachel's picture he wanted her and that it was clear from her application that she had no family to speak of. She had put that she was an orphan and just wanted a chance at a family. There was even a copy of the report he got back from a hired detective telling about her "career" and police record in New York. He had put in gross detail telling what he had done to her and even how he planned to kill her once he came up with a believable story to tell those nosey friends of hers. He wrote of his hate for Allie and how she had ruined his plans. His writing had taken on a different persona and it was clear he was losing control. He had even played with the idea of killing all the women who had befriended Rachel, but could not come up with a plan that would not convict him. He became sloppy and irrational, rambling on and on about his need to kill Rachel and his fury over the people he felt were keeping him from doing it. It was the best piece of evidence Luke could ask for.

Surely with Kevin's own handwritten confession of what he had done to her there would be no problem getting Rachel off on a defense of temporary insanity caused by the stress she was living under from the daily torture. Luke had been afraid if he used self-defense as her motive it would be pointed out that she had the gun and they were in a store full of people. All she would have had to do was ask Officer Sims, who was standing behind her, to arrest Kevin.

Old Harbor - Sisters of Circumstance ~ P.J. Rhea

She wouldn't have to shoot him to escape. But Luke truly felt she did lose her mind for a while. No one could live through what she had for two months and not go a little insane from it. He would make the judge see that Rachel saw no other way of escape in her fragile frame of mind. If it went to a jury he had no doubt they would understand how she would feel that way after seeing pictures of her tortured body and hearing what Kevin had done to her.

Luke had hoped to keep as much as possible away from Rachel. For her to hear the horrible torture the other women had suffered would only hurt her already fragile state of mind. Luke wanted more than anything to protect Rachel from any more hurt, but with bodies being discovered so many places it soon became national news and there was little he could do to keep it from her. The media was in a frenzy trying to find out as much detail as they could and put it on the news. They were trying to find a way to ask Rachel about her time with Kevin. The paper had headlined "The Only Surviving Victim," and that would have sounded like a good thing had they not also put details about all his victims being prostitutes and reminding the readers of Rachel's past. Just as Luke had feared, her nightmares came more often and she would dream in great detail about what could have happened to her. She would wake up screaming, and if the doctors tried to sedate her she would fight them, thinking they were Kevin. It broke Luke's heart, and still he was afraid to take her in his arms and comfort her as he desperately wanted to do.

Luke was making trips back and forth to Old Harbor several times a week to keep Allie and the others updated on Rachel's case and on her condition.

"Please ask her again to let me come see her," Allie would plead with each visit.

Luke would carry her request to Rachel, only to be told again how she was just too ashamed to face her friends. It had been over two months since Rachel killed Kevin. She was both physically and mentally stronger now and would most likely be discharged soon. Luke had been working sixteen hours a day, seven days a week, compiling all he needed to present to the district attorney in an effort to get the charges dropped. He knew a defense of temporary insanity

Old Harbor - Sisters of Circumstance ~ P.J. Rhea

was hard to prove and the percentage of cases where that defense won was small, but he had a very good case. Kevin had proven to be a long-time serial killer and had, in his own words, confessed to his intentions to kill Rachel. Kevin had even supplied them with evidence and a confession as to the torture Rachel suffered for the two months leading up to the shooting.

The media calmed down some and even turned to a more sympathetic approach when telling about Rachel, which in turn gave her an almost celebrity status in town. Women from all over were on her side, but especially in Anchorage, and the district attorney knew it. This being an election year didn't hurt Luke's cause either. What would the voters think of him if he punished a victim for ridding the world of this monster? A couple of days before Rachel was to be brought before the judge and formally charged with second degree murder, Luke had an appointment with Adam Clever, the district attorney, to try to convince him to drop the charges. Luke knew if this case went to a jury trial Rachel would most likely be found not guilty due to the overwhelming evidence against Kevin Marshall and the proof of what he had done to her. But he didn't want to put her through a trial if it were possible to get the charges dropped. It would be humiliating to have to relive all of it in front of her friends, and if he could spare her that pain he would. It would be up to Adam to get the jury to feel, without reasonable doubt, that Rachel killed Kevin out of malice and deserved to be punished for her crime. Once Adam Clever heard all the evidence and he and Luke talked about the possible outcomes for several hours, he agreed to drop the charges. He admitted to Luke, off the record of course, that he too had started to feel sorry for Rachel and really didn't want to punish her for what she had done.

"She should get a medal," Adam admitted. "But you didn't hear that from me."

Luke called Allie while he drove to the hospital to tell Rachel.

"Oh Luke, that is wonderful news. Now she can come home. Tell her we love her and can't wait to see her."

Old Harbor - Sisters of Circumstance ~ P.J. Rhea

Luke agreed to tell Rachel, but he knew how she felt about facing her friends now that everyone knew about her past. He hoped telling her what Allie said would change her mind. The thought that she may leave was hard for Luke to even think about. It was late when he arrived at the hospital and they almost wouldn't let him in to see her. Once he explained to them the reason for the late-night visit they were more than happy to let him wake her. The hospital staff loved Rachel and they were all very happy for her. Luke eased into her room and sat on her bed. He was anxious to tell her the news, but he just sat there for a while and watched her sleep. His heart began to ache at the possibility that she might leave. He wanted to tell her how much he cared for her, and that the past didn't matter to him. He knew every detail of the journey that led her here, including the story of her childhood, and it just made her dearer to him. He wanted to be her protector and her friend and—yes, he wanted to be her lover—but he knew the last thing she needed right now was to feel indebted to him for all he had done for her. He wanted her to love him, not to feel she owed it to him to stay because she didn't want to hurt his feelings. Luke reached out and gently stroked her cheek.

"Rachel," he whispered "I have great news."

∾

Luke arrived at the hospital the next day to drive Rachel to the airport. She was extremely happy and grateful when Luke told her she had been cleared of the charges and could go home. He hoped that meant back to Old Harbor, but Rachel asked him if he would help her get back to New York.

"I promise I'll repay the money for the ticket as soon as I get a job and can save up the money. I hope everyone will understand why I have to go back to New York."

The only person she asked to talk to before leaving was Carl Bible. Luke called him and asked him to come as soon as possible. Maybe Carl could convince her to stay. Carl arrived early the next morning, and Luke made sure to tell him how much everyone wanted her to stay; maybe he could talk some sense into her. Carl went in to see Rachel alone. He knew what Luke wanted, but he was there at

Old Harbor - Sisters of Circumstance ~ P.J. Rhea

Rachel's request and he would just listen and let her say her piece. When Carl left her room he was near tears himself, and he only looked at Luke and shook his head.

"She asked that you come back in an hour and pick her up, Luke. I'm sorry, but she still plans to go to New York."

Rachel looked so sad when he picked her up. The drive to the airport was in complete silence. Luke was afraid to speak for fear he would not be able to control himself and would start begging her not to go.

I won't put that kind of pressure on her.

Rachel was afraid if she opened her mouth she would burst into tears and admit to Luke she wanted to be with him.

He's done enough for me. I won't make him feel sorry for me and ask me to stay out of pity.

When Luke pulled up to the entrance of the airport and started to get out and open Rachel's door she stopped him.

"I'm fine with going in alone. I actually think it will be easier," she half smiled. "Would you please give this letter to Allie for me? She's been a friend, and the closest I have ever had to family. I hope she'll understand why I have to do this. Well…I guess this is goodbye, then. Thank you again for all you've done for me, Luke."

Tears started to burn her eyes and she knew she had better leave quickly if she didn't want to break down in front of him. She rushed into the airport and Luke sat there lost as to what to do next. Finally a horn honked behind him and pulled him back to reality. He pulled away feeling as if he had lost his reason to ever smile again. He held on to the letter as he drove to the other side of the airport where his small plane was kept. It was the last thing she had touched and it gave him some comfort. He would go straight to Old Harbor and take it to Allie. He would not leave until he knew what it said. He could hope she mentioned him and would give him the reason he was looking for to go after her.

130

∞ Chapter Eleven ∞

Heartsick

The grand opening of my studio was a great success. Carl brought Gwen and John for a family portrait a few days before the official opening and I had their beautiful family displayed as an example of my work. Little John had his first two tiny teeth on the bottom and they showed in the pictures when he smiled, which was most of the time. He was a very happy baby. Holding him made me more excited about my own baby growing inside me. I told Gwen our news and she was so happy for us. She was also glad that John would have other children his age to play with. Corinna and Jay would have their baby soon, and all these babies coming made us all feel hopeful for the future of Old Harbor.

I had also taken dozens of pictures of Old Harbor and its people and placed them on the walls of my studio for all to enjoy. After seeing what a great job I did Carl decided the church needed a directory, and requested that I make it my first big project. Of course I told him I would be honored. How could I say no after all this lovely couple had done for me? Trudy and Samuel also came by to have their picture taken. Every time I saw them I was amazed at how wonderful they were both looking. It didn't require any effort on my part to get smiles from them. They were so very happy together.

William was telling all his fishing and hunting tourists they should get a picture made with their trophy catch. And for those who came away empty-handed: "Well, you still need something to remember this vacation by," he would tell them. Luke stopped by and brought me a beautiful bouquet of roses and wished me success. He had been visiting Rachel and working hard on her case. He would come by the studio a couple of times a week to keep us posted on Rachel's progress.

Old Harbor - Sisters of Circumstance ~ P.J. Rhea

"She's getting better slowly, Allie. I'm afraid she's thinking about going back to New York if everything goes well at her hearing. She isn't sure if she can handle seeing this place again."

I wanted to see her. I didn't want to be selfish, but I wanted my sister back.

"Please, Luke, ask her to let me come visit. I want to see her so badly."

Rachel had requested no visitors for now. She was so ashamed of what had happened and that she had considered taking her own life in front of us.

"Give her time Allie, she'll come around. I'll relay the message and ask her again if you can come for a visit."

She had been away for six weeks now and would be released from the hospital soon. That should have been the end of the story, but once she was taken to Anchorage the district attorney wanted to place formal charges against her. Luke was able to keep her out of jail only because of the evidence of the horrible abuse she had endured and the doctor's confirmation that she needed physical and mental help as soon as possible. Luke felt her best defense would be temporary insanity. He didn't think self-defense would work, due to the fact that she had shot an unarmed man in front of witnesses.

"Luke, it seems it should be cut and dried once the evidence of his abuse is presented. Plus, I thought the fact that there was a skeleton in his basement and proof of other victims found in his house should make them want to thank her, not punish her."

"I completely agree with you, Allie, but the prosecuting attorney in Anchorage ran a criminal check on Rachel and decided that her past record implied she may have stayed with Kevin willingly."

"What? How insane is that? Luke, you don't believe that for a second, do you?"

"Of course I don't feel that way, and I have no doubt that if this goes to trial a jury will also see she had no choice in the matter."

Old Harbor - Sisters of Circumstance ~ P.J. Rhea

Luke spent every day possible working on Rachel's case and just encouraging her in her recovery. She still would not allow any of us to visit her. The newspaper wrote about the case for weeks and mentioned Rachel's past. They implied her past was possible proof that the killing wasn't self-defense. Rachel was so ashamed she just didn't want to face any of us. I was so furious that those vultures were looking at this case as a stepping stone to further their careers. This was big news in a tiny town that until now wasn't even on many maps. News crews had flown over the "House of Torture" as they called it, and at times almost made it sound as if Rachel was some type of sadomasochist who enjoyed what Kevin did to her. That because of her past profession it could be assumed she liked it. My heart was breaking for her. I knew she was scared and embarrassed and needed a friend desperately, but she refused to talk to any of us. Not even to me, and I already knew about her past.

It was beginning to look as if this horrible injustice might actually go to trial. We were all afraid we might be called as witnesses against our dear friend. Luke was still certain the plea of temporary insanity was the best way to go. He spent most of his waking hours looking into Kevin Marshall's past. He was aware that the FBI found a long trail behind Kevin leading to the discovery of other victims of his cruel nature. It even became a big story on national news due to the fact that his victims came from several different states. With each new development in the history of Kevin Marshall I was more and more convinced they could never punish Rachel for this obvious attempt to save her own life.

Luke called the day before Rachel was to be released from the hospital.

"I have wonderful news, Allie!"

Luke explained how he had gotten the charges dropped and Rachel would be free to go.

"And now that she's free she'll just have to come back to us," I reasoned. "If she can find the courage to return, she'd have resources here to provide for herself. All of Kevin Marshall's property is hers, as his widow, to do with as she pleases."

Old Harbor - Sisters of Circumstance ~ P.J. Rhea

Luke didn't seem impressed with my suggestion. He hated the idea of Kevin helping Rachel, even in a monetary way, after his death. This animal had ruined her life. Had almost taken her life from her, and Luke wanted nothing of him left behind to touch Rachel. I had a feeling she felt the same way.

Luke was supposed to pick Rachel up from the hospital the following day. He told us he wasn't sure where she would want him to take her.

"She's still thinking about going back to New York, but maybe that will change."

She asked to see Carl, as her spiritual advisor, and I guess we were all hoping he could talk her into coming back to Old Harbor. I think she felt she needed to be forgiven for all that had happened. I wanted to see her so desperately; to get her to understand that none of the things that had happened to her in New York or in Old Harbor were her fault. Corinna was also very upset about Rachel's lack of self-worth.

"She helped me tremendously when I told about what happened to me. Rachel lifted my spirits so much after we told our stories that first night. She's been a good friend to me, to all of us. She just has to come back Allie, we need her!"

When Carl and Luke returned from their visit with Rachel, I could tell instantly something was wrong. Both men looked as if they were coming to inform a family of a death. Corinna and Trudy were with me at the studio, looking over their proofs, when the men walked in. William followed behind them and I could tell as soon as I saw his face that he had already been told the results of the visit. He came over and sat next to me as if to brace me for what was coming.

"What's wrong? Has Rachel had some kind of setback?"

I examined the faces that were looking back at me for a clue.

"Carl?"

I looked at him, waiting for some answer to my question. He finally spoke.

Old Harbor - Sisters of Circumstance ~ P.J. Rhea

"Rachel went back to New York, Allie. She just couldn't face the memories of this town. She said she couldn't stand the idea of the people of Old Harbor knowing about her past. She said they would look at her differently."

William knew this would be a hard blow, and wrapped his arms around me from behind. I couldn't find words. I just sat there, staring at them as if waiting for the punch line. This was a joke, right? Rachel would not leave without even talking to me. We were friends, sisters, family. Corinna and Trudy were both chattering about how terrible it was and how they would miss her. How they hoped they would hear from her from time to time and that her life would take a turn for the better. NO, I was thinking loudly in my head, but still not speaking. Luke looked as upset as I did when he handed me an envelope.

"She asked me to give this to you."

On the front it said "To my Sister," and my heart sank at the idea of never seeing her again.

I held the letter close to me, not ready to read it. Carl stood up and started toward the door, but then stopped and turned to speak before leaving.

"Do you know why she wanted me to come to see her? She was worried about me! Can you believe that? After all she went through she was thinking about how I might be feeling! Before she left to go back to New York, she wanted to be certain I wasn't blaming myself for matching them together."

I lied on my application, Brother Carl, and I'm pretty sure Kevin lied too, so you can't feel bad about putting us together.

Carl was silent for a while.

"I admit I was feeling very guilty about what happened to her. What a special person she is for even thinking of me right now!"

Carl's eyes were getting wet and I knew he was about to cry. He left quickly and Trudy and Corinna followed soon after. Luke seemed to be waiting to see what was in the letter. He just kept looking at me, and I could tell her leaving was hard on him as well.

Old Harbor - Sisters of Circumstance ~ P.J. Rhea

Maybe there would be a reasonable explanation in this letter as to why she had to go. I stared at the envelope for a minute more, and then pulled out the contents.

Dear Allie,

I hope you can forgive me for leaving without coming to see you first. I can still see the fear on your face when we were in the store and I worry you feel you are at fault for what happened to me. Don't, I have always had bad things happen to me, but you were the one good thing. You were my friend, even after knowing the truth, and you made me feel like I truly had family for the first time in my life. Maybe I'll be able to visit someday. Keep in touch and send pictures of the baby.

Your sister, Rachel

William hugged me to remind me he was there for me. Luke just stared at the door unsure if he should leave or stay. As I watched Luke to see what he would do next the truth suddenly hit me right in the face. How did I not see it before? Luke had feelings for Rachel. I could see it in his eyes. He was in love with her and was as heartsick over her leaving as I was. I looked at William, as if to question my own assumption and he gave my shoulders a squeeze and smiled in agreement. He knew what I was thinking. That's why he was so eager to help her. Why he wasn't upset when Lynn left.

"Luke, are you okay?" I asked.

"I should have tried harder to get her to come back to Old Harbor. She needs to be here with people who care about her, like…well, like me."

"Luke, did you tell her you had feelings for her?"

He made no attempt to deny the feelings I had just accused him of having, but instead very sadly began to explain how he felt.

Old Harbor - Sisters of Circumstance ~ P.J. Rhea

"Allie, I knew she was meant for me the first time I laid eyes on her in the basement of the church. I wanted to tell them they had made a mistake, that Lynn was the wrong choice for me. Rachel was so beautiful that night. I kept trying to listen to Lynn, to get to know her and make it work, but I couldn't take my eyes off of Rachel. When Lynn left, I hoped Rachel would back out of her marriage to Kevin and I'd have a chance. Now she's gone and she'll never know how I feel."

He took the doorknob in his hand as if he were about to leave, but I called out to him.

"Luke, it's not too late, you should go after her, tell her how you feel!"

He looked sad and frustrated. "After what she's been through, how could I tell her now?"

I tried to reassure him. "Luke, she'll feel so alone in New York, she has no family there. I know what it's like to be all alone in a place that big. The only reason she left is because she thinks we all feel guilty about what happened to her. Please Luke, you have to try."

He just stood there looking out the small window in the door of my studio. He never replied, he just opened the door and walked away. William helped me to my feet and on with my jacket.

"Let's go home, love. Give him time to think about it. If he loves her he'll go after her. I'm sure of it," William assured me.

Several weeks passed and I did not hear another word from Rachel. Her cell phone had been left behind in the prison she shared with Kevin Marshall. The men who searched Kevin's house told William it looked as if it had been smashed with a hammer, or maybe a fist. The letter she sent to me by way of Luke had no hint of where she would be staying in New York, and of course she would not want to return to her former address. I prayed she wouldn't return to it, that she would come to her senses and return to Old Harbor. I would not let myself believe for a second that she would consider going back to that line of work.

No one had seen Luke Fowler, either. I left a couple of messages on his business phone, but he never returned my calls and I had no idea what his private cell number was.

"Maybe he went to find her," I wished out loud several times.

William was patient with my sad mood. He knew how much Rachel felt like family to me. I'm not sure if it was his intention to get my mind on other things or if he just decided it was time, but he came in one morning to announce he had spoken to his parents and they were coming for a visit. There is nothing like a good case of sheer panic to get your mind off your troubles.

"Exactly what have you told them about me? Do they know how we met? Do they know I'm pregnant?"

I was coming at William with one question after the other. They had known Mary most of her life, and now their son had married a total stranger and had not mentioned me to them until recently. I was sure they would hate me, think I had seduced their son, become pregnant and forced him into marriage. What other possible conclusion could they come to? William just laughed at my frenzy and tried to reassure me.

"Allie, they'll love you and they'll be excited about the baby, believe me. Now, I guess we need to start preparing that nursery so we can show it off when they come."

William was trying very hard not to let his face give away the pain in his suggestion. He knew it needed to be done, but the room had been a shrine to the memory of Mary, and also to the son he had prepared it for. The son he had dreamed about. I'm sure he had imagined them fishing and hunting together, maybe playing ball in the front yard, or just wrestling on the floor in front of the fireplace on those cold nights at home. I knew there was an ache in his heart at the thought, but he was trying hard to be brave.

"William, before we do anything to that room, I want you to go and pack away the things that belonged to Mary and baby William for safekeeping. I noticed a beautiful old trunk in the barn; you could clean it up and keep it somewhere safe. I think you should do that alone before we start any decorating for this baby."

Old Harbor - Sisters of Circumstance ~ P.J. Rhea

He looked at me with so much appreciation that we needed no other words. I really don't think he could have said anything at that moment anyway. William took my shoulders and pulled me toward him; he kissed me on my forehead and again softly on my lips. Then he took a deep breath as if gathering his emotions, and walked out the door and toward the barn. I was confident in the fact that William loved me now, but I knew he still struggled with his loss. This would just be another painful step toward healing.

As excited as I was about fixing up the nursery, I knew we still had plenty of time and we could take it slow. Besides, I had a baby shower for Corinna to plan. Trudy, Gwen, and I were going to decorate the church basement and invite all the ladies, plus all of Jay's family. It would be so much fun, and I knew Corinna was excited about it. She was getting closer to her due date in late July, so the baby shower would have to be top priority for now. Corinna wrote her mom after her marriage and invited her to visit. She told her she was expecting a baby, but did not share with her how it came to be. Her mother sent a short note in response that simply said "Pray for forgiveness." I know it hurt her very much, but Jay's family certainly made up for any pain her mother caused. Her judgmental rejection would assure her a lonely winter. Jay's family absolutely loved Corinna and they were all so happy about the baby; you would have never guessed they knew it wasn't Jay's child. In his heart and in theirs, it was his. Corinna knew this child would be loved like she never was, unconditionally. No matter what this child looked like, and that would be a true mystery until the birth, it would be accepted into the Ellis family with open arms. Jay would tease her when she became weepy over how things had turned out for her.

"I don't deserve you, Jay. I can't believe you still wanted to marry me."

He would just put his thumbs under his suspenders and say, "Don't ya just love a happy ending?" And then, he'd smile from ear to ear.

It got her every time. She could not stay sad when he did that, and it always brought on a smile.

Old Harbor - Sisters of Circumstance ~ P.J. Rhea

William's parents would not be arriving until after Corinna's shower, and I was glad. I wanted to make a good impression and I wanted time to prepare myself for them; find out as much as I could about them from William.

"They always like to visit in July because there are more daylight hours. Not to mention that my dad loves to fish and hunt, so you'll have time to bond with my mom."

"Oh, great," I said with obvious sarcasm. "So you're going to desert me in my time of need!"

William just laughed and shrugged his shoulders. I could never be upset with him when he flashed that dimple of his, and that crooked smile was my undoing. I still thought about the little picture of his family in the nursery, and the smile he had as he looked down at Mary with his hand on her pregnant belly. I hoped for the day when I would see him look at me that way. A smile that said, "I'm complete and there is nothing more I need in life than this."

Corinna was glowing. She was one of those women who never looked pregnant until the last few months. No one would have guessed when she walked down the aisle on March fifth that she was already twenty weeks along in her pregnancy. But you could certainly tell it now. William said she looked like she had swallowed a beach ball. I told him I would be fine if he did not use those descriptions when I started showing. Gwen and Trudy helped me decorate the church basement with blue streamers and baby bottle centerpieces on every table. I had to go to Kodiak for my monthly doctor's appointment the morning of the shower, which made it easy to pick up the cake and ingredients for punch. Trudy made little sandwiches and Gwen prepared a fruit tray and a vegetable tray. Jay's mom made the cutest corsage out of baby socks, pacifiers, and blue ribbon. The last baby shower in this little town had been Gwen's and the ladies from the church were excited to finally be having another one. Little John Bible was almost four months old now and was passed around among all the women at the shower as if he were the grand prize. Gwen whispered to Corinna and I that she was glad there would soon be two more babies in church, or John would never learn to crawl.

"They never let him touch the floor," she laughed.

Old Harbor - Sisters of Circumstance ~ P.J. Rhea

All the tiny clothes and baby things made me more excited for my own baby. I was barely starting to notice the bump under my tummy, but I had already started placing my hands on my stomach all the time. I had seen pregnant women do that a lot, rub and pat their own belly as their child grows inside. I had wondered why they did it, but now I realize it's the early effort to caress and love that little child who is already completely dependent on you. I caught myself talking to the baby, as if he or she knew what I was saying. William would talk to my tummy every morning, kiss it, and tell his child he loved it. He would be such a good father. I was thankful I could give him a child. I hoped it would help fill that empty place in his heart that had been prepared to love a child and then had it ripped from him.

Chapter Twelve

A Love for Rachel

Rachel walked out of the airport with her bags. She left the hospital with little more than a few articles of clothing and some toiletry items. It was not even enough to have to check her luggage. It was just a small overnight bag and a large purse. She had left everything she owned in the prison she lived in with Kevin Marshall and refused to go back for any of it.

"I will never go back to that house of horror," she told Luke when he helped her arrange her trip back to New York.

She left everything in Old Harbor, Alaska; everything including her heart. Luke had appeared to be sorry she was leaving but didn't try to talk her out of it.

"Luke, if you had just asked me to stay I would have," she said out loud, and then in almost a whisper, "I miss my family."

"Excuse me, but are you all right?"

Brother Carl had asked a friend of his, a fellow minister who lived in New York, to pick Rachel up at the airport. He was reluctant to take her to the area of town she requested but she knew it would be more in her budget for now.

He seemed very kind and she was sure he was sincerely concerned, but she didn't respond to him and just continued to cry. She was in no mood to talk.

She had only been away from this city for about three months, but it felt like years. This was no longer home to her. She would have to stay away from the areas she once frequented and avoid any temptation to return to her old lifestyle.

That's not me anymore and I will work four jobs before I do that again.

Old Harbor - Sisters of Circumstance ~ P.J. Rhea

Having other people love her had taught her to love herself enough to want better than that.

Maybe I shouldn't have come back to New York, she thought. *I know my friends, my family, would have helped me if I had returned to Old Harbor.*

Her heart was broken, not because of the terrible thing that had happened to her and not because so many people now knew about her not-so-pristine past, but because for the first time in her life she felt like part of a family and she had walked away from it.

I just couldn't be a burden on them. I would have been a fifth wheel, always the extra person.

Her new sisters were all happily married, ready to start families. She just couldn't bear being a reminder of such a dark time. All of them had witnessed her breakdown at the Trading Post. They had pleaded with her not to take her life and watched in horror as she shot Kevin Marshall. How could she possibly show her face in that town again? It wasn't like New York, where you could get lost in a crowd and never be recognized. A person could get lost here and stay lost for the rest of their life. In Old Harbor everyone knew what happened and everyone would see her for what she was. Well, for what she had been.

She asked the minister to help her find somewhere with a weekly rate that wasn't too high. Luke had insisted on giving her money to live on until she could get settled. She tried to refuse his offer, but he pushed something into her purse as she exited his car. She had assumed he had given her a little money to help her out, but hadn't realized until she was in her seat that it was eight hundred dollars in an envelope. He also gave her his card and made her promise to call him if she needed anything.

"I need you, Luke," is what she wanted to say, but only managed a low thank you and a quick goodbye.

She got a room in a place called the Restful Night Inn, but a more fitting name would have been the Bed Bug Dive. She had slept in worse places, and was just grateful to have a roof over her head and a door with several deadbolt locks. She still pushed a chair under the

Old Harbor - Sisters of Circumstance ~ P.J. Rhea

doorknob for extra measure. The man at the counter wasn't exactly the type who made you feel secure, either. After a restless night she walked two blocks down to the Burger Prince for breakfast, and as luck would have it there was a help wanted sign in the window. It was not exactly a glamorous job, but it was a job. A way to survive day-to-day, and for now that was all she wanted.

∼⌣∽

Luke Fowler was a man with a mission. The plane landed at LaGuardia in the early morning hours just before the city began to wake up for another work week.

I'll hail a taxi and find a room first. I need to sleep for a few hours and clear my head before I start trying to find Rachel.

Luke had tried to sleep on the plane but his mind was whirling.

Allie was right. If I love her, and I do, I have to find her and bring her back. But how exactly am I going to find her? Carl had given him the phone number of the minister who picked her up from the airport. Maybe he would know where she was staying.

He checked into the Plaza, which had always been a favorite of his family. While tipping the man who carried his one suitcase to the room for him it occurred to him that Rachel wasn't the only one who had not been completely truthful about their past.

I mean, my past isn't exactly sordid or shameful. I've done nothing illegal, or even immoral, but I haven't let my friends in Old Harbor know who I really am. The first person I'll be honest with is Rachel, and if she doesn't want me then it really won't matter what the others think. Her opinion is the only one I value right now.

Luke couldn't help but laugh to himself and think of Lynn.

If she had known I was very rich and she would have wanted for nothing, she might have tried harder to impress me. Of course, she never would have believed it anyway. Would Rachel believe it? I mean, let's face it, how many Harvard Law graduates choose to move to a town as small and backward as Old Harbor, Alaska? Who in

144

Old Harbor - Sisters of Circumstance ~ P.J. Rhea

their right mind would live there when their family had left them a fortune, a beautiful home in Connecticut, and another home in Beverly Hills, California? *Now that would really make Lynn mad,* he laughed.

Once he was settled in he called Carl's friend.

"She was so sad and said nothing to me except to tell me where to drop her and to say thank you as she left my car. I hated to leave her there; it's not the best part of town for a young lady to be all alone."

Luke wrote down the address and thanked the minister for the kindness he had shown Rachel. When his taxi pulled up to the hotel he had to agree with Carl's friend. It was a dump. No other word for it.

Luke had a picture of Rachel that had been taken the first night he saw her. He had ripped it in half and burned the half with Kevin on it. *It should have been me sitting there with you, Rachel, and you never would have had to go through all the hell you suffered.* Luke was full of regret and chastised himself as he looked at her picture. He walked into the office and a very grungy-looking man was sitting behind the counter eating a large burger that dripped with grease and some equally greasy looking fries. The large round stomach he had stretched his threadbare tee shirt over gave the impression that this was probably a good representation of most of his meals. Luke started to show him the picture to see if he recognized Rachel, but when he started to take it with his dirty hand Luke pulled it away quickly.

"What's your problem buddy?" he asked, and then burped a very loud and smelly burp in Luke's direction.

"It's the only photo I have so please accept my apology." Luke wanted answers and knew this man would give him little or no help if he felt insulted.

"Yeah, I know her. That's Rachel somebody. Don't remember the last name. She works a few doors down at the Burger Prince. Just came from there myself."

Old Harbor - Sisters of Circumstance ~ P.J. Rhea

Luke could have kissed the man he was so happy. Could it really have been this easy? Not even a full day of searching and he had found her. He gave the man a twenty dollar bill for his information and headed in the direction of the Burger Prince.

Why am I so nervous? I saw her three days ago. I feel like a schoolboy working up the nerve to ask a girl on a first date.

Luke paced the sidewalk for a minute to calm down and think about what he wanted to say. He stepped in through the door of the Burger Prince and there she was. She was dressed in one of those awful, bright purple uniforms they had to wear, with a visor made to look like a crown holding back the hair from her face. She had very little makeup on and there was no smile on her face, but she was still the most beautiful woman he had ever laid eyes on. She wasn't looking up at the customers when taking their orders but just stared at the cash register and handed them their change in a robotic motion. Even when she spoke the words she had been instructed to say, she sounded so very sad and impersonal. Luke watched her for a few minutes, hoping she might look up and notice him. Wanting to see if she looked happy to see him, or angry that he was following her.

After all, this was her choice. She wanted to come back to New York. Maybe she didn't want to be found. Maybe she didn't feel the same way about him as he did about her. He was just a nice man who showed her kindness in her time of need. He was her attorney when she needed one but could not afford one.

I have to take a chance. She is so wonderful, so beautiful and...well, if I am honest with myself, I have never felt this way about a woman in my life. Well, here goes nothing, Luke thought.

"Welcome to Burger Prince, would you like to try a Royal Burger today?" Rachel asked, not looking up to see who stood in front of her.

"No, I'm just here to take you home," was his reply.

Rachel looked up, ready to ask him to move on with an obvious look of resentment on her face; but then her honey brown eyes got as big as half dollars and a smile took over her face that was brighter than the snow of Old Harbor.

Old Harbor - Sisters of Circumstance ~ P.J. Rhea

"Luke!"

The people in the Burger Prince stopped dead in their tracks and all was silent for a minute as they looked to see why the girl behind the counter had screamed; once they realized it was just because she was talking to someone the noise and movement started right back up.

"Rachel, may I please escort you home?"

Luke extended his hand and smiled his most charming smile. Rachel looked almost afraid to answer, and Luke feared she might not be as happy to see him as he first thought.

"Can you come back in an hour and a half, Luke? I have to finish my shift."

Her voice was pleading. She couldn't be sure why he was here and didn't want to take a chance on losing her job after only one day.

"Oh...yeah, sure thing," Luke replied. "I knew that."

Luke checked his watch and promised to return at exactly nine o'clock.

Rachel smiled for the rest of her shift, to the point where her cheeks were sore. She went to the restroom before leaving to freshen up. There was no way to remove the smell of greasy burgers, but she did comb her hair and used the toothbrush she kept in her purse. She wasn't about to leave it in the room where she was staying, not knowing what might crawl on it while she was away. She also applied a little makeup and wiped off her grease-splattered shoes.

O.K., that's as good as it is going to get for now, she thought, and went out front to wait for Luke. As she waited her mind began to race. *I can't believe he is here. But why is he here?*

It suddenly occurred to her that he could just be here on business. Maybe doing something for a client. After all, he is an attorney. Maybe he had even forgotten he was going to come by and walk her home. It was five minutes past nine and she didn't see him.

Old Harbor - Sisters of Circumstance ~ P.J. Rhea

Rachel, how stupid can you be? He wasn't here for you, at least not in the way you hoped he was. I am as bad as Allie, letting my imagination take over like that.

Rachel started to walk in the direction of the hotel when she heard Luke yell at her.

"Hey, beautiful, do you need a lift?"

There stood Luke beside a horse-drawn carriage with a large sunflower in his hand.

"Do you have any idea how hard it is to find a sunflower? Couldn't you like roses like everyone else?" he teased.

"Luke, I only live down about two blocks. We could have walked it in just a few minutes. Thank you for the flower, by the way." She grinned at him and felt herself blush.

"I thought we could take the long way home if that's okay with you?" Luke helped her into the carriage and covered their legs with the blanket provided. "Give us the longest route you have and then back to this area if you please, sir."

The driver was a young man and gave them a grin and a wink before instructing the horse to go by making a clicking noise with his cheek.

Rachel had lived in New York most of her life but had never been on a carriage ride. It was magical, and the way Rachel felt right now she could have been wearing a ball gown and tiara instead of this nasty uniform. She was Cinderella on her way to the ball. Luke and Rachel talked nonstop as the clip-clop of the horse kept rhythm with the beating of their two hearts. It was as if they were both afraid of what might happen if it got too quiet between them. Both of them wanted the same thing, but both were too afraid to say so just yet. Luke was not going to risk scaring her off. He would take it slow and let her get to know him.

Rachel asked about Allie and the other ladies she missed so deeply. They talked about the people she cared about, but Luke was cautious when talking about Old Harbor. He knew her memories of

Old Harbor - Sisters of Circumstance ~ P.J. Rhea

that place were still very raw and unhappy and he was enjoying her smile and laughter too much to risk ending it.

Finally, as the carriage neared her hotel he worked up enough nerve to admit why he had come.

"Rachel I regretted letting you leave from the minute you stepped on that plane, and I'm here to try and win your trust and hopefully your affection."

It would have been easy for her to throw her arms around him and tell him she regretted leaving too, and that he already had her trust and affection—but she wanted to hear all he had to say. Besides, she didn't want to scare him away by being too eager.

"I'd like you to give me a chance," he continued. "Let you get to know me a little better and maybe we could…" He wasn't sure what word he needed to use, and his hesitation seem to concern her. "Ah, I was thinking maybe we could…date?"

Rachel just looked at him for a few seconds and then as a smile crossed her lips.

"Date. No one has ever asked me on a date before. I would love to go on a date with you, Luke Fowler!" She was as giddy as a school girl.

Until now he had not so much as held her hand. He had wanted to embrace and kiss her from the very second he saw her, but Rachel had been abused by men her entire life. Been used like an object and tossed away. Luke loved her to the core of his soul and he never wanted to make her feel that way, so he would be careful about how fast things moved. He wanted to be sure she wanted his attention, and he could not assume anything. When the carriage stopped to let them out, he jumped out first and put his hand out to help her down. Once she was on the sidewalk she put her fingers between his and gave his arm a kind of hug.

"Luke, I'm so glad you're here and I can't wait to see you again, but I hope you'll understand if I don't ask you in just yet."

He gave her a gentle kiss on the cheek and then another one on her forehead.

149

Old Harbor - Sisters of Circumstance ~ P.J. Rhea

"I'll pick you up in the morning for breakfast, if that's acceptable," he grinned.

"I'll be ready and waiting, sir," she grinned back.

The next three weeks were filled with "dates." Luke took her to everything he thought she might enjoy. They attended a play. They went to the ballet and the opera. He took her to the best restaurants New York had to offer. They also went to the zoo and to the ice-skating rink. They took several long walks in the park and ate hot dogs and pretzels with lots of mustard. And with each day they grew closer and closer to each other. She had told him everything there was to know about her past, from her earliest memories as a child to the horror at the hands of Kevin Marshall only a few months ago. Luke already knew most of it from the information made available to him when he was to defend her on the murder charges. He had even seen pictures of her body after Kevin had tortured her. It was part of the evidence that would have been offered if the case had gone before a jury. He didn't let on that he knew any of it, because he knew she needed to tell him herself. That it was important for her to know she had been honest with him.

Luke knew he needed to tell her the truth about himself, too, but was trying to figure a way to do it that didn't sound arrogant or conceited. How do you tell someone you are rich as a king and not sound like you are bragging? Luke had been away from his law practice for almost a month now, and it was time for him to go back and check on things. He had clients who were counting on him, so he knew it was now or never and he hoped it had been long enough.

"Rachel I'm going to have to return to Kodiak the day after tomorrow."

She looked as if I had shot her in the heart. "What, so soon Luke? I mean, you really just got here a few days ago. Do you have to go already?"

Rachel was trying not to sound desperate, trying not to cry, but she wanted to wrap her arms around him and plead with

150

Old Harbor - Sisters of Circumstance ~ P.J. Rhea

him not to go. Had she been fooling herself this whole time? Thinking something would come from this?

He hasn't even tried anything, Rachel. You stupid girl, thinking he might love you. He was just a friend here on a visit. That's all it was and you've built up some fantasy that could never happen.

"Well, it's been really nice having you here, Luke. Maybe you can visit me again some time."

He knew he was causing her to panic but he didn't want to lose his nerve so he didn't try to console her.

"Rachel, I have a few things I need to tell you before I return home, and one important question to ask."

Rachel looked at him and braced herself for the speech she expected. How he had come to realize they could only be friends because of her sordid past, and would she not tell people she knew him because he had his reputation as a lawyer to uphold. Luke took her hand in his and kissed her gently on the lips for the first time since he had arrived in New York. He asked her to sit on the bench with him, took a deep breath and started from the beginning. He told Rachel of his parents, who were killed ten years ago in a plane crash. That he was their only child and heir to their fortune. He told her he graduated with honors from Harvard Law and could have worked with almost any firm. That for a while he lived in New York and worked for one of the largest law firms in the state, but he was just not happy.

"I went to Alaska on a vacation. I had always loved to fish, and as it happened, my guide was a nice man named William Hickman." He smiled at her and they both gave each other a look of appreciation for who William was. "His first wife Mary was still living then and I had never seen such a happy man. I wanted what he had. I wanted to live a simple life away from the crowds, and deal with people on a more personal level. Most of my clients were hard-hearted corporation heads. Their only agenda was to get more of what they already had, and they didn't care who they had to hurt to get there. I helped William

Old Harbor - Sisters of Circumstance ~ P.J. Rhea

with the purchase of his tour-guide business. He was buying the rights from an old gentleman who was ready to call it quits. I watched as they shook hands and conducted their business in a friendly and honest way. I had never felt such a sense of contentment. I shocked everyone who knew me when I left the firm in New York and moved, as they put it, to the end of the earth. I didn't need to work for money. My parents left me well taken care of, even if I never wanted to work again. I fished all I wanted and worked from my small office in Kodiak at the pace I wanted. It was perfect except for one thing. There was one thing missing."

"What else could you want, Luke? It sounds to me like you had it all plus some," Rachel concluded.

"I wanted someone to share this perfect life with. I wanted someone to love and to have children with. I wanted someone to grow old with."

Rachel held her breath hoping this was going in the direction it sounded like it was.

"I thought I had found her but things got a little confused and messed up and then she left and went back home."

Was he talking about Lynn? Had he felt more for her than any of us thought? Had it broke his heart when she went back home? Rachel felt a slight panic at what he might say next. Suddenly Luke jumped up from the bench they were sharing and dropped to one knee. He opened a tiny box to reveal a beautiful diamond ring in what appeared to be an antique setting.

"Rachel, I have loved you from the moment I saw you in that church basement. Would you please do me the great honor of becoming my bride?"

Rachel was in shock and simply could not get the word out of her mouth. Luke started to get a little concerned at her delay, and closed the box while getting up from his kneeling position. Rachel noticed his smile had left and realized he was thinking her silence was rejection.

152

Old Harbor - Sisters of Circumstance ~ P.J. Rhea

"OH, YES LUKE!"

Rachel threw her arms around his neck and repeated her answer.

"I would love to marry you. Luke, I love you so much and I've dreamed of this from that day, too. The whole time I was sitting there with Kevin I was wishing Lynn would just leave and I could have a chance to get to know you. But then...well, as you know, things got complicated to say the least, and..."

"Rachel, I need to know something else."

She stopped her rambling and listened, hoping he wasn't taking back his proposal.

"What is it Luke?"

"Will you come back to Old Harbor with me? If you don't think you can, I'll move back to New York. I'd move to the end of the world for you, but if you think you can be happy there with me I want to take you back home."

"Home," she repeated. No word had ever sounded so wonderful to her. "Yes, Luke, I want to go home," she smiled.

Rachel was so happy—and even more so when she realized she would arrive back in Old Harbor just in time for the baby shower honoring Corinna. Luke took her shopping before they left New York, not only because she needed so many things but because she wanted to find the perfect gift for Corinna.

"I guess there is a slight advantage to being in New York over Old Harbor when it comes to shopping. The Trading Post and the gift shop at The Lodge have limited choices," Luke said. They both had to laugh at the reality he pointed out.

Luke arranged first class passage to Anchorage, and like before there would be a short layover in Chicago. Once they arrived in Anchorage a small plane would take them to Old Harbor.

When Rachel and Luke arrived at the church they could hear the laughter and commotion from the shower in the

153

Old Harbor - Sisters of Circumstance ~ P.J. Rhea

basement. They slipped down the stairs and were glad no one spotted them when Luke placed the gift on the table closest to the doorway. Rachel listened as her sisters went on and on over the cute little baby clothes. It was apparent the shower was a success and everyone had a great time. From the looks of the table across the room, Corinna had received a lot of nice things. Every woman who attended the little church was there for the shower, along with Jay's family and Trudy's mom, who had come from Kodiak. Rachel almost gave away that she was hidden in the stairway, but she couldn't help but laugh when she heard Trudy's mom making future plans for when she became a grandmother. She made no secret of the fact that she hoped Trudy and Samuel would be next to have a child. Luke had told her William and Allie had not talked to people a lot about their pregnancy, not wanting to take the spotlight off of Corinna. It seemed that with all the commotion in the Trading Post that day no one but Rachel and William had heard what she said about a baby, and the few who did know were respectful of their request to keep it quiet just a little while longer. The two ladies who had been the waitresses that first night were at the shower and made several comments about how William and Allie would make good parents and what a good father they felt William would be. Allie had a soft spot for those two ladies and there was no doubt that after telling her new family the news, those two would be among the first to be told. They were about to start cleaning up when they noticed an unopened gift sitting on the end of a table.

"How in the world did we miss this one?"

Rachel was just waiting for her cue before making her return known. Allie carried the gift to Corinna and she looked for a card, with no luck.

"Maybe it's inside the box," Trudy suggested.

She tore open the gift and looked inside to find a picture frame with the words "My Aunts are the Best" across the bottom of the frame. It was a picture of Trudy, Rachel, and Allie.

"Is there a card in the box? Who could it be from?"

Old Harbor - Sisters of Circumstance ~ P.J. Rhea

As they all searched for a card, Luke and Rachel emerged from the doorway.

"Guess I forgot to get a card."

Rachel. Allie could not believe her eyes. Rachel was back and Luke was standing beside her, both smiling back at them, but Rachel's eyes had that wet look you have when you are trying not to cry. Everyone ran toward her—well, except for Corinna—she waddled over to her a little slower and Rachel couldn't help but laugh.

"Are you back home for good?" the sisters asked at the exact same time.

"Yes, I'm back," she hesitated, "back home."

They hugged, cried, and laughed all at once.

"Oh Rachel I'm so glad you're back. I've missed you so much. How are you? Are you all right, where have you been?"

"Allie, I'll answer all your questions soon, but for now, how about some cake?"

Everyone in the room laughed at Allie's barrage of questions but she didn't care—she could not wait to hear what Rachel had to say. Rachel knew Allie was anxious to hear about what had happened. Luke had his arm around Rachel, who could tell Allie wanted to hear about that more than anything. Rachel tried to assure her they had plenty of time. She wasn't going anywhere. She was finally home.

❦ Chapter Thirteen ❧

Visitors

It was the first time Rachel had been to our cabin. Despite the fact that we felt as close as family and referred to ourselves as sisters, the truth was we had only spent a little over a month together. During all the other months Rachel had been in her prison created by Kevin Marshall, then in a hospital to help her heal from the things he had put her through. For the last few weeks she had been in New York, apparently with Luke. I was hoping that if she told me nothing else, she would tell me about the time they were in New York. Rachel had stayed in a room at The Lodge the night before and Luke was back at his house in Kodiak, so there was no obvious answer to my burning question: are they together or not? There had been no opportunity to talk alone since her return. Rachel asked me if she could come over and talk to me privately at my cabin. I was hoping all of my questions would soon have answers. William was taking a group of fisherman out for the day and Luke was working at his law office in Kodiak, so we had the day to catch up.

I was so excited to finally have my friend in my home. I beamed with pride as I gave her a tour of the paradise William and I shared, and the tour was almost identical to the one William gave me that first night. She loved the rustic great room with its large stone fireplace and bearskin rug. I showed her my wonderful clawfoot bathtub and the one-of-a-kind bed we now shared so perfectly. I also included things in my tour William had not felt ready to share with me that night. I showed her the nursery, which was in total disarray because of William packing away the old memories to make room for the new ones. I also took her to see Mary's garden and showed her where Mary and William Jr. were buried. It was June and the flowers were in full bloom with a rainbow of vibrant colors and symphony of fragrances. We sat there in silence for a long while. I hoped she would tell me about New York, but she seemed to need the time to

Old Harbor - Sisters of Circumstance ~ P.J. Rhea

think in this small sanctuary, so I just sat quietly until she stood and walked back toward the cabin.

We hadn't exchanged ten words since she arrived, aside from my descriptions as we toured the house. I let the nervous silence between us linger, wondering where to start. We sat in the two rocking chairs on my front porch. They were comfortable, and I knew from my time with William that it was a place that seemed to invite conversation. I brought out coffee and muffins I prepared earlier for us. Rachel seemed lost in her own thoughts and I wasn't sure what she would feel comfortable talking about, so I just started out with filling her in on my own life since arriving in Old Harbor. I told Rachel about Mary and the baby William had lost, about the bear that could have taken me from him as well. I told her about the night after the bear, when William made me feel so loved and desired, and said his goodbyes to Mary. She listened intently as I told her about my studio and my pregnancy, and that William's parents were coming in a few days and how I was a nervous wreck about meeting them.

I was almost afraid to stop talking because she seemed to be staring out at a memory as I spoke. She hardly said a word the entire time, but would occasionally look at me and smile or sip her coffee. I could not believe how nervous I was around her today. I was trying so hard to make her feel at ease that I made myself tense. Now that I was totally exhausted with my effort to fill her in on every possible detail she had missed, I just sat there waiting, hoping she would have some news to share with me. Hoping she would trust me the way she did on the plane when we made our way to this small island town. I wanted her to tell me about Kevin, and then thought to myself, *Allie, you're crazy for thinking she would want to talk about such a horrific experience.* I was ashamed of my curiosity, but I realized that my obsession to know was about to be met. Rachel finally looked up from her cup, where she had focused for several minutes, and started to speak.

"Allie, I want to show you something, if you're willing to look. I need you to know why I acted as I did that day at the Trading Post. The things that happened to me are too horrible to be put in words. I'm not sure if there's any other way to help you understand, so I want you to see my body after Kevin…" Her voice trailed off and

157

she tried to think of the proper word for what he had done. "…after he tortured me," she finally concluded. "I think once you see what's under my clothes, there'll be no further need to talk about what led up to the scene in the Trading Post."

"If that's what you want Rachel. I do want to know what happened to you, what kept you from us for so long."

Rachel got up from her chair and walked into my house, so I followed. Once she was inside, she started to unbutton her dress while still standing with her back to me. I could hear her taking deep breaths, trying to work up the nerve to continue. I knew this was not easy for her and I was scared myself about what I was about to witness, worried about my reaction. I didn't want to react in a way that would hurt Rachel. She should never be hurt again by anything that monster had done.

Finally, she turned around to face me, tilted her head back, and closed her eyes. I could tell she was trying to brace herself, and I took a deep breath at the same time she did in an attempt to prepare myself for what was about to happen. After standing there clutching the collar of her dress for a few minutes, she finally allowed her dress to fall, leaving herself exposed; completely naked except for her panties.

What I saw horrified me. It took all my restraint not to run to the bathroom and be sick from the thought of what he must have done to her in those two months she spent in hell. I had seen Rachel before our weddings as we women would run around our basement dorm in underwear or even less, getting ready for our different functions. Rachel had taken good care of her body and she was beautiful. Her skin had been a beautiful soft brown, smooth and silky, and the envy of the other ladies there. She didn't have so much as a mole or scar on her body, and I could easily understand how she had been a favorite of her clients.

But now that once-perfect body was covered almost entirely with scars. He had shown no mercy at all in his torture. The pattern of his teeth where he had bitten her in an effort to cause the pain that aroused him was well documented in her skin. Some of the scars implied the bites may have been deep enough to tear her flesh and make her bleed. Some were possibly so deep they were close to the bone. He had been careful to avoid any area that could be seen by others, especially once he realized we were going to keep checking on her. She had only one small scar on her face, just below her lip. She explained that he hit her so hard across the face that first night it cut her lip and loosened a tooth. There were also places that looked as if he had burned her with objects; branded her with whatever pleased him at the time. She had marks made by knives as he would outline her nipples and panty line while he reminded her of the things she had let other men do to her, she explained. Rachel shook almost violently as she told me of the things Kevin had done and said to her every day of their marriage.

Then once she covered herself back up with her dress, she looked at me and declared, "Allie, you're the reason I survived it!"

I started to cry; despite my effort to keep it together I just couldn't stop myself. To know that while I was experiencing the most wonderful time of my life getting to know my new husband she was going through something too repulsive to comprehend was heartbreaking. And then to tell me I was what got her through it. I began to cry in loud sobs, which in turn made her cry. We both cried so hard, for such a long time, that we were weak when we were finally able to stop. We moved to the couch and just sat there in an embrace that seemed to make us both feel secure and relieved.

"Rachel, I'm so sorry. I knew something wasn't right and I should have tried harder to get to you. Can you forgive me?"

"Allie, it was your calling and coming by that kept me alive. He knew someone would find out about it if he killed me; possibly find the other body in the cellar, and that was something he hadn't counted on. That first night he told me no one would ever miss me; no one would ever come looking for me. As bad as it was, it would have been worse. Your attempts to talk to me, they gave me hope and a will to hang on. Otherwise I would have died in that cellar. No one ever cared before if I lived or died. Not the men I 'dated' or the man who paid me; not the other ladies I met in my line of work, not even my own mother. Death almost seemed like a welcome relief on more than one occasion in my life. But you...cared. You love me like

Old Harbor - Sisters of Circumstance ~ P.J. Rhea

family. I never had that before, Allie. You were lonely in New York, but you felt loved in your life. Knowing someone finally loved me, I just had to hang on."

I was absorbing everything she'd said, but I had to ask, "What about the day in the Trading Post? Rachel, were you thinking of taking your life that day?"

I instantly regretted asking the question. Rachel flushed with embarrassment and looked away, not wanting to look me in the eyes when talking about it.

"I was crazy by that point" she said. "Kevin had drugged me on several occasions and I was suffering from withdrawal, plus the daily torture had become almost too much to handle. When I saw my family there in the store, I suddenly felt such shame for the things I had done. I knew I couldn't have stopped him but all the same, I was embarrassed to see all of you."

Rachel got quiet and stared off in space for a few minutes; then an almost peaceful look came over her. She focused on me again and a very slight smile crossed her lips before she continued.

"But then the strangest thing happened; I started hearing this voice whisper in my head. I could tell it was coming from that old woman in the store."

"That's Mama," I interrupted, "one of the eldest members of the Alutiiq tribe. She's very spiritual and her children say she can hear the spirits of animals. William told me she was the reason he applied for a bride. She only speaks to people when she's been given a message for them. The first time I met her, she told me I was pregnant, but I didn't realize she could send messages to you without speaking. What did she say to you? I mean in your head, that is?"

"It's hard to explain, but it was like a calm came over me, and I could picture the outcome if I turned the gun and shot toward Kevin. For a while the room seemed to be frozen in time and it was just Mama and me in that room. It was like I was dreaming or something. Her voice was just a whisper in my ear and I just kept hearing the whisper saying, 'Freedom is yours, you're safe at home.' I just knew I had to do it."

Old Harbor - Sisters of Circumstance ~ P.J. Rhea

She looked at me as if she was hoping I understood. That I didn't think she was terrible for having taken a life, even under such circumstances. "I was like a robot when I turned the gun and pulled the trigger. It wasn't real to me. It was like I was in a trance. I barely remember doing it."

"Why did you go back to New York?" I asked. "No one blamed you for what you did, Rachel, why didn't you stay here with us so we could help you? Why did you leave me without saying goodbye?"

Allie what is wrong with you? Stop asking her so many questions. The last thing she needs is a guilt trip from you for putting her needs before yours.

"I'm so sorry, Rachel. I don't mean to pry. I'm just happy you're here now."

"It's all right Allie; I want to answer your question. I was embarrassed that the others knew about my past. I didn't know how I could face them. I worried they would think I got what I deserved for living that way, for being with all those men. Maybe they would think I asked for it. And even once I realized they would forgive me and still accept me as one of the sisters, I guess I just felt I wouldn't fit in here. All of you were happy and building a life with someone special, but I felt like my chance for a new life ended on the day I married. There was no reason for me to come back here and have all of you feeling sorry for me. I just figured it was better to go back to where I came from."

For the first time since she called me into the living room, I smiled a questioning little grin. I placed my hands as if I were thinking really hard on something and started my next question off slowly and with a bit of a teasing tone.

"So Rachel, what, or should I say who, made you come back to Old Harbor?"

Rachel smiled back and I could see in her eyes that the rest of her story would be a much happier tale. There was suddenly a spark in her eye as she thought of who had rescued her and brought her back to us, to her family.

Old Harbor - Sisters of Circumstance ~ P.J. Rhea

"Well, when I got to New York, I took the first job I could find, which was at a Burger Prince; ya know, the fast food place. A few weeks ago I was standing at my station waiting on customers and not really paying much attention to them. I was focusing on the cash register and all the people were just kinda, ya'know, there. I realized someone had approached my station and I just said, 'Welcome to Burger Prince, would you like a royal burger today?' The reply was, 'no thanks, I'm just here to take you home.' I figured it was some guy hitting on me and I looked up to tell him to move on, but stopped in mid-sentence when I realized it was Luke Fowler. He was standing there with a big goofy grin on his face."

Rachel was staring in space, going to a place in her mind, remembering how good that moment felt, and she smiled a goofy smile. I reached out and placed my hand on hers to encourage her to continue.

"So what happened next?"

"He wanted to know if he could escort me home. He had to leave and return when my shift was over, and believe me when I say that was the longest hour and a half of my life. I was so afraid he wouldn't return, but when he did he had rented a horse and carriage to take us all over the city."

We both sighed one of those "how romantic" sighs women do when they are really impressed by something a man has done for them.

"Luke wanted to know if we could get to know each other. He told me he had been attracted to me when we first arrived in Old Harbor, and that he never gave Lynn a fair chance because he was so interested in me. That he still was interested and wanted me to give him a chance. He asked me to consider spending time with him and get to know him better. Oh, I admit I wouldn't let myself believe it at first, because no matter how bad I wanted it, he just couldn't possibly want me. Not with my past and what had happened to me at the house in Old Harbor. No one would ever want these damaged goods. He just wouldn't give up, Allie. He said my past didn't matter to him and I knew he had learned plenty while working on my case, but I wanted him to hear it from me. I wanted him to understand what

Old Harbor - Sisters of Circumstance ~ P.J. Rhea

led me to that lifestyle in the first place. I wanted him to know about the little girl who was abandoned as a baby and passed around from place-to-place and person-to-person her entire life. He listened as I told him about my past, every bit of it, and I filled him in on what happened to me at Kevin's house. What he knew from working on my defense was only what was on the surface. I figured once he knew the whole truth, he would run like a rabbit back here and never want to see me again. Actually, I was afraid he would do that, but I was clinging to a little hope that he wouldn't."

Rachel's eyes started to fill with tears and she looked at me with a pride I had never seen her display before.

"He stayed, Allie, and he came to see me every day and we actually went on dates. He took me out to dinner in nice restaurants. We went to a few plays and even the ballet. Can you just picture that? Me. At the ballet…and I loved it. We'd go for long walks in the park and talked for hours on end. He told me more about his past, which is pretty tame in comparison, and how he just felt such a connection with me. How he loved my eyes and my hair, and my smile just drove him wild."

She giggled with the pleasure that brought her.

"Oh, Allie, I never dreamed there was such a man as Luke Fowler in this world who could actually make me feel loved, and I love him, too. When it was time for him to leave I was devastated. He encouraged me to return with him, so I agreed to come back to Old Harbor and to become his wife."

"What?" I screamed like a kid who just heard they were going to Disneyland. "Oh, Rachel, that's so wonderful, why didn't you tell me sooner? When are you getting married?"

She couldn't help but laugh at my reaction.

"We talked to Carl and he said he would marry us as soon as we were ready."

Rachel picked up her purse from the floor beside the couch and took a ring from it, placing it on her finger and holding her hand out for me to see.

"I didn't want you to see this until I told you everything. I was afraid you might be too distracted to listen."

We both laughed at how true that statement was.

"Oh, Rachel! It's so beautiful, and I'm so happy for you."

"We want you and William to stand up for us, and I'm hoping Trudy and Samuel can be there, and Jay and Corinna, if we hurry before she explodes!" she chuckled.

Never has a wedding come together with such speed. Partly because we were all so excited about Rachel and Luke; also because we didn't want Corinna and Jay to miss it. It was a beautiful ceremony and I can say with confidence that there was not a dry eye in the place. Carl was so emotional he could barely ask them to repeat their vows. The tears were not from sympathy or sadness for what happened to her. These were tears of overwhelming joy and relief for the happiness she had finally found. The happiness they found with each other. It was definitely a different feeling than the other wedding she had only a few months back. When she and Kevin married, there were no emotions; it was almost robotic. But today with Luke, she beamed with joy and excitement. Her eyes were sparkling with the love she had for Luke, and he was proud she was becoming his wife. Nothing would ever let her forget the terrible things she had been through, but Luke made her believe she was worthy of happiness.

She told me that day at my cabin, "Allie, with Luke it's different than it's ever been with anyone before."

"Because you feel love," I presumed, and finished her sentence.

"No," she answered. "I mean yes, I do feel loved, but there's more. I feel appreciated and even respected for who I am. My ideas and opinions actually matter to him. That's something I never felt before. With Luke, I matter."

I knew exactly what she meant. It took more than just love. You had to matter. That seemed to be the difference in all our stories. I came to realize that was what made the difference with Jay and Corinna. Samuel loved Trudy for who she was and not how she

Old Harbor - Sisters of Circumstance ~ P.J. Rhea

looked. And of course my sweet William had loved me enough to wait and be sure he could give himself completely to me. The difference for us all was that we mattered to them. I smiled as Luke kissed his bride and the church erupted in applause.

We were all enjoying the reception in the basement of our church. That room was a special place for us. There was so much laughter and happiness filling the room, but then came a sudden panicked yell.

"I think my water just broke!" Corinna announced.

Jay dropped his cake on the floor and ran to her side. No sitcom could have played it out funnier than the reaction of this group. Jay and his family surrounded Corinna like the wagons of a western movie and all were talking at the same time. Gwen remained calm and knelt in front of Corinna.

"Are you having any pains yet?"

Corinna nodded her head to imply she had. "I had several but I didn't want to ruin the party," she admitted.

"How close together are the contractions, dear?"

Corinna had been having pains all morning and they had been coming about five minutes apart and increasingly uncomfortable for the past hour, but she kept thinking she could hold off until the reception ended before asking Jay to take her to the hospital. As usual, Corinna hated to be a bother to her friends, but once her water broke all over the basement floor there was no more suffering in silence. She began to express her pain with loud sighs. Carl came in and announced that the van was out front, warmed up and ready to lead the way. It was like a parade leading to the ferry, and they had to make two crossings to accommodate all of us. I have to admit, we were a little concerned that Jay might have to deliver the baby in the van because it takes almost thirty minutes to get across, but Corinna made it just fine.

I'm sure the hospital in Kodiak remembered this unusual group from when Gwen had little John a few months back, but in addition to our newly formed family, all of Jay's family was there, as well as several church members who happened to be at the reception. We filled the waiting room to the max and overflowed into the cafeteria. Several of the men were even hanging out in the parking lot. This was a special baby to all of us and despite the fact that no one said anything out loud, we were curious to see what this child would look like. The biological father of this baby was a total mystery, even to Corinna, and I guess human nature just made us all anxious to find out more.

Her labor was only a few hours, much shorter than Gwen's had been. After only five hours, Jay came out holding a beautiful little boy in his arms. He turned him toward the group of family and friends and pulled the blanket away from his tiny face. The sound from the crowd was a unanimous sigh of relief, I suppose, but also of happiness. This tiny little boy was the spitting image of his beautiful mother. It was almost as if God didn't want her to be reminded of how this miracle came to be, just that he was her child; a beautiful, healthy blessing to be loved and cherished. Jay was the proudest father anyone had ever seen, and his family could not have been happier. Once we knew all was well, the wedding party decided it was time to leave and let this little family bask in their joy.

Luke and Rachel left the hospital for the airport and a short honeymoon. William and I drove them to the airport. I asked them where they were going and they both answered at the same time.

"Hawaii," they said, and then they laughed.

"We decided we needed some warm sunny days for a while," Luke added.

I couldn't help but think that my dear sister would be having sunny days from now on regardless of how much snow may fall, as long as she had Luke by her side.

ઠ Chapter Fourteen ભ

Mom and Dad

*L*ater at home, I lay in bed beside my husband, thinking back on all the wonderful things that had taken place on this day. William's parents were due to arrive in a few days, and I was just hoping the lucky streak would continue.

"Do you really think they'll like me?" I asked for about the one-hundredth time.

"They'll love you, I promise," he assured me for the one-hundredth time.

I knew I was driving him crazy with my insecurity, but I knew how much his family meant to him. I wanted them to accept me, and yes, to like me. William had been working hard the last couple of weeks on the nursery, packing away the things that belonged to Mary and baby William. It was an emotional time and I tried to stay out from under his feet. Not to pry or make him feel self-conscious. I knew he was crying at times as he put them to rest in the trunk he had retrieved from the barn and prepared so lovingly for their things. The only thing he really shared with me was a lovely family Bible that her family had given her as a wedding gift. She had made notes in it, and written down their wedding date. She had even put William Junior's information in, with the exception of the date of birth. William had not been able to complete it or to put the dates of their death in the proper place until now. I knew this was a big milestone for him and another sign to me that he was happily moving forward. I would never expect him to forget them, but I could tell he was ready to lay them to rest and move forward with his new life with me and our child.

"I'm going to ask Mom to return this to Mary's parents for me. They always blamed me for her death, and never forgave me for not bringing her back to Texas to be buried in the family plot. I'm hoping this will help mend some fences. Maybe it will bring them some comfort."

I told him I thought that would be a wonderful thing to do. He is always thinking of others; that's just the kind of man he is. One of the many reasons I love him so much.

Time passed quickly leading up to their visit and William went to the airport to pick up his parents. He was very excited they were coming and could not wait for them to meet me. I, on the other hand, was terrified and not ready to meet them.

"What if they ask how we met, what are you going to tell them?" I asked him.

"I'll tell them the truth, I guess. I've never been dishonest with them before, so I'm not starting now."

I could only imagine how that conversation would go: "Oh, Mom, this is the bride I ordered a few months back. I got her all the way from New York City."

"Well son, she must be a crazy loser to actually answer an ad to be the bride of a total stranger."

Maybe they would think I was a prostitute or a criminal trying to hide out by changing my last name. I was starting to feel sick to my stomach. I knew their opinion of me was very important to William and I didn't want to disappoint him. I had never done a lot of cooking, but I found a lot of cookbooks in the kitchen, so I assumed Mary was a cook. They knew so much about Mary, and I was afraid they would compare me to her.

William, I think you need to ask for another wife, this one can't even cook. But she apparently has an active imagination, I scolded myself. *Allie, you have got to get a grip on yourself. What would Mom have done when meeting someone for the first time? 'Love yourself, baby girl, and others will love you back. If you're yourself and they don't like you, tell them to kiss off.' Okay, maybe I won't look to Mom for advice this time. I can't tell the new in-laws to kiss off, even if they hate me.*

168

Old Harbor - Sisters of Circumstance ~ P.J. Rhea

I was starting to wish I had gone to the Trading Post to ask Mama if she had a feeling on this meeting, but I was told she would not talk to you if she hadn't been sent a message for you by the spirits she believed in. Some tourists, and even townspeople, had tried to get her to advise them, tell their fortune, I guess, but she would just sit silent unless she called you to her and whispered to you. It was amazing how she knew when you entered the store, even though she was blind. I hadn't been to the Trading Post since the episode with Rachel and now I was regretting it. *Well, it's too late now, they're on their way and I'm on my own with this one.*

I heard the truck pull up out front and I had to fight the urge to flee to the back and hide. I took quick inventory of the cabin. I had cleaned it from one end to the other, made what I hoped would be a delicious meal, and I wasn't looking too shabby myself, so here goes nothing, I smiled to myself. I heard lots of chatter as the threesome came up on the porch, and the creak of the door as it opened. William's mother Glenda entered first, a short, slender woman with dark hair and tan skin. William had told me she loved to work in her garden, so I was expecting the tan. Right behind her was his father, Mike. I was shocked at how much William looked like him. It was as if I were looking at an older version of my husband. His hair was salt-and-pepper, and much shorter than William's. He also had a mustache, and it looked very nice with his face. If William ever talks about growing one, I will definitely encourage it. They just stood there for a few minutes and I was frozen in my tracks, not really sure what to do, when William bounced in behind them, set down their two suitcases, and put his arms around them both. He was smiling so big, his dimple was deep into his cheek.

"Well, Mom, Dad, this is Allison Ruth Hickman, my lovely bride, but call her Allie."

I just stood there, still unable to speak or move. *For goodness sake, Allie, they'll think you're mentally ill; would you say something already!*

"Welcome, Mr. and Mrs. Hickman, it's so nice to meet you."

Old Harbor - Sisters of Circumstance ~ P.J. Rhea

They looked at each other and then at William, like they were not sure what to say to that stiff, rehearsed greeting. Then they both kind of chuckled and started to speak.

"Good grief, William, did you make her think we were monsters or something?"

They both approached me at the same time and hugged me like we were old buddies.

"Allie, you are so beautiful, I love the color of your hair, you have this place looking great, I smell something good, and I'm starving!"

They were both talking at the same time and hugging me and patting my back.

"Got yourself a real looker, son, bet that baby is gonna be beautiful with two good-looking parents, not to mention such a good looking grandpa."

"Oh, Mike, you're acting a fool," his mother scolded.

"Well, it may get some of its good looks from you too, Glenda, after all, you're quite the looker too." He teased and gave her a wink.

She lightly hit his arm and turned red as a tomato and we all had to laugh. They were wonderful people and I felt silly now for all my concern. We gave them our room while they were with us and William and I took the bed that pulled out from our couch.

"You know, Mrs. Hickman, we may have to add on a room or two now that our family is starting to grow."

The idea of a large family was wonderful, but I also wanted my new parents to feel they had a place here any time they wanted to visit. It took a lot of persuading to convince his parents to take our room and not go to The Lodge.

Glenda actually reminded me of my Grandmother Ruth. At least, what I thought she may have been like when she was younger. William's mother was a very gentle and caring person and she never made me feel like she was comparing me to Mary or that she was

170

Old Harbor - Sisters of Circumstance ~ P.J. Rhea

concerned about how William and I had met. I concluded that though William looked exactly like his dad, he had his mother's spirit. They were both gentle and kind. They were both patient, loving people and I quickly formed a true bond with her. His parents asked if I would please call them Mom and Dad, because as far as they were concerned I was their new daughter. I almost cried at the request but managed to hold myself together. A flood of memories waved over me at those special titles, and an ache filled my heart and made my chest almost hurt from the effort to keep my emotions in check. William knew how honored I was by the request and gave my shoulders a squeeze.

William and his dad spent most of the next few days fishing and touring this beautiful area, while Glenda and I went shopping for things for the baby or the house. She said she had to get us a wedding gift, after all.

"I might as well throw in a baby gift or two while I'm at it," she added.

Other times we would just sit and talk for hours. It reminded me of the many long talks I had with my mother. Glenda and my mom would have been friends if they had ever met. I took her to see Gwen and the baby. She had met Gwen when they visited before and was thrilled about her being a mother. While Glenda sat holding little John she admitted she had the same fear William had when he first told her about the pregnancy. She was afraid something could go wrong, but she also knew if all went well, it would be a healing for William and for them as well. I guess I hadn't thought about it until now; that they had lost a grandchild. I found out that she had helped Mary decorate the nursery and they were heartbroken when the grandchild they dreamed of died before they could even meet him.

I was thrilled when she wanted to help me plan a nursery for our baby. We looked at the now bare nursery and talked about different ideas for decorating it, depending on the sex of the child. She wanted to know if I would mind her coming up to help with the baby for a couple of weeks after the birth. I told her I would be thrilled for the help and I meant it. She talked about how they had looked forward to being grandparents and how worried they had been

Old Harbor - Sisters of Circumstance ~ P.J. Rhea

about their son, cutting himself off from his family and almost grieving himself to death. I think she was actually grateful I came along, and it didn't matter how he met me. I told William how much I was enjoying their visit and that they made me feel so welcome into the family. He simply beamed with pride and smiled at me as if to say, "I told you they'd love you."

Rachel and Luke returned in time to meet them, and William's parents fell in love with Rachel. I explained to them she was like a sister to me, so they insisted she call them Mom and Dad as well. I don't think they will ever understand what that meant to her. Rachel almost seemed to be looking for reasons to call on them.

"Oh, Mom could you pass the tea? Dad, do you think I'll need my sweater, if I go on the porch?"

The Hickmans seemed a little bewildered by her abundance of odd questions, but I knew exactly what was behind them. Rachel never had parents and right now she was an excited little girl who had finally been adopted. When Luke said they needed to head home, I could tell it was difficult for her to leave them. They were special people, and Rachel and I both had fallen in love with our new parents. Their visit ended way too soon. William's parents agreed it was the right thing to do when asked to return the family Bible to Mary's family.

"They miss her so much, William, and if you don't mind, I'd like to encourage them to come see her grave sometime in the future. I think they need the closure."

William looked at me as if asking if I would mind and I nodded and smiled in agreement.

"That would be good, Mom, tell them they are welcome to come."

I went with William to the airport to say goodbye and I could honestly say I couldn't wait until they came back.

"Maybe a few months after the baby comes, we can take a trip to Texas and let them show off their grandbaby. After all, I haven't been home in several years," William suggested.

172

Old Harbor - Sisters of Circumstance ~ P.J. Rhea

"That is an excellent idea, Mr. Hickman!" I replied with a smile.

I knew I truly would miss them. My family was growing and I loved it. Those lonely years in New York were dim memories now and my insecurities were going away. Except for the years I had with Mom, I had never felt so loved.

✄ Chapter Fifteen ✄

Thankful

It was unreal how business at my little studio had flourished over the last few months. It seemed both my business and my belly were growing rapidly and getting harder to keep up with. I finished the church directory for Carl. It was a beautiful job, if I do say so myself. There was a picture of our vibrant church building on the front cover with the entire congregation standing on the steps and sidewalk out front, and inside was an individual picture of each family who attended there. The first page had a picture of Carl and Gwen with little John in her lap and above it the words *Our Minister and his Family.* The rest of the members were pictured in alphabetical order. Trudy and Samuel looked like totally different people than they had last March when they first married. They shared with me that they hoped the next directory would include a picture of their family with a child or two, depending on how much time passed between directories.

I didn't tell them, but I was going to try and update the new directory as children came along. I had a feeling that would be often. I knew Rachel and Luke wanted to have a child soon. Both were in their mid-thirties and they said the biological clock was ticking.

Jay and Corinna were happy to be getting a family picture that included their perfect little boy, David Matthew Ellis. David because it means "beloved," and Matthew, which means "gift from the Lord." That is exactly how they both saw him. I was amazed at how someone could have the kind of mother Corinna had, have something so terrible happen to them, and still be so gentle, sweet, and forgiving. She held no hate for the men who had raped her and said she had forgiven them a long time ago. I asked her how she could possibly forgive them and she told me it was not for their sake she had forgiven them, it was for her sake.

174

Old Harbor - Sisters of Circumstance ~ P.J. Rhea

"Holding hate in my heart will only hurt me, not them. They'll never know the difference either way, but I will. It made me free to love others completely, because I have no space in my heart for hate to grow."

She could only feel grateful to be in the place God led her to.

"I'm not saying God wanted that awful thing to happen to me, but once it did he led me to a place of love and healing. I think my being able to forgive them is why God blessed me so much."

Rachel heard Corinna's explanation and I think it helped her a lot in letting go of the past. She would not let the hate and pain stop her from moving forward with her life.

Toward the back of the book, I had pictures of the events that took place, especially all those wonderful times in the church basement. And of course, there were pictures of four couples on their wedding day. The new directory was small. It was only eight pages due to the small population of our town, but I had great expectations for this church and for this haven we had found. The next directory could be twice this size and full of pictures of children and activities surrounding the four new families our church's minister had helped create.

I was also hired to take pictures of the forty-nine students of Old Harbor Academy, including the six seniors. It had been several years since the school offered pictures for the students, and the children's parents were thrilled. The families of Old Harbor welcomed my business with open arms, getting pictures made of many occasions: birthday parties, anniversaries, sports teams, and even kids with their first hunting kill or first catch.

I hired Rachel as my assistant and was teaching her photography. We added a newer digital camera and printer, which helped a lot. Rachel didn't really have to work, but she was like me in that she needed to stay busy. She was keeping a picture diary of my ever-growing tummy. The same day every week she would have me pose with my bare belly in front of a picture of a big yellow moon. She would joke that soon I would be bigger than the moon.

Old Harbor - Sisters of Circumstance ~ P.J. Rhea

"You're going to be a great mom, Allie, and I'm going to be an awesome aunt," she'd laugh.

Rachel was prepared to run the studio for several weeks until I was ready to return to work, and we had a little nursery set up in what had been a storage room. William built a small storage building behind the studio to help keep down the clutter.

Poor William was becoming more and more worried as the pregnancy progressed. He would question the doctor unmercifully at every visit. The only time he was speechless was when we had the ultrasound done. He sat there holding my hand and swallowed hard when the doctor told us we were having a little girl. I saw a tear run down his cheek, but he couldn't speak.

Once we left the office, he said, "I hope she's beautiful, like her mother."

All I knew was that there would never be a little girl more loved.

The ladies quickly went to work planning another baby shower as soon as they heard it was a girl. The ladies at church, who loved William so much, started having a quilting party once a week to make a quilt for the nursery. I wondered if some of these same ladies had made the little quilt that was spread across the rocking chair the first time I went into the nursery. I had assumed Mary made it but now I wasn't so sure. I was due the middle of December, so the shower was set for December fourth, following worship service.

"I know that's cutting it a little close, but I figured everyone would want to wait until after Thanksgiving. You'll still have around two weeks after the shower before the baby is due."

She was excited about hosting the shower—with the help of Gwen, Trudy and Corinna, of course.

We all agreed that our first Thanksgiving in Old Harbor should include a meal together. Of course, it would be in our church basement. We knew Trudy and Samuel would want to have dinner with their families, as would Jay and Corinna, so we had our meal on the Friday after Thanksgiving. Gwen and Carl set up a beautiful table, with her wedding china, linen tablecloth, and napkins. She placed a

176

Old Harbor - Sisters of Circumstance ~ P.J. Rhea

large horn-of-plenty in the center of the table, and it overflowed with small pumpkins, squash, and apples, some of which had come from her garden. We all pitched in to cook the food. Corinna and Trudy brought pies left from their family gatherings the day before. I was more emotional than I wanted to be and blamed it on the pregnancy when others would act concerned, but I knew it wasn't the pregnancy that was making me emotional. I had not had a real Thanksgiving feast since I was about nine years old at Grandma Ruth's house. Mom usually had to work at the restaurant on Thanksgiving and we would eat there. We'd watch the parade on the big-screen TV they had for customers.

"We can't really have a family Thanksgiving with two people, kiddo, and I might as well make some extra cash."

I never told her how much I wanted the dinner they showed on the movies, with a dad to carve the turkey and lots of people around the table. Having a big family had always been a dream of mine. I felt cheated as a child when it came to holidays or birthdays. I think that is why this meant so much to me. I finally had the big family I dreamed of. I had a lump in my throat as we sat around the long table. Carl asked us to all hold hands while he said a prayer to thank God for this bounty. Rachel was on my left and William on my right, and I think they were both struggling to keep their composure as much as I was. As Carl continued to express how blessed we'd been this year and thanked God for family and friends, the tears flowed uncontrolled down everyone's faces. The lives of every person at the table had changed drastically this past year, and though some had taken a much harder path than others, all of us felt so grateful for what we had now and for each other. Carl said "Amen" but no one looked up or stopped holding hands. We were all fighting to gain our composure when little John helped us break the silence with a hard slap on his high chair tray followed by a burp.

"Son, that's for after we eat," Carl teased.

We all laughed and were able to relax and enjoy our time together. Carl and Jay teased William about how his daughter would have two older men to choose from when she was old enough to get married. William would tease back about cleaning his gun when they came to call and how his little girl couldn't date until she was at least twenty-five. Rachel and Trudy looked at their new husbands with wishful eyes, hoping they too could join in these types of conversations by Thanksgiving next year.

I was glad to see Rachel happy and very much in love. I knew her scarred body would never let her completely forget what happened to her at the hands of Kevin Marshall, but Luke did all he could to make her feel beautiful and loved. They had sold Kevin's house and business to a couple who were looking to start over after losing their jobs at a plant in Kentucky. They were an older couple and looked at it as early retirement and an extended vacation. They both loved to fish, so it was a good business for them to be in. Rachel gave them a price they could not resist. She only wanted to be rid of that place. To never have to enter those doors again as long as she lived.

We stayed and visited for several hours in our little church, the women cleaning up and packing away leftovers to take home. We played with babies while talking about the upcoming baby shower. We talked about how much we all were looking forward to our first Christmas with our new husbands, who were all gathered around a small TV watching football and talking about fishing and hunting, while debating on whether or not they should get just one more piece of pie before heading home.

When we left the basement, it was starting to snow. In November, the daylight hours are growing shorter. That was one thing I was still trying to get used to. In this area of Alaska, there were only about eight hours of daylight in November and even less in December. By January, after the baby came, we would only see six hours of daylight. This past summer I had to get used to days with eighteen to nineteen hours of daylight, and it was hard to make myself get enough sleep. It just didn't seem right to go to bed when it was daylight. William warned me we could get some severe snowstorms from December until February, and since the only way out of Old Harbor was by plane or boat during those months, he was really concerned about getting me to the hospital. He even suggested that after the baby shower, we might want to rent a room in Kodiak until after the birth. I agreed to do anything that would bring him peace of

Old Harbor - Sisters of Circumstance ~ P.J. Rhea

mind. He had been reading books on childbirth just in case he had to deliver the baby himself, but I told him he was just worrying for nothing. December was good for duck hunting and blacktail deer in this area, but William had turned down recent work, afraid for me to be left alone. I hated that he was in such a panic, but I understood why he was. I tried to be patient and cooperative with his wishes.

The nursery was ready, except for the gifts I was sure to receive at my shower next weekend. We had kept the same crib and dresser, but painted it white, and the border was now teddy bears instead of boats. There was a lamp on the dresser with a base that was a chubby white bear with a pink bowtie, and the little jewelry box my dad gave me when I was a child. We hung pink curtains on the one window, replacing the blue ones. Gwen assured me the new quilt would match the décor because she had hinted strongly that I was fond of teddy bears. William bought a big stuffed teddy bear, which sat on top of a trunk in the far corner with a white lace shawl draped over it like a tablecloth. I knew the trunk contained the memories of his little son, but I never said a word about it. I just told him how much I loved the teddy bear and that it looked good there. I couldn't wait until the shower so I could fill the dresser with little pink gowns and bibs that said "Mama's Angel" and "Daddy's Little Girl." The doctor seemed to think I would not go before my due date.

"William, there's no sign she'll go into labor early. Everything looks fine, son, you've got to calm down."

The doctor would try to reason with him at every visit, but there was no way he was letting me out of his sight. I felt sorry for him and wished I could somehow calm his fears, but I knew it was pretty hopeless until this baby was safe in her crib. Poor William would jump if I so much as moved. He would rush to my side to be sure I didn't need something. I would have enjoyed the attention had it not been at the expense of poor William's sanity. I hoped he would be able to relax once the baby shower was over and we were in Kodiak near the hospital. At least with Rachel to help watch over me, he would allow some time for himself to mentally prepare for his new role. His arms had felt so empty for such a long time. We both dreamed of the day I could place our little girl in his arms. She already lived in his heart.

❦ Chapter Sixteen ❧

Not Again

December came to Old Harbor and a blanket of white covered the lush green I had admired for those three short summer months. Alaska only seemed to have two seasons. The spring and autumn months were never obvious. Alaska seemed to only have a short summer and a very long winter. Old Harbor was on the edge of Kodiak Island, the second largest island in the United States; and in the summer it was covered in green vegetation, not the snow and igloos so many think of when speaking of Alaska. Kodiak is known as "Alaska's Emerald Isle" and for those summer months it was a beautiful sight to behold. It was almost overwhelming at times: the massive area of untouched land. There were miles of green surrounded by massive tall mountains, and this was as much of a draw for tourists as the hunting and fishing opportunities. But the locals knew it was only a matter of days until the snow would be so deep it would leave us secluded from everything besides the small band of people who lived on this short strip of land called Old Harbor. All of us knew we had to use the summer months to stock up and prepare for a harsh winter. It wasn't always possible to get to Kodiak to shop, and the Trading Post could not supply everyone if the plane carrying our supplies was delayed.

The tourist business slowed down from November until February, but even now that the snow covered all that green, tourists could still enjoy the crystal waters filled with fish, the pristine land, and endless sky. I knew William had to be missing his beloved outdoors, and I was getting a little case of cabin fever myself. I had grown to love the beauty of this place, which provided unequalled exposure to the gifts of Mother Nature and the Alaskan wildlife. I missed taking pictures of everything this place had to offer a photographer, but William would not let me venture out. I sat in front of our fireplace on the creamy, soft, leather couch, covered in a

Old Harbor - Sisters of Circumstance ~ P.J. Rhea

blanket and listening to William hum as he prepared our dinner. He was taking good care of me as we waited for our daughter to make her entrance into this world. He insisted I not go in to work anymore with the snow and ice such a hazard. We put up our Christmas tree, knowing we may not be here to enjoy it on Christmas day. I promised William that once the baby shower was over, we would make arrangements to stay in Kodiak until the baby arrived. He was taking no chances that anything would happen to me or this baby. We chose an artificial tree this year because it would be left unattended for so long.

"But next year," he declared, "we'll cut down a real one and give our little girl the best Christmas a kid ever had."

I couldn't help but laugh, thinking she would be less than a year old and wouldn't even understand why Daddy was putting a tree in the living room, but I let him fantasize about our life with children; it was, after all, a dream come true for both of us.

The day before the baby shower, as we were working on packing for Kodiak, there was a knock at the door. It was Mark Sims and Carl Bible, asking if William would help them in a search. A newcomer to the area had ventured out to sightsee early in the day, and his wife was frantic because he has not returned; it was going to be dark in a couple of hours. William refused, saying he was not leaving me alone.

"He has his two children with him, William, and they won't last all night in this cold! You know this area like the back of your hand, otherwise we wouldn't ask you."

"William, you have to help," I pleaded, "you know those children will be helpless in this weather!"

He nodded at the men and went in the mud room to put on his warm coveralls and boots. He came out with a large flashlight and his rifle.

"Okay, let's get this done, so I can get back to Allie."

He kissed me and told me to stay put and not do anything foolish.

181

Old Harbor - Sisters of Circumstance ~ P.J. Rhea

I pointed at my large pregnant belly and, with the usual sarcasm he had learned to expect, I said, "What am I going to do, go mountain climbing?"

He laughed and seemed relieved at my joking mood.

After William left, I became bored and uneasy, wandering around the house looking out the different windows at the beautiful color-filled sky as it touched the horizon of snow surrounding my yard. I was used to snow in New York, but this was a different snow than what I had known: clean, white, and as smooth as a white sheet across the land. I stepped out on my porch to enjoy a few minutes of the freshness in the air. It was very cold and the wind was blowing the snow in small whirlwinds across the yard. Living near the ocean not only made it seem that much colder, it added to the windy conditions as well. The icicles that hung off my roof grew sideways, as if they were all pointing toward our barn. I noticed another big difference from the winters of my past: there was no black-laced dirty snow piled beside the road, and no smog or fumes to hide the smell of snow. I never realized until living in this pure place that snow seemed to have a smell all its own. And of course, there was the quiet of it. To stand outside while the snow fell fluffy and soft all around you; it was a strange but wonderful quiet. I had never minded the snow but never appreciated it in New York. I stood in front of my home just taking in the marvel of it. I felt tranquil, and almost like I was dreaming as the sheets of white circled around me.

As I stood there looking up and watching the glorious shapes fall from an almost purple sky, I heard an unexpected sound. Somewhere behind the quiet curtain came a snort-like noise, as if something had blown a lot of air from its nose to signal its location. I looked in the direction of the sound but could not see anything but white at first. Something moved and distinguished itself from the snow. Once my eyes focused I couldn't believe what was only a short distance from me. It was a majestic albino moose, so white he almost blended in with the snow. Had it not been for his massive antlers, I would never have seen him. I knew they could be dangerous and not to get close, but I had to get a picture of this wonderful animal. How often would this opportunity come along? I hurried into the house, put on my coat and boots, and grabbed the camera I kept close to the door and always loaded and ready.

"Oh, please still be there," I wished out loud.

I eased out into the yard and searched the overwhelming white for those antlers. I finally spotted him near the tree line on the other side of the field, adjacent to our yard.

If I climb the path that leads to our barn, I'll be able to get the perfect picture, I reasoned.

There was a fence between the barn and the field, and I stepped up on the first plank so I could lean over for the angle that would show his massive head and antlers. My pregnant belly made it difficult to lean over, but I placed my feet between the second and third plank and braced myself, hanging my belly over the top of the fence. When I felt it was the best shot possible, I started clicking. The sound must have startled him and he looked right at me, which frightened me and caused me to fall backwards off the fence. My leg caught in the fence when I fell and I hit the ground hard, bumping my head. I must have been knocked out for a little while, but a sudden sharp pain woke me. I lay there, dazed, trying to get my mind to clear.

"The moose."

I panicked, but soon realized he had gone. I started to get up, but a pain in my leg that was almost enough to render me unconscious again stopped me. My leg was broken.

Oh great, Allie. I chastised myself. *William is going to be so mad at me. I promised not to do anything foolish and now here I am, several feet from a warm house, with a broken leg, lying in several feet of snow, and the sun going down, which means temperatures are going to drop rapidly.*

I decided my best course of action was to ease my leg from its trap and drag myself to the house. Not easy in itself, but assuredly made harder by the huge stomach I had to be careful with. I pulled as gingerly as possible at my useless limb and screamed so loud from the pain, I thought maybe someone would hear me and come to my rescue. After several attempts, I was exhausted but had managed to free my leg. The pain was unbearable as I tried to drag myself toward the porch. My useless leg lay in an unnatural position from the break, the foot lying to the side as if I had removed it and attached it sideways to my ankle. As cold as it was, I broke into a sweat from the effort, but had only covered a few inches. The porch almost seemed as if it was teasing me and moving farther away. I was trying to catch my breath when another pain brought me out of my unconsciousness, shooting through my back and around into my stomach.

Oh no, please don't let this mean what I think it does; I cannot be going into labor. The barn, I remembered, I'm closer to the barn, plus the two-way radio is in there. I have to crawl to the barn.

I worked with all the strength I had to drag myself toward the opening to our barn. It was more of a workshop for William and contained his fishing gear, ATV, lawn mower, and tools. It was not to provide shelter for animals, but it would shield me from the constantly falling snow. The snow was falling rapidly now and the temperature started to fall drastically. I was moving so slowly I was being covered in snow, and I felt as if I may be going into shock. I was freezing and my teeth started to chatter. I felt dizzy and faint, and the pain was so intense I screamed with every movement I tried to make. The contractions were still coming as well. Not too close together yet, but I had experienced enough of them now to know I was in labor. I kept trying to reach the opening of the building that would give me shelter, and I hoped I could somehow reach the radio that would bring me help.

"Oh, William," I moaned out loud, "I am so very sorry. This cannot happen to you again. You're so good and so dear and you've been through so much. Oh, dear God in heaven, please don't let this happen to him again. If you can only spare one of us, please let our daughter live!"

I tried to cry, but didn't have strength left to do it. I could hear the overwhelming quiet as the snow fell. I heard tree branches as they cracked from the weight of the snow and I could hear my

Old Harbor - Sisters of Circumstance ~ P.J. Rhea

own heart beating, pounding loudly at first, but as I felt myself grow weaker the pounding grew softer and harder to hear. I also noticed a change in my breathing. I could hear my breath as it raggedly went in and out of my lungs. Each breathe was deliberate and purposeful. The cold air hurt my lungs as I lay there helpless against it with no way to cover myself, but I kept reminding myself of my daughter who needed the oxygen I supplied and of my dear William who would be hurt beyond words if he lost another child.

I lay there watching the snow as it came down on me, as I was enveloped in the quiet and the darkness. The only light was the pale light given by the fire in the living room I so recklessly abandoned. I ached for the warmth that would meet me in front of that fireplace. I imagined myself on the soft inviting couch, covered with my warm blanket, drinking hot cocoa and waiting for my William to come home and hold me. To see his beautiful crooked smile and the deep dimple I adored. Would he have to bury another wife, another baby in the garden? And if he did, would his grief be so impossible to bear a second time that he would die from his broken heart and be placed in the ground between his two lost families? I could tell I was growing very weak, and it was as if a wall of darkness was creeping closer and closer around me. I no longer chattered with the cold, no longer winced with the pain, but felt calm, as if drifting off to sleep. Just before my eyelids closed, I saw a figure beside me. It was a beautiful angel, with short black hair and deep blue eyes, and she seemed to be telling me to hold on, not to leave William. I looked into the pleading eyes of this angel I assumed had come for me, but I realized she was trying to get me to hold on to life. Not to give up. It was Mary. It felt as if she laid herself over me, perhaps to keep me warm, and as this soft black blanket surrounded me I fell asleep.

185

∞ Chapter Seventeen ∞

Mary

"*H*ope you enjoy your picture," Rachel called to one of the many tourists who used the little cabin studio to capture a memory of their Alaskan adventure.

She had to admit she loved working there, but she missed Allie now that she was on William-ordered rest. Luke and Rachel lived in Kodiak. They had a nice house and had insisted that Allie and William stay with them once they came to Kodiak to await the baby's arrival. Rachel was amazed at their friendship and how much like sisters they had become. She decided to close the shop a little early so she could apply finishing touches to the basement for the baby shower. She also wanted to get home before the snow got deeper. Like Allie, Rachel was accustomed to snow, but here it could get pretty deep before anything was done to clear a street. Old Harbor was not equipped with machines to clear streets like the big city. She also knew she would have to leave in time to catch the last ferry of the night to get home to Kodiak.

When she arrived at the basement, Trudy and Gwen were already busy making the preparations for an event the whole town was looking forward to. Everyone in this small village had personally known Mary and William, or at least heard of their tragedy, so it was a healing of sorts to everyone when the news of his marriage and baby daughter reached their ears. Gifts arrived at the church from people throughout the town, from people who were not personally invited to the shower but just wanted to join in the celebration of this happy event. Even some of the tourists who had known William for years as his return clients wanted to give gifts and words of congratulations to this lovely couple. The basement was so pink it was almost sickening, but the ladies all agreed with a chuckle that they just couldn't help themselves. All three of them were taping pink

Old Harbor - Sisters of Circumstance ~ P.J. Rhea

streamers and big pink bows on everything when Corinna walked in with baby David.

She said, "Man, I hope the ultrasound was right," which stopped them all in their tracks.

They looked at each other with stunned faces for several seconds, holding themselves like children playing freeze tag, unwilling to move a muscle.

Corinna laughingly added, "Just kidding."

"What if she's right?" Trudy inserted with a whining tone.

"Well, then the little guy will have to learn to like pink and learn to fight," announced Rachel.

They all laughed and finished the preparations for Allie's shower. Just as they were about to call it done and leave for home, one of the Alutiiq people who worked at the Trading Post came in with a gift from Mama. Rachel had seen her at a festival the Alutiiq tribe held every summer in Old Harbor. She was part of the dance group that performed, and had asked Allie if she could display some of her paintings at the studio, which Allie gladly agreed to do. The girl, who was named Cougar, rushed over to Rachel to relay a message.

"You must go to Mama; she asked me to find you," she declared, while pulling on Rachel's arm.

Rachel had not been in the Trading Post since that horrible day when she was put on display by Kevin and consequently shot him dead.

"I'm not sure I can go there yet, it holds some pretty bad memories for me and I'm just not ready to..."

"You must go when Mama summons you, she only does that when she needs to tell you something important!" the girl pleaded, sounding almost desperate.

Rachel was stunned, but nodded her head as if agreeing to the command of the old woman.

Old Harbor - Sisters of Circumstance ~ P.J. Rhea

"I guess I should go see what she wants," she announced to the other ladies.

They all volunteered to go along with her for support, but Rachel wanted to do this on her own.

Rachel bundled up to face the cold, deep snow and headed toward the little store. This was going to be hard, but she remembered the things Allie had told her about the old woman's predictions. That she only relayed things she was told by animal spirits and otherwise sat silent to all those who tried to pull predictions or advice from her. She also remembered very vividly the day she, by some mental messaging, told her it was the right thing to do to shoot her abusive husband. She remembered the calm that came over her when she listened to the voice in her head that she somehow knew belonged to the old Native woman she had never met before that day. As she approached the front of the building, she stood there staring at the large wooden bear that guarded the door and the totem pole that kept watch on the opposite side of the wide stairs.

"Come on, Rachel, you know he isn't in there, so just get in there and see what she wants," she said softly to herself to work up her courage.

Rachel slowly climbed the stairs and stood with her hand on the door handle, unable to go in. Her stomach was in knots and she could hear her heart pounding in her ears. She was about to turn and retreat, thinking it was foolish to come running because this old woman commanded it.

I'm not a slave to someone's demands anymore, why should I go in if I don't want to?

A customer pulled open the door, pulling Rachel inside.

"Sorry, lady; didn't know you were there."

"That's okay, no problem."

Rachel let the door close and stood in front of it, just taking in the familiar room. She started to feel dizzy and felt a sense of panic. She found herself staring at the floor as if Kevin's body still lay there

188

Old Harbor - Sisters of Circumstance ~ P.J. Rhea

with his shirt soaked in blood. She thought she could still smell the gunpowder and hear that one loud pop.

"Child, come here to me quickly." Mama motioned with her feeble hand. "There is no time to waste, come now."

Rachel walked over to where Mama sat in her chair at the end of the counter. It made her uneasy when Mama stared at her through eyes that could not see; those eyes that appeared almost a milky white. When Rachel got close enough, Mama reached out for her arm and pulled her down where she could talk in her ear.

"You must help them before it's too late."

"Help who?" Rachel asked.

"Your friend and her baby are in trouble, you must go to the barn."

Rachel was confused and thought the old woman may have finally gone mad, or senile, maybe.

"What makes you think she needs me?"

"The spirit of the white moose told me she was in need, but Mary is with her, waiting to see if help comes in time."

Mary. The minute Rachel heard that name she knew Allie needed her. She rushed out of the store and went to find help. There was a lot of snow on the ground and she would need someone to drive her to the cabin. She was able to find Jay at the restaurant and tell him what had happened. He knew of Mama's ability and sprinted from the diner, despite the large crowd. Corinna was frantic, but knew she had to stay there and watch after the baby.

"Please find her in time," she prayed as they fled.

Jay had a truck with large tires that was perfect for the snow-covered road, and they hurried as fast as was safe to find Allie. When they arrived at the cabin it was very dark, as if no one were home. The fire that had once glowed in the fireplace had burned down to ashes. Since it was light out when Allie left the cabin, there were no lights on in the house. Jay and Rachel went to the door, which was slightly open, and rushed in.

189

Old Harbor - Sisters of Circumstance ~ P.J. Rhea

"Allie, where are you?" they both frantically called out, running from room to room, flipping on lights.

"The barn," Rachel screamed, "Mama said to look in the barn!"

The two of them almost crashed into each other trying to race out the door. Jay had a flashlight he carried in his truck and together they searched the path to the barn. At first they didn't see her laying there, because the snow had completely covered her with the exception of the top of her head, which was the only part of her she had managed to get into the barn. Rachel noticed her strawberry blonde hair and screamed a shrill plea,

"Oh, Allie no! Jay, we have to get her to the hospital!"

Both Rachel and Jay worked frantically to remove the snow from their friend. Allie was so quiet and cold that Rachel wasn't sure they had made it in time. As they pushed the snow away, Rachel feared that once the snow blanket was lifted she might see the beautiful little baby dead in a horrific replay of William's first child's end. Jay looked at Rachel and they both sighed with relief when her still very pregnant belly was finally exposed. Allie let out a soft moan and brought them back to the reality that it was urgent to get her to the hospital as quickly as possible. The only way to get her there would be by boat. Jay ran to the dock to be sure William's boat was there. It was, and Jay knew where he kept the key. People in a small town watch out for each other and usually know everything about their neighbors, including where they would hide the key to anything they had. Rachel was rubbing Allie's arms, trying to warm her up. She mumbled only one thing and then blacked out again.

"Mary…"

Rachel could not help but think back to what Mama had said: "Mary is watching over her."

It caused a shiver that had nothing to do with the cold to run down Rachel's back. Jay came back to get Allie, but when he lifted her, the leg she had broken went limp and she moaned from the pain.

190

Old Harbor - Sisters of Circumstance ~ P.J. Rhea

"Her leg is broken," Jay informed Rachel, "try to hold it as still as possible while I carry her to the boat."

They placed Allie on the floor of the boat and covered her with blankets they found in the house. Rachel left a note for William in case he came home before they could reach him by radio, and sped through the dark water toward Kodiak.

❧ Chapter Eighteen ❧

Reflection

What is that beeping noise?

I was starting to wake up, but had no idea where I was or what had happened to me during the night. As the sound of the heart monitor and IV pump started to nudge me awake, I tried to focus on where I was. The snow had stopped and the sun was shining in the window, making the all-white room, combined with the glare from the light, feel as if I was still out in the snow.

If I'm still in the snow why am I so warm, and what are those strange noises I keep hearing?

Aside from the beeping sound, I could hear people mumbling close by and heavy steps in the distance, as if someone were walking on a hard floor and not the snow. All at once, a dark shadow moved between me and the bright light and I could better open my eyes.

"William, is that you?"

"Allie, you're awake! Do you have any idea how worried I have been?" William took my hand and kissed it.

"Where am I?"

"You're in the hospital in Kodiak, don't you remember what happened?"

I remembered being outside watching it snow. I remembered seeing the moose and wanting to take its picture. But after that, things were a little confused. William proceeded to fill me in on the rescue and told me I had broken my leg pretty badly. *My baby! Did I lose my baby?* Out of habit, I reached down to touch my belly.

"The baby, where is my baby! Oh William, did I lose our baby?"

Old Harbor - Sisters of Circumstance ~ P.J. Rhea

Before he could answer my panicked questions, a nurse walked in the door pushing one of those carts with the clear basket on top. There was a pink blanket wrapped around something like a tight cocoon.

"I have someone who wants to meet you" the nurse said, almost as if singing a tune.

William helped me sit up in the bed and asked if I felt steady enough to hold her. I reached out for her. William picked up the bundle very gently and passed it to me. Never had anything taken my breath away like this. She was so tiny and yet so magnificent, and I was instantly in love with her. William pulled the blanket back to reveal our little girl's perfection.

"See, ten fingers and ten toes and the tiniest bit of reddish hair, just like her beautiful mother."

I smiled through tears at his enthusiasm over our baby girl, and it was obvious William had already taken inventory before I woke up, maybe more than once.

"Oh William, I'm so sorry for putting you through this. I should have stayed in the house like I promised, but I saw a moose and wanted a picture, and…"

"Shhhh," he silenced me, "I know you didn't mean for any of it to happen. I'm just grateful Rachel and Jay found you in time."

"How did they know to come and look for me?"

William proceeded to tell the story as it had been told to him; all about Mama and her urgent message for Rachel. How I had been completely covered in snow and they might have never found me if not for Mama telling them to look in the barn. That the only reason they knew it was me under that snowbank was because of the red hair that remained uncovered just inside the entrance to the barn. He told me they had to deliver the baby by Cesarean because I was too weak to help deliver it naturally and they repaired my leg while I was sedated.

"The doctors said you wouldn't have lasted much longer if they hadn't found you when they did."

193

Old Harbor - Sisters of Circumstance ~ P.J. Rhea

William could barely get the words out and I could tell he was blaming himself for leaving me alone. I wanted to pull him out of that sadness.

"We should dwell on this beautiful miracle and not on what could have happened," I told him.

We couldn't take our eyes off our beautiful little girl.

"Did they reach you by radio or did you come home to find me gone?" Allie asked.

"Well, that's the weirdest part. You're going to think I've gone crazy when I tell you this..." he hesitated before admitting to me, "...but Mary told me you needed me. I was hunting for those kids and their dad when I saw her in the woods. She didn't say anything, but when I saw her, I knew. That's when I rushed home and found the note Rachel left."

He stood there waiting for me to laugh or accuse him of being nuts, but I didn't do either.

I placed my hand on his and smiled, "I saw her too, William. She was making sure you didn't suffer another loss. I thought I was dying and that's when I saw her, but I know now she wanted to tell me to hang on for your sake and the sake of our daughter."

William and I embraced around our daughter and just held each other, unable to say another word. Our quiet was finally broken when Jay couldn't take the suspense any longer.

"Well, did you find them?"

We looked at him a little confused by his question.

"Who?" we both asked.

"The man and his kids, did you find them?"

William couldn't help but laugh. "Yes, Jay, we found them and they're back at The Lodge safe and sound."

I was in the hospital several days due to the surgery on my leg and healing from the Cesarean; because the baby had been two weeks early, she needed a little extra time in the hospital as well. The

194

Old Harbor - Sisters of Circumstance ~ P.J. Rhea

day we were to be discharged, the nurse came in with the birth certificate paperwork.

"So, what's the baby's name?" she asked.

William and I looked at each other for an answer. We had not decided yet on what to name her. I looked down at my daughter. As I examined her tiny face, it was as if I was really looking at it for the first time. In her face, I saw the eyes of my mother, Carol, and Grandma Ruth looking back at me. They were bright and wide and full of sparkle. She had William's mouth and I could tell she was going to have a dimple on the same cheek he did. Her long fingers and gentle hands reminded me of my dad who, despite his illness, was a kind man and never raised a hand to me in anger. I saw the generations of my family resurrected in this little person and I knew they would all be watching over her as she grew. I thought of the little boy William had wanted with Mary and how sad it was that she never had this moment with her son.

"William, I want to name her Mary Carol Hickman, if that's okay with you."

He looked up at me with wet eyes. "I love it," he said. "And I love you for thinking of it."

Little Mary was born on December third, the day before my baby shower. The ladies of the town had the shower without me, and Rachel and Gwen took all the baby things to my house and put them away for me. They teased me about the party I missed, but took lots of pictures and a video so I could enjoy it later. Rachel left one gift unopened. It was from Mama. She brought it to me in the hospital so I could open it myself. I tore open the box to find a beautiful baby-sized blanket in vivid colors, and weaved into the blanket was the image of an albino moose. Also in the box was a tiny pair of moccasins and on the top of each shoe were beads woven into the fringe, spelling out Mary's name. I looked at Rachel with shock on my face.

"She delivered this to the church the day of my accident, right?"

"Yes" she confirmed, "why?"

Old Harbor - Sisters of Circumstance ~ P.J. Rhea

I held the blanket up for Rachel to see and we both just stared at it with amazement. Had Mama known this was going to happen or was it just a really strange coincidence that Mama's gift told the story of what happened to me, right down to the baby's name on her shoes?

The first place I wanted to go when I left the hospital, even before going home, was to the Trading Post to thank Mama. I also just wanted Mama to meet Mary, perhaps to bless her or something. I wasn't completely sure how Mama's gift worked, but knowing she was somehow watching over us made me feel safe, made me feel connected in my soul with all those who had passed. I hoped that if Mama could receive messages from the animal spirits and apparently knew that William's wife Mary had watched over me, then maybe—well, maybe she also heard from Grandma Ruth and my own mother. I entered the store and hoped she would motion me to her. She smiled big and waved us to her.

"Mama, we wanted you to meet our little girl and to thank you."

She raised her hand as if to stop us from further vocalizing our appreciation. She explained to us that she didn't like it when people thanked her because she felt it was her responsibility to relay the messages that were freely given to her. She placed her hand on the baby and smiled broadly. She leaned down and whispered something we could not hear to Mary, and when she finished she just smiled and looked away from us as if to signal that she was done and we should leave now. As we left the store, I felt a strange emptiness. I turned back to look at Mama and she had gone. I had never known her to get up from that spot, and the empty rocking chair made me feel sad.

We heard the next day that Mama passed away in her sleep. She was one hundred and twelve years old, according to her children. This town will not be the same without her and I will never forget what she did for us and for Rachel.

No one other than the members of her tribe had ever witnessed a funeral in the custom of the Natives who shared their island with us. Most had only quiet services, held privately among their people. They had a cemetery separate from the one used by the other townspeople, but because Mama was a spiritual leader her body

Old Harbor - Sisters of Circumstance ~ P.J. Rhea

would not even be placed in the tribe's cemetery. Their beliefs were that the spirits of their dead would leave their body and enter an animal, which was why they listened for messages from the animal spirits. Since Mama was the last tribal elder and had become so well known and loved by everyone who lived here, her children offered to open the ceremony celebrating her transfiguration to all who wanted to attend. It was a beautiful thing to watch, and I sat in awe as they danced and sang around Mama, who they had placed on a kind of altar. After the long celebration Mama's body was burned in a funeral pyre, and they explained to us the smoke from her would travel into the mountains to join the great bear and moose from which she had received most of her wisdom. Her family explained to us that only one as wise as Mama could enter such an animal. I would truly miss this gentle woman, but next time I see my albino moose—I will send my regards to Mama.

Our first Christmas in Old Harbor came a few days after I returned home from the hospital. William's parents came to help while I recovered and were amazed at their perfect granddaughter. When we told them her name, Glenda could not help but cry.

"You are so sweet, Allie, what a true gesture of love for William!"

I just thanked her. It didn't seem logical to tell her about how Mary helped save my life and warned William that I needed him. It wasn't easy for people to accept the mystery of Mama. All my sisters and their families came to visit over the next few days and with each visit, I felt grateful for the love and family that now surrounded me. It seemed as though the life I had left behind less than a year before was now a faint memory of a past that no longer belonged to me. I had never felt so content and so happy. Rachel took a picture of the three of us on her first visit.

"Never too early for a family portrait," she insisted.

She brought it to me on Christmas day in a beautiful frame, and it was wrapped like a Christmas gift.

"Merry Christmas, Sis," she chimed.

Old Harbor - Sisters of Circumstance ~ P.J. Rhea

When I took the picture from the tissue paper that cushioned it, I gasped and put my hand over my mouth.

"What is it Allie, did I not do a good job on it?"

"Oh, it's perfect, Rachel—absolutely perfect!" I announced, as I hugged her and wiped my eyes.

Rachel placed the picture in the nursery on top of the dresser for me. After everyone left, I went back into the nursery to admire the picture and to confirm to myself what I had seen earlier. William's smile; it was the one I had waited for since the first time I entered this nursery. He looked at me and little Mary and his smile was the one that said: I'm complete. And that was exactly how I felt too. I once felt as if I would never live to grow old and if I did, it would be a lonely, cold existence with no family to love me through my winter. But now I had a large family with sisters and brothers–in–law, nephews, and I felt nieces would someday join that list. I had a wonderful husband, a mom, a dad, and a daughter. William had already said he hoped we would have at least one or two more.

I just laughed and said, "Let's get her out of diapers first, then we'll talk about it."

The truth was I didn't care if we had a dozen. I felt happy and confident that if I lived to see the winter of my life, it would be full of people who would make me feel warm and loved through those years. *Grandma Ruth, I don't fear my winter anymore. I will welcome it.*

Old Harbor - Sisters of Circumstance ~ P.J. Rhea

℘ *Chapter Nineteen* ℘

Goodbye, Old Friend

It's hard to believe that it has been thirty years since I came to Old Harbor. It seems unreal to me now to think back on that sad girl who walked the streets of New York thinking she would be lonely her entire life and most likely die young, as so many of her family had. I stopped by the little church that is such an important part of me now to leave food for later in the basement kitchen. I looked around the empty room, remembering the first night I walked into this basement and the dear man who brought me here. In a short while this room would be filled with people ready to say goodbye to him.

It was cold that day at the cemetery. Gwen could hardly stop shaking. I didn't know if it was the cold, or Carl's death that was chilling her to the bone. He'd gone peacefully in his sleep and we were thankful he had not suffered. The coroner said it was a blood clot that had gone to his heart. Carl had a heart attack a few years earlier and his health had been a concern for a while now. All I knew was someone else I loved had been taken way too soon.

After the burial we gathered in the church basement, as we had on so many occasions, to feast on the delicious food people brought over. I thought back on all the good memories this room held for we "sisters of circumstance." I had to smile at the memory of Carl calling us that. Now we were here to celebrate the life of Carl Dible, the man who brought us together in the first place. I surveyed the crowd that had gathered and realized that so many of the people who had assembled here would never have existed were it not for this dear man. Certainly our lives would have been very different, including my own.

I looked at Rachel and Luke, about to be grandparents for the first time. Rachel, who had never known her own parents, had become a mother of three. First was a little girl, less than a year after

199

Old Harbor - Sisters of Circumstance ~ P.J. Rhea

my own daughter Mary was born. They named her Hope, because that is what she came from. About a year and a half after that she delivered twin boys, whom they named Stephen and Stewart. They were the light of their mother's eyes. Stephen married a girl from Kodiak and they were having a baby boy in a couple of months. Corinna and Jay had been blessed with another son as well, but you would never know Jay wasn't the father of both. He never showed a difference. Trudy and Samuel also had two children, both girls. They lived in Anchorage now but had to be here to say goodbye to our beloved friend. William and I were also blessed with another child, a son we named Roger after my dad. Mary told us when she was only three that Roger would be coming soon. She had apparently been given a gift by Mama that day in the Trading Post when she whispered to our tiny daughter, because Mary had always had a sense of things that were coming. She showed no surprise at Carl's sudden passing. It seemed she knew it was supposed to happen that way.

As my son-in-law, John Carl, was trying to get everyone's attention, I couldn't help but notice the striking resemblance he had to his father. He had the same toothy grin that put people at ease and made you smile. After the room quieted, John Carl began to speak. He thanked everyone for coming and showing their support to his family; hanging onto his daddy's pants leg was little three-year-old Will. John Carl picked him up and kissed him gently on the cheek. I looked over at Mary and could see a tear running down her cheek. She was so proud that John Carl had followed in his father's footsteps and was now the minister of our little church. Carl had given up the ministry just a few short months before he died and John Carl gladly stepped up to the pulpit. In a soft, humble voice, John Carl began to speak again:

"To everything there is a season, and a time to every purpose under the heaven: A time to be born, and a time to die; a time to plant, and a time to pluck up that which is planted; A time to kill, and a time to heal; a time to break down, and a time to build up; A time to weep, and a time to laugh; a time to mourn, and a time to dance; A time to cast away stones, and a time to gather stones together; a time to embrace, and a time to refrain from embracing; A time to get, and a time to lose; a time to keep, and a time to cast away; A time to rend,

Old Harbor - Sisters of Circumstance ~ P.J. Rhea

and a time to sew; a time to keep silence, and a time to speak; A time to love, and a time to hate; a time of war, and a time of peace.

"It is time today to say goodbye to someone who meant different things to all of us. He was a loving husband, a wonderful, patient father and grandfather, and a loved and trusted friend. We will miss you, Carl Bible, but we will see you again someday when this life is over."

After a short prayer, Mary rose and went to stand next to her husband and son. William tightened his arm around my shoulder and gently pulled me to him as I wept quietly. He whispered softly in my ear, "Allie, you have been my season; my purpose under heaven, and I thank God for you and our family every day."

The next afternoon, I was over at John Carl and Mary's house watching little Will. I was straightening up the living room and ran across a stack of papers on the coffee table. *John Carl must be working on next Sunday's lesson.* As I gathered them up to take them into his office, I noticed the heading at the top: Object: Matrimony! I recognized Carl's writing and realized it was his original ad. John must have been going through his dad's papers. I smiled to myself, thinking of all the lives that ad had changed, and placed the papers back on the coffee table. I couldn't help but wonder if John Carl had considered placing that same ad himself. I was hopeful that if he did my son Roger would apply for a bride. I wanted more than anything for my son to be as happy as his sister was, as happy as his father and I were.

I sat down on the couch and little Will came over and crawled in my lap.

"Gran'ma Allie, what's a season?"

I pulled him to me and told him the story Grandma Ruth had told me. Then I cupped his chin in my hand and smiled down at him. "That's my wish for you, little Will: that you live long enough so you can enjoy the winter." I knew he was too young to really understand now, but I would tell him the story several more times and one day he would.

201

Chapter Twenty

Through Mary's Eyes: Frozen in Time

$\mathcal{I}$ came home while my mother, Allie, relayed her wish for her grandson; and it made me remember when Mom told that same story to my brother Roger and me. I felt I probably had the perfect childhood. Old Harbor was like going back in time in many ways. Both my brother and I had been to Texas several times to visit our grandparents and our father's sister Janie and her family. We also traveled to New York once or twice to shop and go sightseeing. Mom wanted us to know about our Grandma Carol. She also told us about her dad and Grandma Ruth, but we never went to Tennessee. After each visit outside of Old Harbor, returning would feel like going back to a place frozen in time, never moving forward. Even now, the school is still small and has only two teachers. The same little businesses still stand, but no new ones ever seem to come here. Kodiak has almost doubled in size since I was a child, but Old Harbor remains untouched and pure and perfect. Not everyone feels that way, of course. Most of the children I grew up with left once they were old enough. My brother and I seem to be among the few who want to live out our lives here—which makes my parents very happy. But things didn't exactly turn out the way they expected.

My mother always assumed I would follow in her footsteps and be a photographer. She tried to groom me from a young age to take over the little studio my father, William, gave her in the early months of their marriage. She and my aunt Rachel built the business as mostly a tourist attraction, because in this small island town there simply wasn't enough business from locals to pay expenses. The little studio was well known for wildlife pictures, paintings by the locals— especially the members of the Alutiiq tribe who share their island with us—and the staged portraits of the tourists with their prize kill or catch from the hunting and fishing trips Old Harbor hosted year round. That was my father's business, to be a tour guide for those tourists, and he in turn groomed my brother Roger to continue in his

Old Harbor - Sisters of Circumstance ~ P.J. Rhea

path, taking him on hunting and fishing trips since he could walk. It was no surprise to me that neither of us followed the path our parents had expected.

Roger wanted nothing more than to please our dad, who happens to be the most loving, caring dad any kid could ask for. He would go every weekend with him to fish or hunt, and when school was not in session he would go to work with him, especially when it was an overnight trip and they could sleep in a tent. Roger loved the outdoors and the beautiful landscapes of Alaska. He also loved looking for wildlife or that big fish everyone dreamed of catching, but he only wanted to take pictures of them. At first it was hard for dad to understand Rogers's feelings on killing the animals; after all, he had made his living from just that for all his adult life. The first and only time Roger killed a deer he cried for several days about it. He was only nine, so they assumed it was just his age and because he was tenderhearted, but his willingness to participate in hunting stopped after that. He still wanted desperately to go with them, but only to take pictures of the animals. He would try to keep a distance when he knew they were about to kill. Once our dad saw what works of art his pictures were, he no longer questioned him about it. He had a true gift, and when he was in his teens he would sometimes stay perched in a tree or slumped in a cave for hours, or even days, to capture that perfect picture. My mother would protest, saying she was worried about him being eaten by a grizzly, and would often remind him of her close call with one. But he would tease her and tell her he wouldn't stop until he captured a picture that would outdo her close-up of that grizzly.

Roger has traveled to several different countries to shoot pictures of the wildlife and scenery this world contains, but his heart is in Alaska and I doubt he would ever consider moving away. The longest he ever stayed away was when he was doing a tour for a book he had published containing some of his most beautiful pictures. He and Mom could spend hours and hours talking photography. It is their passion. The only other time he stayed away was when our mother would start trying to find him a wife. It is true that my parent's story of how they met was like a fairy tale. It is full of romance and tragedy right up there with Romeo and Juliet. But it's impossible to convince

Old Harbor - Sisters of Circumstance ~ P.J. Rhea

Allie Hickman that not everyone is desperate to find someone. Roger has no problem meeting women. He's smart, handsome, and a real charmer. We live in a tiny town, and my parents are adored for their story of overcoming and having their happily ever after. That makes Roger the prince charming of the community and considered a real catch. The thing is that Roger is in no hurry to be caught. He has probably been on at least one date with every unattached female from Old Harbor to Anchorage, not to mention those he dated while on his travels, but no one has captured his heart.

As for me, I chose to be a healer of sorts. I went to college in Anchorage with all intentions of becoming a doctor, but found myself wanting to be home and near the man I loved for my whole life. John Bible was my other half for as long as I could remember. We were childhood friends, and then he became my boyfriend once we were teenagers. Only seeing him a couple of weekends a month was not enough, so I went a route that would take a few less years and became a nurse practitioner. I felt the need to help others in some way from the time I was a very small child. I don't like to talk about it much, but I seem to have a gift that allows me to know things. I always felt a sort of connection with animals and could sense things when they were near me. They didn't talk to me or anything crazy like that, but it was almost as if they were sending me messages in some spiritual way. I never really understood it and never really tried to explain it to anyone except Roger. I think that is why it bothered him so much to see the animals killed, because of my connection to them.

Sometimes it seemed they would give me insight to what was wrong with someone. I would be listening to a patient as they told me about their complaint and suddenly I would just feel the answer, and I would know exactly what test to run to confirm it. I didn't really need to run the test to be sure, but I couldn't exactly tell the patient I had a "feeling" I knew what was wrong. The doctors I reported to as my consultants and advisors were often amazed by my ability to diagnose my patients. I tried to keep my ability a secret even from them, to avoid becoming a freak show, but the local natives knew, and mine was the only medical advice they would listen to. Because of the great need for some sort of medical facility, I agreed to run a small clinic in

Old Harbor - Sisters of Circumstance ~ P.J. Rhea

Old Harbor so the locals would only have to go the distance to Kodiak for more serious medical needs.

My mother told me long ago about the old woman named Mama who gave me some kind of power by whispering to me when I was only a few days old. I heard all the stories of Mama and how she listened to the animal spirits. How she had saved not only my aunt Rachel but my mom, and actually me as well. In the beginning I have to admit I thought my parents were a little crazy to buy into all that spiritual guide stuff, but as I grew older and saw for myself the gift I possessed, I had no choice but to embrace it and use it for the good I feel it was intended to give. I don't think Mama would have passed it along to me, someone who was not of their tribe, if she had not known I would use it properly.

My mother asked me several times what it was like for me. It was really difficult to explain exactly what I was able to do. I didn't see visions or have dreams, never went into any kind of trance, or had others talk through me. I couldn't tell the future or predict what the winning lottery number would be. I just—knew. I could look at someone, and without really understanding why, I knew if something was going to happen. Sometimes it would be very specific. For example, when I was three I looked at my parents one day and in my mind I knew they would soon be holding a baby boy, so I told my mom she would be having a little boy soon. Roger was born about ten months later and I felt as if I knew him before he arrived.

Most of the time my "feelings" were just that: something was about to happen that would either be very good or very bad. My last awareness was a few weeks ago when I glanced at a picture of my wonderful in-laws, Carl and Gwen Bible, and Carl's face seemed to be fading away. I felt an almost unbearable sadness because I knew what it meant, and within minutes we received a call that he had passed in his sleep. My husband had only recently taken over the position of minister in the little church Carl led for almost forty years. He was a big reason for my even existing, because he brought my mother and father together. I loved him as much as I loved my own father, and I would forever have an empty place in my heart that no other could fill.

Old Harbor - Sisters of Circumstance ~ P.J. Rhea

Gwen would be lost without Carl, but she continued on as the church's secretary so I could put more time into the clinic, and she was also babysitting our son Will for us when we needed her. Since the house she and Carl had shared was actually meant for the minister and his family, we asked Gwen to please stay there with us. She agreed to it, on the condition that we would allow her to make the basement of the house into a small apartment. It had not been used in thirty years for anything but storage. The last time it was slept in was when my mother and my aunts Rachel, Corinna, and Trudy came to be brides for men they had only met by way of phone and email. There was one other woman named Lynn who changed her mind and left, and Aunt Rachel married my uncle Luke, who had originally been matched up with Lynn. I knew something horrible had happened to Aunt Rachel and the man she had married was killed, but it was kind of a forbidden subject no one would talk about. Mom would just say, "It is as it should be," and I knew she was right.

It was a little confusing when I was younger, trying to understand how people who were not related to us by family ties, who looked so different from us and from each other could be my mother's sisters. But as I grew up I began to realize that these four women were closer than most families. They came together because of some life in the past they could not bear, and found support and love from each other. Their stories were never shared with anyone outside of the four women and the husbands they found, and I knew some of it was better left buried. It was, after all, that secret past that made them sisters. It made them family. They were, truly and forever, "Sisters of Circumstance."

The End

Old Harbor - Sisters of Circumstance ~ P.J. Rhea

ℬ About P.J. Rhea ℛ

*A*uthor P.J. Rhea is a southern preacher's wife. Married for thirty-eight years, she and her husband, Mike, live in her Tennessee childhood home. There, she is surrounded by the memories and dreams of her youth in the very place where she's watched her children and grandchildren grow. And there, amid the sweet, summer breezes over the fertile land between the Duck and Piney Rivers, P.J. Rhea listened to her heart and the echoes of history. It was from those enchanting melodies that ideas sprang forth which would become *Old Harbor, Sisters of Circumstance*. A mother of three, a grandmother of six, and a friend to many, Rhea's knack for telling stories comes through in this, her first novel.

CPSIA information can be obtained at www.ICGtesting.com
Printed in the USA
LVOW100113261012

304383LV00001B/3/P